SANTA CRUZ MUMBAI

By

DAVID RAY

Published by Slingshot Publishing

Dedicated to the funky beautiful part of you that comes alive when you're really alive and showing that world you!

TABLE OF CONTENTS

Enkida

"The Revolution has arrived!" a sign invited in hundreds of unwashed hippies, laid back surfers just out of their wetsuits, Patagonia vest wearing software engineers, loose clothing yoga connoisseurs, edgy alternative education teachers, and funky University of California Santa Cruz students. They all meandered in half-purposefully under the all-too-prophetic glittering sign-"The Revolution has arrived."

Yes, a revolution was landing. Things had long been weird in Santa Cruz but they were about to get much weirder. Those flowing into the eco-conference didn't expect much of a revolution. They anticipated a chill afternoon, a mildly anti-establishment meeting of eco-conscious ideas, people, smells, and gadgets. Of course, there was also the expectation of free acai flavored mouthwash samples, opportunities for flirting, and some talks on environmentally hot issues.

Then the wild card was called into the mix, "Enkida, please come to the main stage." The request was blasted from speakers of Santa Cruz's Kaiser Permanente auditorium. *I'm up,* Enkida smiled to herself mischievously. Enkida had practically fallen into this speaking opportunity. With her ancient dreadlocks and self-righteous strut, she blended right in here. She had been invited to be one of the conference's last minute keynote talk additions (due to the cancellation of a renowned "eco-futurist" who had been slated to do a talk titled "How smartphone's apps will save the trees AND nourish our hearts!")

Enkida and her dreads floated by the many kiosks, kiosks which sold solar powered dancing Greta Thurnberg toys, biodegradable toothbrushes, and an "Earth Mama" board game. Unfortunately, all of these products were made in China. Enkida, the soon-to-be messianic sexy pagan, pushed through the dense smell of patchouli doused eco-warriors. She wasn't there to sell any app but, rather, to call on a regiment of militant pranksters. As if she were a general, people naturally made way for Enkida as she headed to the stage. Enkida's immodest leather dress revealed radiant deep brown skin of her legs well above the knees.

Enkida and her dreadlocks ascended the steps of the auditorium's stage and approached the podium. Then she pivoted confidently, her thin shawl draped over dark skinned shoulders. And she looked out at the large audience. From her perspective, the crowd looked smugly and pathetically content with whatever screens or gadgets they suckled, zombie cows more concerned with paying bills, getting to tai chi classes, and boasting to their friends that they'd attended an eco-conference. Enkida judged all this as the obstacles of her cause.

She whispered at first, "are you ready to be turned on." The words and the way she said it sounded sexual. Her tone seductively disrupted the selling of Atlantean books, "natural" beauty care products, certified fair trade coffee, and holistic cell phone accessories.

Enkida pushed a dreadlock up off her face, glared out disdainfully, and asked more loudly, "are you ready to get turned on and bare some of your fangs?"

As if a police raid had just busted a high school party, the people at the conference now became fully alert. This speaker was clearly different from the ones who'd already rambled on "soil quality" and "making money with an eco-podcast." Everyone stopped mulling around the kiosks. They gave their attention to this speaker.

Now Enkida spoke with force, "you came to this conference looking for the revolution, looking for change, looking for your cause! Listen, you already know your cause! To the corporations, you've smilingly begged for change. Then you waited. You put on your patchouli and waited. You bought your groceries at Whole Foods and waited. You bought hybrid or electric cars and waited. You watched shows about global warming and waited. You listened to

Bernie Sanders and waited. You signed the petitions and waited. You went to a few protests and waited. That's too much damned waiting. I am here to let you know you've waited long enough."

The crowd was in full attention, "you've sat on the sidelines with your computers and your aikido classes hoping for some tiny hint that powerful people care for the rivers and trees, care for the air, care for you. You wanted to be the change you wanted to see. But you waited for even that to happen! Well, unless you're a fool who doesn't really want change., I'm here to say 'stop waiting.'"

She continued, "while you've waited, they've ransacked our hopes, our rights, our bodies, all that is sacred to us. Going the safe route, you've groveled and tried to convince them with scientific data and documentaries. Still, they out-lawyered and out-played you. They laughed at you and continued to cut down the forests you sang songs about, pollute the river you swam in, and start stupid wars despite your ineffective little douchey protests."

The eco-conference crowd listening to Enkida's rant became both nervous and excited. She went on, "follow me and we will no longer be ignored, no longer be discarded as dreamy purple crystal unicorn worshiping idiots. Ignore me if you prefer to remain slaves of buying stupid crap like the stuff they sell here. If you think this eco-sellout bullshit is enough, don't follow me. Let me make myself perfectly clear, this so-called eco-conference is scamming you out of real purpose! This is part of your shackles! If this is enough you are the feeble-minded tree hugger they claim you to be. Are you really sheepish impotent flowery morons?"

Her microphone was turned off.

Now, she yelled: "We must rise up. Follow me and we will spur on a real revolution instead of this pathetic wank off."

Burly security guards walked up the stairs of the stage to Enkida. It wasn't the first time guards crashed a pivotal moment of Enkida's life. They grabbed her wrists and aggressively dragged her from the podium. The organizers of the Eco-revolution conference expected something entirely different from her presentation. They'd wanted Enkida to say things like "many drops of small change culminate in an ocean of difference." They wanted her to preach on "the power of non-violence to make shifts in the *paradigm of consciousness*." The expected new age phrases about "respecting Mother Earth's sanctity." Instead, Enkida had beckoned an army. The audience gasped as the security guards hauled Enkida away, turning Enkida into an instant underdog.

Enkida struggled just enough to make herself look oppressed. While maintaining her poise, she half-allowed the security guards to shove her towards an emergency exit adjacent to the stage of the auditorium. Before their final shove out of the building, she screamed, "they don't care about me. They don't care about you. They just want to keep you on their email list. Stop waiting!"

Two thousand years earlier...

In her massive limestone palace bedroom, Enkida pulled down an intricately embroidered soft cloth blanket and rubbed her eyes awake. Having always slept nude, she picked up and slipped on a jewel encrusted cloth robe. And, as if her dressed body gave the cue, servants quickly brought in ladles of camel milk, figs, and her crying baby.

The baby's legs were unusually skinny but Enkida lovingly embraced and held the noisy babe. The thick smell of frankincense oil in her dreadlocks and her magnanimous eyes instantly soothed the child. The child was wrapped in a blue cloth and wore a simple anklet- a leather strip with three rare beads on it. Each of those stone beads had an orange dot on it. Wearing this anklet was a longstanding tradition calling on the blessing of the goddess Ishtar's protection.

Enkida hummed an affectionate melody and kissed the child's face and shoulders. The child was nameless because royal children in Uruk are not named until they are a year old. She didn't know this nameless child was about to be taken away from her. She didn't suspect the wheels of time were revolving towards a hateful coup. On that morning, after feeding her child, Enkida placed him on a pile of palm leaves servants had put in the center of her straw mattress. Then it began! A dozen well-armed guards barged into her serene palace room.

It didn't take long for her to figure out what was happening-the guards pulling Enkida screaming from her palace room were her brother's most trusted goons. Her brother was disposing of her so he could reign without any other monarch's influence.

At first, Enkida naturally commanded, "I am your queen. Remove your hands from me!"

The guard/ goon grunted, "you are no longer my queen or anyone's queen. Get out of your royal gown and then get out of this kingdom." With a knife at her throat, she was forced to remove her jewel encrusted cloth and put on a common peasant's short leather dress.

Enkida tried chanting spells but felt some force instantly dissolving their power. So, she was pulled along from her palace to a walkway outside. Under early morning's darkness, she was shoved past ziggurats, temples, and well built mud brick homes. They passed merchants pulling camels but it was largely quiet. She knew the sun would rise shortly and multi-colored tents would be bustling with the haggling that makes up Uruk's bazaar. The roadways were lined with countless palm trees, stone walls adorned with mosaics, and statues of Uruk's many gods.

Enkida's scream was muffled by the guards until they arrived at the gateway through which one leaves Uruk's well fortified and cultivated oasis. Beyond Uruk's walls was a harsh barren world, a vast desert. Enkida's brother waited there at the gateway. With a victorious smirk, he stated,"I'm sorry, Enkida. It's time for you to go?"

Enkida nodded. There wasn't a choice here. She only stated, "you're chasing after power, brother."

"Poor sister, you've been chasing after witches and shamans, your versions of power. Now I'm just releasing you to be true to yourself. And, of course, I am not alone in thinking your influence over our people is unhelpful. I am freeing you from a burden beyond your abilities. This is a gift."

"Then let me take my child with me," she pleaded.

"I'm sorry. That won't happen," her brother's eyes drew dark, "as long as that boy is safe and well here, I stand unquestioned as the sole ruler of this land. Yes, I do seek power. Good leaders know there is no shame in seeking power."

"What about loyalty? Is there shame in having none?"

"The leaders of our army will fight for me alone," her brother was unshaken.."There's plenty of loyalty here, sister."

"Then why am I still here? Why have I not already been killed?"

"Efauu read the stars and decided it would be most auspicious to let you live until you walk outside these walls for at least a day. Lucky you!" Efaau, a tall fair skinned foreigner with long black hair and beard, had recently been embraced as a High Sorcerer and Counselor to Enkida's brother. As an advisor, Effau almost always lurked nearby.

"You and your pale faced wizard fear the ghost of a weak-minded witch like me?" Enkida was crying.

Maka, her brother, growled back, "you gave our kingdom the legitimacy of an heir, your son. And, in return, we must let you live, at least long enough to walk into a sandstorm. And," Maka added one last thing to his departing sister, "if you return, both you and your child will be killed in a very unpleasant way."

Enkida turned away from the walls of Uruk. She stepped into the sands outside Ururk's walls.

Just like so much of history, this fairytale begins by things going wrong. She'd been queen, full of hope alongside her beautiful baby boy, surrounded by fragrant gardens, dutiful servants and rich savory cuisines. Now she was an outcast, wearing only a cheap peasant's leather dress, simple sandals, and a thin veil (which she now wrapped over her arms and head due to the scorching sun.)

Enkida guessed her boy would be entrusted to nursemaid-slaves, who would keep the child alive and nourished as any royal child of this land. By the law of Ur, this newborn male heir gave Enkida's brother rights to sole political rule until the boy was 5 (as long as Enkida wasn't around and the boy remained well). For five years, her son would serve as a placeholder. Then her brother would fully usurp control over all law... and ruthlessly dispose of that child.

Enkida walked for hours away from Uruk on the nearly white sand. There were small holes where desert rats, foxes, and turtles made their home. But there was no safe shady place for Enkida to crawl into. She knew it was unlikely she would survive outside Uruk's walls much more than a day. There just wasn't enough cover.

The worst was the thinking of her son...*how can I survive and gather enough power to free my son?* With that burden weighing on her, she walked for hours through the increasing heat.

"My brother was right," she admitted out loud to a rock. "I have overlooked enemies, been too interested in herbs and healing. I'd have been wiser to pay more attention to my political power."

So much heat and no food or water. Her skin felt like it was melting. Then a lizard scurried through a pile of sand near her feet. It was scorching hot. And that type of heat can make anyone a little nutty. The lizard looked up and Enkida thought she heard, "in thousands of years, you will live near a vast ocean in a town full of strange people. There you will be reunited with your son. This is not the end." Enkida rubbed her eyes and the lizard was gone.

It got even hotter. Somewhere along the way, she collapsed onto hard rocky earth. She passed out.

Later, just as the sun descended below the horizon, a scorpion crawled up onto her arm before she flung it off. In the distance beasts yelped loudly. She pushed her aching body back up. The darkening desert quickly shifted from too hot to too cold. Enkida wrapped the thin shawl tightly around her body. She worried whether every tickle in her dreadlocks wasn't the breeze but another scorpion. Beasts howled again but now they sounded closer. *Efaau must have conjured magic to draw all the hungry monsters of the world to me.*

Enkida again thought about the talking lizard that scurried under a rock. It had seemed to say, "in thousands of years, you will live near a vast ocean in a town full of strange people. There you will be reunited with your son. This is not the end." *What a strange delusion.* But it was better than thinking about the yelping beasts, the darkness, and the cold.

Enkida was ripped violently from her thoughts, sharp teeth digging into the flesh of her right shoulder.. Enkida whipped around and pulled off a spastic coyote whose teeth had grinded into her shoulder. Her back seared with pain; and, even in the darkness, she saw at least a dozen more pairs of coyote eyes glowing around her. They all looked possessed with a hunger for her.

Enkida quickly whispered some words of power.. The chant she whispered was a mantra to invoke deep sleep. She whispered the words with all the strength and calm she could gather. In working with a shaman, she'd been taught this spell to put someone into a deep sleep if she had to scalpel a growth from a person. She was trying to use this spell on herself. She wanted to make herself fall deeply asleep so she didn't feel her body torn apart by these beasts circling her. She closed her eyes and waited.

Of course, as the lizard had said, it wasn't the end. She waited with closed eyes for many minutes. When curiosity opened her eyes, she saw the whole pack of coyotes still around her, but instead of looking hungrily at her flesh, they were sleeping. Her incantation had worked, but not as she expected. Only one coyote had managed to stay awake, and it was wobbling away from her as if drunkenly resisting an overwhelming grogginess.

Not sure if she was happy to still be alive, Enkida walked away from the pack. In the cold of the night, she walked and walked until she was unbearably sleepy. She lowered herself to rest on the rocky ground, whispering the most powerful incantation of protection she knew before blacking out in sleep.

In a restless dreamworld, Enkida was with her baby. She was flying like lightning across the sky with that warm, brown-eyed child. There was a sandstorm throwing up sharp blades and hateful poisoned arrows, all of which she was able to skillfully dodge.

Still dreaming, she landed on a mountaintop and then had to leap up along floating boulders like a staircase to the sky. Along the way, the baby somehow slipped from her fingers. She didn't know where it had gone. She was screaming. And a big flying boulder smashed into her back.

She woke up screaming in the desert alone and childless. Where the coyote had bitten her back was bleeding and radiating pain, the theft of her son was still not a dream, and, perhaps most imminently significant, a large purple lion with a grand mane stood over her.

Enkida's cousin had kept lions in cages in one of his pleasure gardens. Her cousin collected exotic wildlife from kingdoms they raided (her cousin thought praying to those animals gave him power). But the lions in that cousin's care were never purple. And she didn't know that lions of any color had been previously seen roaming the deserts of Ur.

An intense full moon lit the desert so she could see the gigantic beast's gray eyes staring deeply into her. The beast towered over her, and she knew it could rip her to shreds with one effortless swipe of his paw.

"Another monster sent by Efaau," Enkida didn't even try to fight. She didn't even stand up. She quickly prayed to Ishtar that she might be killed quickly, so misery would not further wither her soul before going into the beyond.

But the lion didn't attack. It brushed up against Enkida's nose and pushed its clawed paw gently against her shoulder. Enkida had seen cats play with their prey, taking little harmless swipes at mice for hours before the lethal bite. She smelled and felt the lion's breath on hers. Even under the moonlight, she saw its large teeth. When the big cat licked her face, she decided she would not endure hours of this agony. She'd had enough.

"Kill me, damned beast," she cried and swung her arms uselessly at the monster's whiskered face. The cat absorbed her hits as if they nothing. She flailed again and again, hitting and screaming with all her might, "Kill me. Please!"

Her throat grew dry and raspy. Her arms grew tired and sore. Then, as if to sacrifice herself, Enkida bowed to the lion before passing out, overwhelmed by fear of the pain she expected to follow.

It wasn't a particularly restful sleep, but when she woke again it was not night. It was already warm and bright. She was alive and the only wound she felt was the coyote's bite at her right shoulder. She didn't see or hear the lion.

Still, her limbs and thoughts were overwhelmed by too much fear, too much grief and shock. It had all happened so quickly – her child being taken away, her brother's betrayal, being ousted from her home to face the heat of the desert, and facing the beasts of the night. Now even the morning sun rays made her wince in pain. She just didn't have the energy to fight through another day of the desert again.

She expected the lion to jump from every rock. But when it didn't, she wondered if she'd imagined that beast (as she must have imagined the talking lizard).

Enkida rolled onto her right side. And she watched the sun climb further into the sky before pulling the veil down over her face. Under that veil she smelled sweat from her own overheated body. She even thirstily licked some of her own perspiration. Then she closed her eyes and waited for death in the heat capsule within her shawl.

She didn't wait long. Eyes closed, minutes later she heard the shuffling of feet and a man's voice. "There she is, laying on her side. Looks like something bit her back."

"Is the bitch dead already?"

"I see her veil moving a bit and there's no breeze, so she's breathing." His voice was uncaring.

"But she won't be alive for much longer." A few men laughed.

Enkida knew these soldiers were sent to make sure the desert had finished her (or kill her themselves). Their only task was Maka's recently adopted tradition of having his enemy's bowels cut out. She knew one of these men would have a small-bladed shovel to scoop out her gut (while she was still alive). Her brother would later cook and eat that flesh, thinking this cannibalistic entree gave him her power.

The men's well-made sandals stomped over to her. Seeing she wouldn't resist, they quieted down for their duty and one pair of sandals kicked up sand only inches from her head. She didn't resist at all. Humbled and defeated, she just accepted what was happening.

Enkida heard a metal object pulled from a leather satchel. She knew the sharp shovel digging into her body would hurt before she died, but afterwards there would at least be the relief of the next world.

She waited. In what was probably an accident, before they pierced her abdomen with the shovel-knife, one of the men's knees hit against Enkida's shoulder as he positioned himself to cut into her. Enkida frowned nervously.

Then, just as she thought she felt the tip of the sharp metal-bladed shovel touch the lower end of her navel, what sounded like a mountain of wind blazed above her. Sand rushed over her whole body like there'd been an instant sandstorm. She heard the men gasping or swinging. Completely confused, Enkida pulled the veil down from her face and peered around her. Two of the men were already down and covered with blood. She saw the third getting his face ripped off by the giant lion. Afterwards, the big feline laid down next to her with its deep raspy breath.

She looked into its massive eyes. The lion's paws were covered with blood. In the daylight, the lion's eyes were greenish-yellow. She thought they even looked sad, remorseful about what it had just done. The cat wasn't actually purple. What she saw as purple the night before was a trick of the moonlight. The beast was a light brown similar to the color of the sea of sand all around them. Still, the beast was even larger than she had thought. Like the night before, the lion gently brushed up against her.

She didn't yell and swing this time. She asked, "What do you want?" The lion didn't answer. Like the night before, the lion gently brushed up against her. She looked around at the three dead soldiers, their noses, eyes and mouths scraped bloodily from their heads, streaming claw marks bleeding down each of their chests. She looked back at the lion, unsure of what was next.

She didn't yell and swing this time. She asked, "What do you want?"

The lion didn't answer. It was getting hotter but she noticed that her would-be assassins had brought a ridiculously generous supply for their murderous hunting expedition into the desert. They had expected a hunting trip more than being mauled to death by this panther. She grabbed a satchel of their water and drank it freely. She grabbed some pomegranates and pistachios, olives and salted fish from their supply. She cried gratefully for the nourishment, stuffing it into her mouth. She felt mischievous, like she cheated death.

Enkida found a set of sticks and a thick cloth which were meant to be used as a tent. From those she made shade from the sun. She set it up and even welcomed the lion to join her under the makeshift tent. The lion curled up next to her like a house cat.

I will find an army and return to save my son. She wanted to go directly back to her son but could not imagine how that could end well. So, with this unexpected stash of good supplies and a surprisingly powerful friend at her side, she schemed her next steps for surviving the desert banishment before her.

Nariah

Many weeks later at the sea of Galilee, a lake near Tiberias, Judea. Tiberias was an unofficial outpost of the Roman Empire. It was a day's walk from the town of Nazareth.

As she headed East, Enkida wasn't sure if the lake was another mirage like so many she had seen during her long walk across countless sandy deserts. Then she got to the water's edge, took her sandals off, and dipped her toes in the glistening clear water. Yes, it was genuine water. The water wrapped its cool sweetness around Enkida's strong feet. Then she slipped her leather dress off and dipped her legs, her belly, her breasts, then her whole body in. Not knowing how to swim, she didn't go far, but she squirmed in delight.

The lion followed her, radiating a soft purring sound. It, too, was grateful for relief from the countless hours of heat that had been on their path through the days and weeks across the deserts to the east. Enkida splashed the cat like a child playing with her pet and the lion's eyes seemed to smile, but he mostly ignored her, swimming a short distance out into the lake, deeper into the refuge of the water's embrace.

As she sat with the lower half of her body in the water, Enkida felt ecstatic. She watched the glittering light of the sun on the lake's surface, thinking *water is a miracle.* Having been raised in the desert, this large body of water invoked awe and even a little fear in Enkida. She let this fear wash off as she soaked her body in the cool water. And she looked around at the landscape around this lake, rolling green hills with a few orchards of young olive trees.

As she sat there in the water, she saw a lot of movement across the lake. She couldn't tell for sure, but it seemed to be hundreds of people gathering for some reason. Looking there, she felt the hairs on the back of her neck bristle, apparently something special was happening in that place. It even drew her there. She got out of the water, put her clothes back on, and led the lion along the coastline toward the gathering.

Along her way to the gathering, it was mostly just sand, but she passed some huts made of little more than twigs and palm leaves. Near one small hut, she saw a fisherman who'd recently pulled in his humble boat and unloaded his fish. Speaking some Greek she learned as a child, she asked, "What is going on at the hill over there? So many people. Are they preparing for war?" Enkida thought maybe she would find her army there.

The fisherman saw Enkida and the lion at her side. He grew pale. Then he stumbled over the fish he had just unloaded, landing on his behind before running to push his boat hastily back out into the waters.

Enkida had not meant to scare him, but she laughed at the fisherman's cowardice. She had spent many months coursing through the barren sands of the desert with only the lion as an ally. Unless someone meant her harm, it now seemed outrageous for anyone to fear her cat.

Enkida turned to her friend, the lion, "I guess the fisherman has offered you a dinner."

The cat understood, his powerful shoulders rolling almost like wheels as he sauntered down to the pile of fish on the sandy coastline. He ate dozens of them. It seemed like the lion was laughing, even enjoying that his status as a terrifying beast garnered the reward of such a good feast.

As she waited for her feasting feline ally, Enkida's eyes were again drawn to the gathering across the lake. She had always been pulled to people and places that were full of what people in Uruk called Tash – which translates loosely as spirit power. The people with abundant Tash were often shamans, the readers of stars, or knowers of hidden knowledge. The places with Tash were the temples, mountain summits, and burial places of holy men and women. What Enkida sensed across this lake radiated more Tash than any person or place she'd sensed before.

After the big cat had his fill, Enkida climbed on her lion, and was carried towards the meeting place full of Tash. She did not ride the cat all the way to the gathering. Next to a stream flowing into the lake, Enkida got off the cat and whispered, "go into the hills while I see what is happening on this hill. You're a big cat and will most likely not be safe there. They will feel too threatened by you. Find me later." The cat looked grieved, but slowly turned around before dashing up into the hills and leaving her behind alone (for the first time in many days).

Enkida sent the cat away for its safety. The commotion of a large cat might understandably provoke unnecessary defenses. She knew mobs were stupid and impulsively violent when intoxicated with fear.

So Enkida walked for a while along the lake's coastline in solitude. Eventually, Enkida saw four men and two women heading in the same direction. These men and women all had bows and arrows, were strong and muscular, and had lighter skin than most people Enkida had known. Hoping they might help her blend in, as being a foreigner rarely worked instantly to one's advantage, she slipped in among them inquiring, "Is this the way?"

"You mean to Capernaum, to see him?" one of these archers responded.

Enkida nodded, "Yes, to Capernaum."

"Then this is the way. Come with us," they encouraged, curiously eyeing Enkida and the mess of dreadlocks on her head. The group was quiet and walked carefully, as if they'd learned to expect battle at every turn. They climbed up and down hills without even a comment. This little band seemed more delicate than their stout muscles and large bows might suggest.

Then, after climbing to the last tall peak, Enkida saw the meadow and the many people gathered there. Their focal point was clearly a seated unarmed man wearing a simple tan robe. The man was sitting quietly and somberly, apparently unaffected by those gathered around him. As Enkida approached, he closed his eyes and seemed to disappear deep into his soul.

The rest of the crowd excitedly talked among themselves; they expressed anticipation for all sorts of things. Enkida heard some exalt the man as a political leader, "He will lead the nation to a revolution," while others suggested, "he isa prophet for our time." And a few declared, "He is a heretic. We will prove it soon and be done with him."

Among them all there was a visceral roaring silence, a presence that filled Enkida. The force of this presence was like a vortex, a confidence that everything Enkida knew could completely shift.

Enkida connected this intensity with being physically close to this shaman at the center of it all. She wanted to ask, "Who is this man? Is he a great healer? Is he a god-king leading you all to battle? Will he turn you all against me if it's learned I'm a foreigner? What is it you all expect from him? How does he radiate such vastness?"

Still, she sat very quietly, peering at those who had gathered, waiting with open ears.

She overheard more conversations. "Even more than John the Baptist, he is making Rome nervous." "Is it true he studied with the Essenes and with the holy men in the lands to the East?" "Is he earning money doing all this? Is he still a carpenter?" "He healed my brother, and so many others.." It was clear to Enkida this man was the center of many controversies, questions, and wonders.

Then this man opened his eyes, stood up and spoke, his voice calm but immensely strong, "You who have ears, listen to what I have to say. But even more than listening to the words, if God's Will permits, may you discover that which is in between my words for, it is there that you might find actual wisdom. And, just as a carpenter etches words upon his woodwork at times, may this wisdom be etched upon your hearts."

As he spoke the crowd was quiet. Enkida felt an indescribable buzzing. The man was, without question, radiant. His eyes poured something of himself out in all directions. Though she was in the back of this crowd, it seemed he was directly in front of her. She tingled at the base of her spine. Her muscles, still lazy from the cool waters she'd bathed in, became even heavier. This man told a story about a plant that didn't realize it had roots, "How overjoyed the plant was upon finding this hidden part of itself..."

Enkida lost interest in the words and felt what seemed like gentle hands pull her eyelids down over her eyes. She contentedly fell into a deep trance dream.

In this state, Enkida had something of a vision – her brother, Maka, stood before her with his protruding belly and bald shaved head. She wanted to kill him, to rip him apart like she was the lion she'd traveled so far with. Then a cool wind blew in through her fury and she saw what a broken man her brother was. Enkida saw their father beating her brother until he was covered in purple bruises and almost dead. She saw her brother being instructed by cold overbearing priests to take power at any cost. She saw a mysterious beautiful woman telling her brother she would love him only if he managed to take control of the kingdom all for himself. Enkida felt empathy and, in empathy's warmth, her hatred struggled to remain intact.

As the memories of her brother thinned out into an echo, she saw other images that invoked hatred inside her. She saw the faces of those whom she'd considered friends but had allied with her brother over the years – a General Twan, her cousin Lars, and even one of her servants. The same thing happened with them – she could see into their pain, their hidden shame and wounds she never fully knew. She saw how life had crushed them and made them traitorous, hungry for power and privilege. Her yearning for revenge thinned out.

And then Enkida felt a warm sweetness wash through her unceasing worry for her son,a trust that he would be well. It was like a seed rippling out through an ocean within her, leaving her with a knowing that her beloved son would thrive, that he would grow strong and wise and learn the truth of why she left the kingdom of Uruk. Then she saw the mild-mannered man from the meadow directly before her in this vision.

"I promise your son will be taken care of," the man gently assured her.

The intensity of the sight and the strength of this being's words seemed more lucid than waking reality.

Still, she pushed back against the vision, "You are tricking me, trying to seduce me with this magic so that I will follow you. You want me to be your slave."

"I do not want a slave. I am here only to help you move forward."

"Move forward! I wish I could be thrown far into the future, to a time when this disgraced life of mine is long forgotten…"

The image of the calm man before her smiled with unconditional love and light and then faded away. Then Enkida woke up back in the meadow next to the lake. But it was many hours later and there was no man at the bottom of the meadow, no big crowd huddled eagerly, and no sunlight.

In the darkness of a crescent moon, all Enkida could see was the outline of the hills where so many people had been sitting when she arrived at that meadow. She heard frogs at the sea of galilee and a wind rustling. She listened a little more and heard someone snoring, on the hill not far from her.

Scared by the magic she just experienced, Enkida wanted to find her cat and get away from here. She pulled herself up and started the trek back to where she had parted with her lion. She hoped the lion would return to that place during the night. She was shaky, and even her hands were clammy.

Enkida had studied healing with all the medicine men and women of the kingdom where she had lived most of her life. She'd witnessed magic over weather and the elements and other hidden forces. Still, she had never experienced anything close to the vision she had just been immersed in. The experience had touched her depths.

She walked up over the hill. She walked back to where she left her cat but it was not there. This scared her. The lion had been her companion but also her primary protection for the hundreds of miles it took for her to get across the desert. Before arriving at this lake, the lion had been an ally through dozens of desert towns. Without the lion's protection, she might have been raped, killed, enslaved, or given up to despair.

Having been raised as a monarch, Enkida was well educated and knew four languages – that of her native Uruk as well as Greek, Persian, and Safaitic. These languages all proved useful along the way west, but not one of these tongues was so useful as the cat friend she could no longer find.

She'd had no intention of ever giving up on her journey. She intended to go west until she found an army or she made it to the end of the horizon and faced the goddess Ishtar herself. But she didn't want to go on alone. Instead of the lion coming to her side, Enkida heard a bubbly female voice yelling, "Wait, wait! Please!"

Enkida turned around and stood on guard. A plump woman came heaving and running as fast as she could toward Enkida.

"What is it? Who are you? What do you want?" Enkida yelled aggressively at this woman who seemed to chase her.

The plump woman tripped over herself some distance from Enkida. She clumsily picked herself back up, laughing hard and finishing the final sprint to Enkida. As she caught her breath, she announced, "I am Nariah."

"And?" Enkida countered sharply, not trusting or particularly interested in this jovial buffoon.

"Well, I am a friend of Mary's."

"I don't know who Mary is and don't care if you're her friend!"

"Mary of Magdalene. And while Jesus was speaking," this woman clearly enjoyed talking. "Mary saw you and she said 'that woman is special. That one knows mysteries hidden to most of us.' You were meditating, and looked like you were going very deep. I've gone deep in prayer before. It's very nice, wake up all refreshed and the world looks so nice again," she talked and talked, "anyway, Mary saw you sitting like that even after Jesus left and she asked me to wait on the hill until you woke up. She said you should stay with us tonight, that you've had a rough time recently. This world can be so rough." Nariah started tearing up. "So many people come to Jesus with diseases and problems with money and shame. There's too much suffering…"

"What do you want from me?" Enkida impatiently interrupted.

"Jesus said, 'God is Love and…'"

"I'm not interested in your Jesus. I'm no follower. I am nobody's slave."

Nariah looked hurt, like she was going to break down in tears, then burst out laughing. "Yes, yes. You're sick of men who are hungry for power. I'm glad you said that. So much revenge and most of it is led by men. Hmm… well, women are usually playing some role in these things, too. It's just often behind the scenes. Anyway, I don't think Jesus wants slaves but, anyway Mary told me to invite you to our home. Come eat some nice food, rest safely, and be with us. I offer a refuge."

Enkida had just arrived in this region. Her cat, her protection, was gone and it was late and she was tired and hungry. It sounded wise to take the gift of staying wherever Nariah called her home. Maybe there would be something to learn there or at just some sanctuary from this region's dangers.

"Okay, Nariah," Enkida said, "I will join you. But, please, let us walk in silence from here on."

"Yes!" Nariah exclaimed as she instantly took Enkida's hand in hers and pulled her along. "Jesus is always saying 'Nariah needs to explore silence more.' I know I talk a lot. I'm very excited about all the excitement of this movement. By the way, we're not Essenes exactly. We pray throughout the day together. We eat together. We disagree about what we should and should not eatt. Some of us are very keen on not mixing meat and dairy. Some say no meat at all. Some say it doesn't matter. Some say we have to do really long Hebrew prayers before every meal. Some say those prayers are for the old times. I'll tell you, I like the prayers but…"

She didn't stop talking. She barely gave Enkida a single minute of silence as they walked for a little while longer to Nariah's home. Nariah talked about how her father had been a fisherman but, when she was a young lady, a storm flipped his boat and he drowned in the big lake they walked around, Nariah called this lake, Galilee. After living a life alongside the lake, her poor father still couldn't swim. And neither could Nariah.

Nariah shared that, not long after her father's death, she had to sell her body for sex to pay for things. Nariah was very open and honest about this. "I met Mary, another prostitute. But Mary's life changed completely when we met Jesus. And I was right there with her. I saw a good thing as a good thing. So I no longer sold my body. Instead, I found miracles happening everywhere."

Enkida listened with some irritation to this tale, but, after the long walk, she was grateful to find a solid stone home welcoming her to sleep in.

It was quiet in the home. Everyone was apparently already asleep or away, and Nariah gave her delicious sweet apricots, a tall mug of wine, and some soft fresh bread before leading her up some stone stairs, where she could sleep on the second floor of the home. Left all to herself, Enkida gratefully wrapped herself in a warm sheepskin blanket and sank into a peaceful deep rest.

Kle and the Turning of the Wheel

As the group of eight Greek seamen walked up over the hill, the largest among them, Euty, complained,"There's just a bunch of damned sheep everywhere. There's way too many sheep in this land. I'm hungry for substance, for gold. We should go back to the boat."

They stood on a summit looking over rolling grassy hills with at least a dozen small flocks of gray and white sheep with their unkempt shepherds. Dotted along the hills, there was little more than the sheep, olive trees, and some small makeshift huts. In the distance, the large lake of Galilee had a few small villages around it. The lake was glaring with the bright blaze of the sun so that they had to squint from the sheen of its light as they headed towards it.

Alos added to Euty's complaint, "I don't want any sheepskin. They better have some shapely women who will keep me warm tonight in exchange for a piece of copper or two."

"Always thinking from your cock," Kle teased, much more as an effort to be part of the conversation than to insult. Kle was the runt of this lot. His arms were still sore and legs wobbly from the long days of rowing. He was grateful to be out of their boat and felt excited about what they might find in this new land. Kle loved the thrill of discovery more than the acquisition of wealth.

"At least I'm thinking, Kle. You haven't found us a single worthy thing to trade for on this whole trip," Alos snapped back at Kle, making it clear he wouldn't welcome any playful taunts from Kle.

"Kle traded nearly a bucket of our copper bars for a pile of ground up roots the Assyrian sold him," another man groaned.

"That pile of roots was saffron powder. It's a very valuable spice in many lands," Kle feebly defended himself, remembering how the other Greeks used the saffron power as kindling. They refused to consider that saffron was worth much.

"And then Kle sold a chest of our textiles to pay for the bones of some old corpse," another man complained about Kle.

"They call those bones ivory. And…"

"And I'm sick of how you waste our resources to trade for junk because you don't know how to make a damned deal," Alos spit out.

"Leave him alone," Euty said. Euty's natural authority shut the other men up. Like the others, old Euty was disappointed with Kle. Still, he knew better than shaming anyone in front of the group. Euty only scolded the boy in private. Euty himself had bitter memories of being humiliated. Still, Euty had already privately commanded Kle not to trade any more items without his approval.

Kle knew Euty's command meant he was just along for the ride and to help with rowing, that he'd been demoted to little more than dead weight on this expedition.

"Thank you, Euty," Kle said weakly. The teasing ate him up inside, made him feel like the black sheep among these other more powerful and entrepreneurial men. The fruits of their trade had been jade, swords, poisons, gold, and maps. They were right, he knew far less about the buying and selling of things. He was too enchanted by silly things.

Euty encouraged him, "Now sing us a song to help us keep good cheer until we get down to that town next to the lake."

Kle smiled. He was good at making up lovely lyrics on the spot and using just about anything as an instrument.

As they continued trekking down the hillside, Kle shook off his shame and sang/spoke lyrics about rowing across the sea past serpents and mermaids and whirlpools and Poseidon's army of fish. He stomped his feet and sang more – of arriving at magical islands with tall homes that reached to the clouds, of magic mirrors that reflected visions of one's fantasies.

His lyrics were spontaneous and came from that mysterious portal of creativity only real artists can access. He occasionally tapped his chest to a beat, whistled to an unexpected, but vibrant, melody, and laughed at the spontaneously discovered lyric. Like a fish at home in the sea, Kle was at home in music. And it gave him an escape from the waves of feelings like a failure in this company.

It was a long hot walk, the olive trees giving little shade. The shepherds along the way avoided these muscular Greeks like a plague. So, the five Greeks just pushed on toward the largest town they could see next to the lake, each relishing their own fantasies of women, riches, or discovery hiding there.

Tiberias

Holding a candle. Nariah shook Enkida trying to wake her up. "Come pray with us," Nariah smiled widely.

After Enkida reluctantly peeked her eyes open, she groaned, "What?"

"Mary Magdalene will read us psalms now," Nariah said.

"Psalms?"

"Yes. The poetry of the prophets. Then we will sit quietly."

Nariah exuded a warmth, a mystical contentment even, which Enkida envied. Furthermore, a broken part of Enkida felt a kinship with Nariah's confident vulnerability. Like Nariah, Enkida had been shunned by her community, shut out to fend for herself. While Enkida faced the desolation of the desert, Nariah faced the desolation of being poor and without a father and having to unwillingly become a prostitute to survive… that is, until she shackled herself to devotions toward this sorcerer-man Jesus.

Still, Enkida didn't want to be enlisted in any community as a pawn in some unspoken plan. While the magic of this Jesus had let a deep sweetness wash through some of her wounds, she did not feel compelled to worship him like a mindless slave.

"We are not praying together," Enkida responded dryly. "I am sleeping and will do so until I decide when my day begins. Or, as my host, do you claim to be my master?"

Enkida didn't see Nariah's reaction in the shadows of the candle. And Nariah didn't say anything. She just faded back down the stairs. And Enkida drifted back into her rest.

Later, when the blue-gold light of morning seeped into the stone walls of that room, Enkida woke up irritated with thoughts of Nariah's jolly servility. On top of that, she had grown quite used to living outside of any community's limitations; she valued the freedom of not being obligated to any tribal customs or persons or even any place. She wouldn't be coerced into some religious practice that was not her own.

Because of all this, Enkida decided to leave. She picked her few things up and slipped down the stone stairs and out of the house. She caught one quick glance of more than a dozen men and women seated around the woman who was obviously Nariah's Mary Magdalene. Mary Magdalene was almost painfully beautiful, not just in terms of her appearance, but she had an inner glow that seemed to burn all the way through Enkida's core.

Enkida snuck out of the home and headed toward what looked like the largest town around the lake. It was not a long walk. When she arrived, Enkida heard people call this town Tiberias and she understood this was where fisherman from all around the lake went to sell their catch.

Tiberias was where all local commerce took place. It was where one could buy carefully painted ceramic pottery depicting Roman gods (great for Roman soldiers stationed in the region). It was where the bathhouses with healing waters were (again, Roman soldiers love it!). Tiberias also housed the only elegant inn of the region, four synagogues, a temple to the god Dionysus, and a well inhabited cave system where people had lived for thousands of years. And, for restless Roman soldiers stationed at that lake, local ladies of the night (as Mary and Nariah had been) were found in Tiberias. While only a few thousand people lived there, it was the closest thing to a metropolis for the northern Judean peoples.

That morning, in the marketplace of Tiberias, Enkida had no money to buy dolmas, olives, apples, fish or sabra fruits strewn across the market. People pushed by her to barter for the lowest price on these items. In the hustle and bustle, Enkida was quick of hand. Enkida swiped a gracious helping of grilled lamb and juicy fruits and fresh bread and salty olives and carried it all down to the lake. There she ate patiently, savoring her meal, feeling like royalty again.

Having lived so much of her life in the most arid of deserts, this lake seemed to her as impossibly beautiful as liquid gold. It blazed with the light of the sun. She watched fishermen push across the lake in their small boats. She saw countless birds flying over the waters. "This lake is like a mother, nourishing all who come to it," she heard herself say. And mentioning the word mother made her think of her son and her stomach hurt, wanting to see him again.

Sitting there, belly full, she suddenly remembered the power object she'd swiped when she was thrown from her kingdom. She took out the pouch with the talisman in it. It had been given to her and the chant taught to her by a magician whose life she saved. She remembered how the magician had been caught in the pleasure garden of her brother's harem.

Her brother would not have hesitated to take the man's head. Being the lone monarch while her brother was away, Enkida had to make the decision of what to do with this nuisance. As the sole authority, she commanded the soldiers there to hold off on executing anyone until she found out more.

"Who are you?" she questioned the trespasser.

The foreigner claimed, "I have lost my way and stumbled here."

Enkida suspected the man was having a forbidden affair with one of his brother's concubines. "Why were you in the pleasure garden of my brother's women?"

"I am a healer," he replied. "And one of these women got a message to me because she was sick and not being cared for."

"Sick? How?" Enkida asked.

"Sick with grief."

"Sick with grief? What do you mean? Why did you not get my brother's permission?"

"Your brother told this woman who called on me that he would never trust another man in his harem's garden with his fruits. She said she's sick of being one of his neglected fruits; that she is fading from lack of love. She went to great lengths to get a healer here."

"Hmm," Enkida actually felt sympathy for such a woman. And it seemed like this man was telling the truth.

"Where are you from and what is your name?" Enkida continued interrogating him...

"I am Surya from Kakamuchee, far to the east of here, from where the river Ganges meets the great Himalayas."

"What gods do you worship?"

"I know God in all things but Hanuman, the monkey god, keeps special watch over me and what I do."

"Monkey god?" Enkida didn't know what a monkey was. This Surya did not respond to her question.

"What will you do with me," Surya asked.

"Leave and never return, even if every fruit in my brother's harem pleads for you with open legs."

"You saved my life," this man looked relieved. "Can I give you anything, merciful queen?"

Enkida replied, "Do you have anything with magical value?"

Surya shared a little about a healing magic called Ayurveda. He told her about the "doshas," the humors of the body, and the "gunas," the subtle qualities of the mind, and "ojas," the reserve of energy that keeps us from getting sick.

Enkida listened attentively but encouraged her captor to share something more dramatic, suspecting he was a magician in addition to a healer.

"Do you know any incantations?" she asked.

"I am a simple man. I heal and I practice wisdom as best I can."

"Yes," she said a bit dismissively. "Perhaps I should hold you in our dungeon until my brother returns, or is there something for me that you don't share?"

The man said, "There is one thing. But it cannot be easily controlled. It is a wild magic."

"Tell me." Enkida's voice sounded hungry, less kind than before.

He took out a talisman with dots on it, "with the right incantation, this can shift seasons and places, throwing open portals and hurling destinies around in response to your fear and desire."

"Throwing open portals?"

"Our fears and desires are magnified and create connections that transcend space and time."

"Tell me more."

"This magic is very dangerous," the man warned. "It's like a dragon once awakened."

"I do not fear dragons," Enkida boasted, straightening her back with pridew. "Why should I fear?"

"Half-knowledge is a burden," Surya warned again.

"And you would be more than half-dead right now if not for me."

"Okay," Surya agreed. "But, again, if you wield this without sufficient mastery, which is almost certainly the case, everything you love may be thrown around. And there are nine openings in this magic, one for each of the souls who the magic wraps around. That is, after it is invoked…"

Enkida spaced out. She didn't understand a lot of what this man said, going on about "the constellations' influences," dimensions, portals and the nine soul shifting stones.

"Please just tell me how to use it," Enkida politely demanded.

"The stars of the moment and your thoughts mix like a potion in this mantra…drawing you closer to those with whom you are strongly connected, whether through love or hatred."

After a while, the man took a piece of what looked like yellowish copper with nine small dots imprinted on it. And he let Enkida take it from him. "You have to be touching this ancient stone somewhere on your body. Then keep your mind as clear as you can. And chant the mantra."

"What is this gem?"

"I am not sure," Surya admitted, without trying to take the gem back.

"Teach me the mantra."

"It is a mantra that awakens the dragon…" his voice got increasingly dramatic.

"TELL ME!" Enkida rolled her eyes, now impatient.

"Please remember, I have warned you."

"Yes, I've heard your warnings."

Surya looked toward the ground as if in shame. But then he recited a long mantra while Enkida's sharp mind listened to each sound and inflection of it.

Enkida shook herself from that memory. She'd never repeated the mantra. But now, looking at the lake, she decided it was time to try the magic she had cajoled from that healer-intruder-foreigner. She would "awaken the dragon." Without her lion friend, she saw no other option, knew no other path that might reunite her and her son through the vast distances and obstacles that separated them. She wasn't afraid of having everything thrown around. Her life was already wrecked.

After the band of Greek sailors made their way to the town by the lake, the Kle was completely shut out of helping to make deals. While the other men had some stock of swords or silks or copper to trade, Kle was told not to even be around them as they put together their deals. Euty was the only one to show Kle sympathy, encouraging him to, "go earn a few coins by making music at the market."

Alos sarcastically whispered to the others, "In two thousand years, Kle will have earned enough coins to justify letting him row across the sea with us again." Interestingly, he was correct. But we'll get to that.

The other sailors said no more to Kle as they excitedly hunted out opportunities for a worthy deal.

Feeling disgraced and unimportant, Kle walked through the village alone. He felt bleak but, as they suggested, Kle called up his musical talents to find some relief. He found some pieces of driftwood on the lakeshore to turn into drums. He took out his penny flute. And he sat himself down at a busy corner of the outdoor market to make music. He was between a man selling carved wooden bowls and another selling dried meats.

And Kle began. No one, even the vile Greeks he traveled with, could trivialize Kle's talent with music. The moment he found a rhythm with his makeshift driftwood drum, he fell into a trancelike state. He closed his eyes, and sang a spontaneous tale, this one about ceaselessly traveling and having no home to return to. He sang about estrangement and isolation. He transformed the small pieces of driftwood into a percussive perfection. And he transformed his pain into beautiful lyrics and lovely melodies on his penny flute.

He sang about being on a ship and then getting thrown off that boat to drown. He sang about a star that was blasted out of the night sky by a jealous moon. He sang again about alienation. And he sang about it beautifully.

After Nariah saw Enkida leave early that morning without saying a single thing to her, Nariah was upset. She knew that Jesus preached about forgiveness and turning the other cheek and not judging others, but she was angry and determined to tell this inconsiderate woman just how inconsiderate she'd been. *She could have just said bye!*

Nariah rushed outside and followed her hunch that Enkida went to Tiberias. All the while, she was steaming out loud to herself, "How can we bring God's love to the world when there's such viciousness out there," and "I am going to spit on her face. Well, maybe I can't do that. No. Jesus would be very disappointed in me. But Jesus turned the temple upside down when they were using it like a market to sell their crap. Maybe I need to turn this woman upside down. Yes, I will spit on her. No. Maybe I won't."

She talked to herself all the way to town until she arrived at the market and saw this beautiful man reciting verse and tapping rhythmically on some driftwood. The poetry she heard was about not fitting in, about being different, about wanting to have a place to call home.

She sat and listened and cried. Not only was his music divine, but she drooled admiring his exotic long blond hair, his strong physique, and his sharp pointed eyes. She wanted to wrap herself around him and disappear. Then, she got an idea: I will convert this foreigner and then become his wife. Maybe I could even preach Jesus's message in whatever kingdom this man came from.

After listening to three of his songs, Nariah built herself up enough courage to approach the man, "welcome, friend, what blessed music comes from your lips."

"Thank you, kind woman. Do you have a coin to spare?"

"I do not presently, but I have something worth far more than any coins."

Kle's eyes lit up. "And what is that?"

"Oh," she said, as excitedly as ever. "Come with me and you will know. You will know so much!" She intended to bring the man directly to Jesus. And if Jesus had slipped away to preach in some other place, she intended to make the man wait with her until they fell in love.

"I agree to see whatever you have if it is worth more than gold!"

Kle needed no further encouragement. This kind lady said she knew of something worth more than gold. Kle picked up his penny flute and followed this woman, leaving the driftwood quietly behind. He didn't earn a single coin but he was being led to something she had said was worth much more!

"Oh, my friend, your music is majestic, intoxicating," Nariah offered more praise.

Then, as they left the market, Nariah spotted the woman who had initially drawn her out that day. Enkida was sitting on the shore, her long dreadlocks uncovered like snakes of a demon woman.

"Are you okay, lady?" Kle asked Nariah.

"That woman took something valuable from me," Nariah replied pointing at Enkida sitting on the shore. "I intend to tell her, uh, to give it back." Nariah didn't know how to explain much more clearly without making herself look petty, but she hurried over toward Enkida.

Kle lit up again at the word valuable. He thought maybe the valued item ("worth more than gold") might have been taken by the dark-skinned woman with dreadlocks. A lot was unclear.

Anyway, Kle planned to get back whatever it was that had been taken from his new friend. And maybe he could convince Euty to trade something for it. *Worth more than gold! The other sailors would finally recognize my value,* Kle thought.

Nariah ran towards Enkida and Kle excitedly followed her. As they got closer to Enkida, they could see the strange woman was talking to herself. Kle saw a small gem thing held up in Enkida's right hand. It had nine stones inlaid upon it. Kle knew this must be it. He needed to see it more closely. He reached out for it.

Nariah was so worked up she could barely see straight. She called out, "Enkida! Enkida!" But Enkida did nothing and continued talking to herself. Nariah was not sure exactly what she should say to Enkida. Then Nariah felt a rush of guilt for having been so angry. She wanted to simply ask Enkida why she had left like that. She reached out for Enkida's hand. An orange-haze seemed to be encapsulating Enkida, but Nariah assumed it was some trick of the sun's light. Nariah reached her hand out and then stumbled.

Kle, feverishly trailing Nariah, didn't notice she had tripped and he, too, fell forwards onto Enkida.

Enkida had just finished the mantra when all three of them managed to be touching that strange copper thing at the same time. "Have I… has my incantation worked?" Enkida whispered, barely audibly.

For Nariah of Galilee, Enkida of Uruk, and Kle of Athens, everything suddenly imploded. They were suspended in space. Nariah noticed even her breath was caught, not allowing her to talk. And then a hole opened up underneath them and they fell- not up or down but there was suddenly no ground and no sky. More than a fall, it was like a feather drifting steadily along on a windless day... Then they collapsed upwards into a space thicker than matter.... And all this was accompanied by high pitched sounds of laughter, slow rolling rumblings of thunder, quick running of many feet, a disturbing chewing sound, and a final stormy wind. In the strange moment that followed nothing could be smelled, felt or anything. That moment stretched and stretched until it snapped!

Then there was a release like the letting go of the arrow by a bow. And they all fell into another world.

Falling

Nariah crashed face first into water. It was cold salty water and she took a big gulp of it. She didn't know how to swim but she knew water and her arms thrashed about, wildly reaching for something.

Calling up all her strength, Nariah managed to pull her head above the water long enough to inhale a gulp of air. Then she was underwater again. She wondered: "Did God make another flood but this time He was so fed up with us it happened in an instant?"

Nariah gasped for another breath, but it was getting harder to propel herself up. She felt heavier, her arms flailing more slowly. She didn't think she could pull herself up from the cold water to breathe again but then powerful arms as strong as stone dug under her armpits. Then these arms lifted Nariah's hefty weight into the air. She gasped, filling her lungs with fresh air. Then this set of powerful arms pulled her along through the water, heaving from the strain of this effort. Nariah's spirit soared high seeing a head of blond curly hair next to her. She knew who that was. Save me, save me, she thought, quite turned on.

A coastline appeared, not more than a few hundred strokes away. "Swim!" she shouted in her delirium. "There is land! Do you see it?"

Kle expended no energy on speech; his task was only to bring himself and this boisterous woman to safety.

As he and Nariah approached the shore and began walking upon the wet sand, there were strange sounds echoing around them. As they got closer, it became clear that these were not simply sounds, but a choir of heavenly voices. At a hundred foot's distance, the words this choir sang became audible: "When I find myself in times of trouble, mother Mary comes to me…" And Nariah, thinking of Jesus's mother Mary, knew this was somehow God's plan. Sluggish and feeble, disoriented to the maximum, Nariah and Kle emerged from the water.

It was then that Kle finally gave into his immeasurable fatigue; in the shin-deep water and, with Nariah's arm still clutching his shoulder, the hero collapsed in pure exhaustion. Nariah fell next to him, wrapping her arms around her rescuer, shedding tears in relief.

As they lay there, it was clear there were not only voices but an orchestra of countless stringed instruments. Stumbling a few steps before falling to her knees, Nariah puked up a steady stream of salty water. Then she looked around and asked the man who delivered her from the wrath of the sea, "What has happened? Are we in heaven?"

"I don't think we're in heaven," the Greek stallion replied angrily. "But I thought you were going to tell me what's happened to us."

She turned away from him and headed toward the music. The words were in a language she'd never heard before but, somehow, she understood it. Just a short walk away from the water, hundreds of people were sitting together in a circle. Dozens of them played small stringed instruments, ukuleles. Most of the people wore strange multi-colored clothes – tie dies. And everybody sang along. Finding herself speaking this same language, Nariah asked a very large man who dwarfed the instrument he held.

"Is this the rapture?"

"Yes, my dear! It's the rapture," the man laughed.

"We're the Santa Cruz Ukulele Club," an older lady explained to Nariah.

Kle grabbed Nariah's arm and insisted, "Tell me where this thing worth more than coins you talked about is."

"I meant Jesus, my spiritual teacher! But I don't know where Jesus is now," she replied.

"You leave her alone, boy," the large man who'd been playing a ukulele hollered at Kle.

Kle ignored the large man and roared furiously at Nariah "What do you mean, spiritual teacher? That's what was so valuable?"

A few ukuleles stopped.

"Jesus is a teacher and his wisdom is worth more than all the gold of the world," Nariah whimpered timidly to Kle. "I was taking you to him."

"You tricked me," Kle grabbed Nariah by the shoulders and shook her angrily.

Every ukulele stopped. At least thirty older men quickly stood up and pushed themselves between Nariah and Kle.

The most wrinkled and ancient of these men fearlessly announced, "We have already called the cops, young man. You are a disgrace shaking a woman like that. Don't try it again around us or you'll find out we're not as old as we look, you'll get your ass whooped."

Wherever he was, however he got there, or whoever these people were, Kle was confused and even intimidated by this mob in strange clothes, wielding ukuleles. Kle didn't challenge their authority or wait for the arrival of whoever the cops were. With adrenaline rushing through his system, he turned away from the Santa Cruz Ukulele Club and ran as fast as he could away from the beach and all of them.

Particularly because they were singing right next to the ocean, Kle thought this big group of people could bedevotees of Poseidon. He knew Poseidon held a grudge against his family line – Kle was descended from a man named Odysseus. Through the stories of family's lore, Kle knew that Odysseus killed the son of Poseidon, a cyclops by the name of Polyphemus. This barrage of Poseidon's folk, Kle guessed, was some unfortunate delayed retribution against his family line. So he ran as fast as he could, knowing the task at hand was evading the vengeance of a long grieving god.

"You okay, honey?" an old woman rolled toward Nariah in a chair with wheels.

"Yes. Thank you."

"Was that your husband?" the woman in a wheelchair asked.

"No. I just met him."

"I'm sure," the woman replied skeptically. "You don't need to protect him. You don't deserve a schmuck like that. Do you have a safe place to stay?"

"I don't even know where I am."

"Well, there's the Crow's Nest and the harbor," the woman pointed to her right. "And East Cliff is that way," she pointed to her left. "How did you get here?"

"I fell through a hole and dropped through the sky into this ocean," Nariah told her.

"She's on some drug," someone whispered.

"Sounds like acid," another speculated.

"Whatever it is, we probably all did it thirty years ago," she said to general laughter.

"Let's get back to the music," another encouraged and, suddenly, Nariah was not the center of attention.

"How about some Grateful Dead?" the large man suggested, mentioning LSD apparently kindled some memories. Right away ukuleles were strumming away and the legion of voices rejoined to the lyrics, "I lit up from Reno, I was trailed by twenty hounds, didn't get to sleep that night till the morning came around, I set out running but I'll take my time, a friend of the devil is a friend of mine."

Nariah heard the words about these people being a "friend of the devil" and knew she, too, had to get away from them. Not wholly unlike Kle, she too dashed away.

Nariah didn't know many of those people had been deadheads in the 70s, that "Friend of the Devil" was a Grateful Dead song, that many of them were, or had been, "Jesus Freaks." She just did her best to get away. As she headed off, it started drizzling and she found she was in a place unlike any she'd seen before. Large gray boxes were everywhere. Nariah could see through holes in these boxes that people were hiding in many of them. It became evident to her that most of them were homes, some were shops, and other, smaller, shiny boxes zoomed along as carriages (but without horse, donkey, or camel!)

While Nariah wore clothes dramatically dissimilar to anybody here, nobody minded her, nobody harassed her for being a foreigner, and one group of people passing by even commented, "cool clothes." Unnerved that the first people she met here were "friends of the devil," she didn't talk to anyone else. She walked through the day until she was drenched and it was dark and cold and she could walk no longer.

Then she lay down outside one of the largest box-homes. It had soft grass and a fence that protected her from the wind. But, most importantly, the large overhanging roof of this box protected her from the rain, even though she was technically still outside. She was tired. She smiled at a lady on the other side of the window-hole peering at her from this particular box. And she lay down on their lawn.

Before five minutes had passed, the palest scrawniest man Nariah had ever seen emerged through a door of the box-house. This man was wearing small rounded sticks around his eyes and asked a bit aggressively "What are you doing in our yard, lady?"

"Sleeping. Thank you, sir," Nariah shared innocently.

"You can't sleep here," he asserted. Nariah suspected this emaciated man was concerned about her, that wolves or some other vicious animal came out at night and would threaten her, even eat her, then.

"I have no option," she confessed. "No matter what dangers are here, sleep is overtaking me and I must rest."

"I'll take you to a place where you can safely sleep," the man said confused.

"That would be so kind of you. You are a blessing from the heavens," Nariah exalted. "Take me to this refuge."

Within a few minutes, Nariah found herself following this man to sit inside one of those moving boxes and then speechlessly fly down the dry black river roads that criss-crossed everywhere. She held so tightly to the car so that her knuckles turned white. Thinking she was a lazy homeless person, the man driving asked her, "Have you ever even had a job?"

"My father never taught me to fish, but I used to be a prostitute," Nariah replied plainly.

This man suddenly felt very humbled and remorseful for having judged her as worthless. He wondered what a hard life she had endured. They drove the rest of the way in silence. After arriving, he said, "Take this. You deserve it."

He pulled out all the cash that had been in his wallet and put it into her hands. He did not make a big show of his generosity. He just gave ninety dollars to her and sped away again.

Enkida realized that something in the magic had gotten twisted. Instead of only the power of her thought-force infusing the gem, there were two other fingers there. That meant two other thought-forces fused into the orange hazy light of the magic she was conjuring.

She'd done everything perfectly – focused her mind's power towards her son while completing the chant with the copper in her left hand the whole time. Then the two other fingers appeared and she knew the portal was influenced by forces she had not intended.

Still, she dropped into the eternal realm where she heard the thousands of tiny feet, the wind, and was then released. Instead of the daunting high walls around the ziggurats of what had been her kingdom in Ur, instead of the precious Euphrates River, instead of stepping forward to confront Efaau and find her son, she found herself standing high in the branches of a supernaturally tall tree. She knew this was no dream and instantly steadied herself as well as she could. She grabbed the branches around her but dropped the talisman as she did so. She watched despairingly as the talisman disappeared hundreds of feet beneath her to where she could not see.

"Oh goddess Ishtar, why?" she cried. In response,it started to rain.Enkida took a break from pleading to her Ishtar. She just flung her legs and then her arms as carefully as she could, climbing down the massive redwood tree. At least to Enkida, the strange massive tree seemed to have a heartbeat. She started to see the ground below her. "You have a special magic," she told the tree when she was halfway down. "Did you pull me here?"

And the tree responded! "I didn't pull you here but how was the view at the top?" The tree spoke, shocking Enkida. She knew some animals could talk but a tree? She'd never heard of such a thing! And, how odd that it would ask her how the "view at the top" was. So exceedingly shocked, Enkida almost slipped the next seventy feet down.

"You okay? I didn't mean to surprise you."

Behind Enkida, on a nearby branch, was a young man. He had hair like hers, hair that rulers, priests and priestesses in Ur often donned – tightly coiled dreadlocks. He wore brown leather pants and a jacket made of a material she'd never seen (nylon). And, like her, he had his arms locked tightly to the branches.

"Oh, good priest, did you come through the portal too?" Enkida asked.

"You mean did I get here from Summit road?"

"No," Enkida was unsure. "Where do you come from?"

"Uh, UCSC. But I parked just off Branciforte Road before walking here."

"UCSC?" she asked, completely unclear what he was talking about…

"Ya. I'm a History of Consciousness major."

Realizing this young man spoke in riddles or did not understand her, she asked something more functional, "I don't know what you mean by saying you're a 'history of consciousness major.' I do not know your religion. But do you have food?" After doing such a powerful magical incantation, she was starving.

"At the place where I live, there's plenty of food. It's kind of a co-op. But I'm not going there for two days."

"You will not go to your co-op for two days?" Enkida repeated some of what the boy said in a question. Enkida guessed this co-op might be a place where priests and priestesses were trained to sacrifice animals to the gods. She didn't believe in animal sacrifice but, having learned from so many different medicine men and women over the years, she had developed an inner-tolerance for other paths. She considered herself open-minded. "I am Enkida. I am from Uruk. I was once a ruler there."

The young man smiled awkwardly. "My name is Santiago."

"San-ti-ago," she sounded it out carefully, trying to figure out why he mentioned the whole history of consciousness major at first.

Thinking she was asking about his name, he added

"Ya. My family's from Argentina."

"Again, why can you not take me to your co-op now, Santiago from Argentina? I am hungry."

He responded proudly, "I can give you some Turkey Jerky, apple juice, and granola right now but I'm staying here for two days. You see, like Julia Butterfly Hill, I'm staying in this tree to protect it from the school's loggers. They're supposed to take it down this week. If you want to stay with me here for two days, afterwards I'll make you a great feast with the rest of my tribe at the co-op. At night time we can sleep in my tent at the bottom of the tree."

"Yes, I will wait here, stay in your tent at night, and then go with you to the co-op and eat with your tribe. I hope they are peaceful and do not eat the flesh of live animals or other humans," she said.

Dreadlocked Santiago laughed, appreciating what he thought was a joke. "I don't think the flesh of live animals or other humans is on the menu today. Is that common in Uruk?"

"No. But to the south of Uruk it is."

"You know I've never heard of Uruk," Santiago said. This Enkdia didn't have an accent he could pin down exactly. No matter where she was from, she was not wearing a bra and from his vantage more than a bit of her breasts was currently being exposed to him. She could've said just about anything right then and he'd have remained quite content.

"And I've never heard of Argentina."

Every moment he grew more enamored with this muscular dreadlocked woman who seemed to come from nowhere. He hadn't expected to meet someone climbing down a tree he was climbing up. He liked that she had so much wit and so few undergarments.

She stayed with him for two days. She ate a lot of his beef jerky. At night she did sleep in the tent with him but she showed no eagerness to get into his sleeping bag and he grew increasingly intimidated by her, so they kept their physical distance.

After two days, they climbed down the rest of the tree together, increasingly careful of their footholds because the constant rain made it more and more slippery. Enkida had never been in a place so wet and with such awe-inspiring trees. In the daze of arriving in this place and meeting Santiago, she completely forgot about the small significant gem that had dropped from her after first arriving. Greatly curious about what his co-op was like, Enkida followed the boy she met in the tree to his tribe's co-op..

Kle kept looking behind him, but none of the people with ukuleles had kept on his track. In relief, he slowed himself to a walk continuing along one of the black dry streams that criss-crossed this whole land. Every once in a while one of the small horseless carriages raced along by him as fast and loud as Zeus's lightning. Calming himself down, Kle thought, I have been to many lands but none like this. I don't even know how I got here, where I am, or how I'll get home. This is a mess, a horrid mess. Oh Poseidon, have mercy upon me.

Still, he tried to find his courage, telling himself *I am descended from Odysseus, the boldest and most enduring of the Greeks. I will find a way to survive. And maybe, like Odysseus, they will tell the stories of my tumultuous journey home. Like*

Odysseus, I will triumph even if I have to go to the underworld or fight the six-headed Scylla beast, or even evade a kingdom of cannibals or a giant whirlpool. Kle imagined the glory of living out the glorified struggles of his forefather's heroic footsteps.

Just then Kle saw a clean white and red bus go by with the words ORACLE written in large white letters on it. It was a company bus bringing a team of Oracle employees to the beach in Santa Cruz for a "team building day." But that didn't matter to Kle. He just saw it as a sign from the gods.

"I need an oracle to guide me home," he told himself out loud. "An oracle will help me know which tasks I have to complete to return to Athens the celebrated hero great Odysseus desires me to be."

Kle eagerly asked a person walking by him, "where is the oracle of this town?"

"Back off, buddy," the extremely tall postman grumbled nervously and kept walking carrying a bag of parcels over his shoulder.

"I'm sorry. I just need an oracle," Kle said and confidently followed the postman. The postman moved with a sense of purpose, something Kle always admired.

"Go to the boardwalk," the postman said anxiously to this muscular man following him eagerly. "If you have a quarter, there's an oracle machine at the Boardwalk."

"A quarter?"

"Twenty-five cents."

"Ah, a coin!"

"Yes. A coin," the postman hurried on, tired of dealing with so many of the crazy people in Santa Cruz.

"Are you a man or a messenger of Athena!" Kle exalted.

Hoping to completely evade this crazy person, the postman clarified, "the Boardwalk's down that way. Two miles down, turn left on Ocean Avenue. The road will end at the Boardwalk and you'll see a roller coaster there."

"I don't know what a roller coaster is but I will find it. Blessings upon you, fine servant of the gods!" Kle leaped into a run. Kle knew what to do – go to the boardwalk, get a quarter, and find the oracle!

Kle was propelled by the self-glorifying idea of himself doing something heroic. Furthermore, in this world he was feeling some relief from being criticized by Euty, Alos, and those other *butt sores* (his thought). Kle asked people along the way about the Boardwalk (to make sure he was heading towards), "Is this the way to the realm of the roller coaster, where the oracle resides."

Kle asked a grungy flannel wearing bearded guy outside of the Mongolian restaurant next to Rio Theater, "Am I going towards the realm of the roller coaster?" And then he asked the same question of a woman wearing oversized green overalls, just outside of the Staff of Life grocery store, "Where is the realm of the roller coast?"

Then he asked a pink-haired lady wearing little more than undergarments outside a hotel on Ocean Avenue. She told him with a smile "I'll be your oracle" but Kle kept walking.

And, lastly, he stood in front of a young man wearing spandex and zipping along on his bicycle on Ocean Ave. The biker freaked out about Kle almost making him crash and yelled, "The roller coaster's that way you stupid asshole! Now get out of my way and be more careful."

Kle deeply appreciated the biker's enthusiasm and cut down through the beach flats.

Then he came to the conglomeration of arcades, bumper cars, a carousel, a haunted house, cotton candy, giant pretzels, laser tag, and, of course, the roller coaster! The wild noise of the place, the flashing colors: it all screamed the finish line to Kle. He had succeeded in navigating to this very strange land. And, upon being asked, a security guard told Kle "the oracle is just through that building."

Unfortunately, the building the security guard pointed towards had a mural of Poseidon painted into the front of it. Poseidon had a trident and smiled proudly. On the mural, Poseidon was surrounded by devious seahorses. It was crystal clear to Kle that this place was firmly under the control of Poseidon, a vindictive god that despises Odysseus as the worst of enemies. Kle wondered, *will the god of the sea strike me down as I try to cross through this temple?*

Kle peeked inside and saw people playing beeping arcade games. To Kle, it just looked like dozens of magic mirrors controlling young zombie warriors. Kle was scared of this magic, the people looked hooked into a joyless hypnosis. They clearly didn't have the illumination of Athena or the power of Zeus infused into their lives. No. These were sad ghosts from Atlantis, Poseidon's underwater ghetto cemetery.

If he dared enter this power center of Poseidon's influence, they'd likely attack him right away or, perhaps, they'd wait until he was deep in their lair? These zombies were likely already aware that an enemy of Poseidon was so close. Kle smelled cigarette smoke and cringed in disgust, suspecting the Marlboros hideous reek was Poseidon's toxic fury.

Kle froze before going in, thinking, Maybe I don't have the courage to be a hero… Does Odysseus see me from the underworld now and does he pretend I am not descended from his seed."

Kle remembered the many times he'd been taunted by the other men on the boat. He'd journeyed with them for six months and they'd never slightly let him be a part of their clique. Maybe they, too, just saw who I really am and were frustrated with being forced to waste their time on someone like me.

He turned away from the task of going into Poseidon's temple. He knew he would just fail.

Then a young girl walked by wearing a beige shirt with a slogan on it that read, "Always Believe in Yourself. And Unicorns."

"Yes," he said out loud and, inspired, shook off his self-doubts. "I already believe in unicorns but it's time to believe in myself, too." Kle turned decisively around and dramatically swung the doors to Poseidon's building open. Then he strutted in. His heart was pounding, fists clenched, and toes curled back to ward off any hexes (as was Greek tradition in suspicious places).

Inside the dark arcade building, nobody approached him. He took a few more steps. And a few more steps. Blinking lights and a lot of shadows. There was a cacophony of horrible beeping sounds that made it hard for him to think, techno-metal music that hurt his ears, and people passing by bumped him thoughtlessly without awareness.

Still, Kle was not blown into a million pieces by a trident wielding servant of Poseidon and he kept walking. He almost made it to the door on the other side of the arcade, which was only feet away from the Oracle, when a boy a couple years younger than Kle grabbed his shoulder and said, "I know you." The guy had a weak attempt at a mustache and a small pointy beard.

"Are you sure you know me?" Kle asked, breaking out in a cold sweat, suspecting this was it, realizing one of Poseidon's pawns had caught him.

"Yes," the kid yelled. "I know you. And you thought you could just strut around this arcade without being recognized!"

"Please have mercy on me," Kle replied, knowing everyone in the arcade probably had a weapon or at least some minor magic at their disposal. And they'd all use it after discovering a major enemy of their Lord, Poseidon, had arrived. Or maybe even this person was Poseidon himself in the guise of a rather stupid looking human mortal adolescent.

"Have mercy on you! That's a laugh. You kicked ass last week at the surf competition. Hey, guys," he hollered to some other young men in the arcade. This is Reggie Shags."

"I am Reggie Shags?" Kle asked.

"Ya, you came out of nowhere and I can't believe how easily you won the O'Neill surf competition last weekend."

Two other young long-haired surfer-skater kooks approached Kle to get their moment in the light of an emerging celebrity. "Whoa! You're awesome!"

"Dude!" one of them added to the 'Whoa. You're awesome.'

"You're not a devotee of Poseidon?" Kle asked them, a little relieved.

The first kid replied, "Poseidon loves you, man. You really know how to work with his waves. Can I get a selfie with you?"

Kle didn't know what a selfie was. But, thinking quickly, he said: "For a quarter, I'll give you a selfie."

Each of the three guys gave a quarter and then got their smiling selfie. Kle followed this with, "May Poseidon be kind to us all!" before walking the final feet out the door of the arcade by himself.

And Kle saw the oracle. He was in a box. He was motionless and quiet. Kle saw a slot to put his quarter in. He put the quarter in and, right away, the box lit up and the oracle said, "You seek your fortune. You seek your way. Read Zolton's card and what it has to say!"

A small gold paper card popped out of a slot under the electronic oracle. Then, once again, it went quiet.

Kle picked up the card. For some reason it didn't seem strange that he could not only speak, but read this language: "A journey of a thousand miles begins with a single step."

He paused to think and then put another quarter in the machine. Again, the machine box Oracle of Santa Cruz lit up, wobbled his head, lights flashed and he said, "You seek your fortune. You seek your way. Read Zolton's card and what it has to say!"

Kle waited for the card and it came. This one said: "You will soon face great challenges."

"Argh," Kle groaned helplessly and put his last quarter into the oracle.

The yellow lights flashed inside the oracle's box, his head turned left and right, as he said a last time, "You seek your fortune. You seek your way. Read Zolton's card and what it has to say!"

A golden card dropped. Kle picked it up and read, "You will find a thing. It may be important to transform your situation."

"Unparalleled praise to Zeus," Kle said, delighted by this profound prophecy. "This oracle speaks from the summit of Mount Olympus." Kle walked away content somehow now knowing exactly what to do.

Where?

While the scrawny man in glasses drove her to the homeless shelter, Nariah saw many strange sights. Among these were buildings with large crosses above them. She had no idea what that was about. Then she noticed the man letting people into the homeless shelter where she arrived wore a similar small silver cross around his neck. She innocently asked the gatekeeper to this homeless shelter, "why do you wear a cross?"

"It reminds me of Jesus," the man said somberly.

"You know Jesus!" Nariah exclaimed, totally thrilled, even thinking maybe she wasn't so far away from the Sea of Galilee as it seemed.

"Yes," he responded.

"Why does a cross remind you of Jesus?" Nariah asked, confused.

The man wasn't exactly sure whether she was mocking him. Still, he humbly answered, "Jesus was crucified for our sins more than two thousand years ago but, I suppose, the cross reminds me that he's in our hearts now."

"He must be talking about a different Jesus. Their Jesus died more than two thousand years ago," Nariah mumbled to herself. Still, the thought of Jesus dying hit Nariah hard. Jesus was Nariah's world. She had spent as much time with Jesus as the apostles did. Her connection to Jesus was non-exclusive and platonic but, still, she adored him with her whole heart. She loved him with all the fervor that a fan loves her favorite rock star, a mother cares for her favorite child, and a lover passionately yearns for her beloved.

Wherever Jesus went, Nariah just showed up like a groupie. And she helped out however she could. He'd welcomed her, been patient with her, and encouraged her. And he tried to teach her the mystical secrets about finding heaven within herself. But Nariah rarely listened to what Jesus said. She just relished bathing in his majestic loving presence. His loving presence had given her permission to live more boldly. After meeting Jesus, not only did she start to speak up but she practically didn't stop talking. Around him, everything felt right and good. Sometimes she felt jealous that Mary was so close to him, but she didn't stagnate in that puddle very often. She was grateful for whatever she was to Jesus. The thought of losing Jesus made Nariah feel meek, delicate, and quiet.

"You can go find a bed," the cross-wearing greeter prodded Nariah, welcoming her to the homeless shelter.

The stress of her situation made Nariah break out into a cold sweat. She plopped down on a mattress and cried into her pillow, "what did Enkida do? What did I do?"

As she lay on her bed, she couldn't stop imagining sweet loving Jesus hanging innocently from a cross. Crucifixions were for thieves and bandits, not wise teachers. The man must have been talking about a different Jesus.

Nariah talked more to her pillow. "What kind of evil is this world? Am I in the future? No! Jesus could not have died. Crucified for our sins? What was that man talking about?" Nariah felt such a sense of loss that her stomach hurt enough to make her throw up in her mouth. She cried into her pillow at the homeless shelter, until she fell asleep.

Another woman at the homeless shelter, wearing a rainbow-colored shirt and rainbow colored pants, whimpered sadly to herself, "The aliens took me through the portal to their world. It was so beautiful and bright. But they made me come back. They said I wasn't ready…"

In the morning, Nariah followed the other homeless people to the cafeteria and took her plate. While ravenous, she didn't like the food. It was an apple that had almost no taste, dry bran flakes with sickly tasting milk, and coffee that made her feel jittery and pukey. "If I am in the future, I guess food has gotten worse over the last two thousand years," she grumbled.

The man who wore the cross was serving the food and asked her, "Did you sleep okay?"

"No. I was just thinking about Jesus all night."

"I know a church just down the street you can go to if you want." The man was hoping to play a part in saving this disoriented strange young woman.

"What's a church?" Nariah asked.

"It's where Christians go to worship," he laughed meekly. "Are you just messing with me?"

"What's a Christian?"

"This is your last answer, because I think you're twisting my arm, lady. And I don't appreciate being mocked. Anyway, Christians are people who know that Jesus Christ is God."

"What? Jesus. He's, uh, God? Is that so? I don't get it but where's this church?" Nariah asked, more than a bit confused. She loved Jesus and saw him as the greatest inspiration, but Jesus always told them, We are all children of God. She didn't understand how that morphed into being like a Roman emperor, or one of the vicious pharaohs she had read about in the Torah.

But the man told her where a church was and she followed the directions down the street. She walked hungry for the uplifting spirit she felt with Thomas, James, and the other apostles when they got together. Inside the church was a very high vaulted ceiling. While not a place she thought Jesus would have designed himself, it was pretty. She thought maybe she could get some relief from everything that confused her.

Instead, a red-faced preacher man strutted in and started with, "why do we think it's okay to hate god?" He passionately went on about the "sinful nature" of the gays, the adulterers, atheists, the socialists, the hedonists, a group called "Muslims," New Ager Crystal Worshippers, and then… the Jews. The Jews? That one completely confused Nariah. Jesus was a Jew. I am a Jew. Even though they referred to little pieces of Jesus's life, she was very confused by how the man of this church interpreted Jesus's words and deeds.

Nariah's jaw dropped trying to understand that this preacher man. Jesus had not judged her once. From what she could remember, she'd only seen Jesus judge a few times and that was because people were hypocrites. He definitely never mentioned anything about gays, socialists, hedonists, or New Age Crystal Worshippers. Thomas had proudly told her how Jesus got mad at the temple once, but Thomas had added as a side note, saying: "I think Jesus was just pretending to be angry to make his point about materialism crystal clear."

Anyway, Nariah never saw Jesus have such a temper tantrum like this preacher. The preacher finished by proclaiming, "Jesus wants every one of you to fight in his army against the devil."

Now Nariah felt pity for this man. She'd never heard Jesus talking about fighting in an army. Jesus used some of his auric light to clear out possessed souls…but that was different. This just made no sense. Jesus was more subtle, a trillion times more uplifting, than this very unstable man.

Nariah left the church and walked without aim. She was just so shocked that Jesus's life had somehow morphed into whatever the guy in that church-thing was talking about. Eventually, she ended up walking to a sidewalk on Westcliff, the road going along the coast of northern Santa Cruz. Massively expensive houses lined the route. But she didn't focus on those big boxes. She just stared at the waves crashing on the beach and its rocks. She didn't like this world. She wanted real tasty bread, fresh fish, and juicy olives like she ate in Nazareth. She didn't want to sleep at that dirty shelter again. She wanted to meet somebody who made sense to her, who helped her understand why she'd been hurled through time and space. She wanted something to clear her head of any horrible images of Jesus on the cross. Perhaps out of habit, she prayed for just a moment.

Then she heard the most amazing thing. It was more beautiful than the sound of any horn, harp, drum or voice her ears had been touched by before. This sound made her body bounce and made her want to yell at the sun so its rays would come dance with her. The flow of sound filled her with happiness. The music came from a boy who looked a few years younger than her. He was sitting on a bench and had oddly skinny legs.

"What is that noise?" Nariah asked him.

"Uh, is it too loud?" the kid replied and timidly picked up a tiny box at his side. He tapped it in a way that made the music much quieter.

"No! Please don't turn it back up," Nariah begged.

The boy turned the music back up. "Okay. It's the Shins." The boy was repeatedly putting a small burning stick into his mouth and breathing it in.

"Why are you inhaling the smoke from that?" she asked.

"Uh, I will assume you're being a smartass," he shrugged, "but you're welcome to have some."

She looked at him blankly.

"Do you want a drag?" He extended his hand with the joint. She took the joint and inhaled like she'd seen the boy had done. Then she passed the little burning bush back to him. It repeated. He took a drag and then passed it back to her again. She liked the taste of the smoke. She did it one more time. And then they just sat for a few minutes quietly.

"Why are your legs so tiny? You're like a grasshopper," Nariah smirked without tact.

"I have muscular dystrophy. It makes my muscles weak," he said without taking offense. A crutch lay beside him.

"You just need a miracle to cure your legs!" Nariah suggested.

"No. I don't need a miracle, I need a good attitude. I'm guessing you're the one that really needs a miracle," he responded unshakably confidently. He had a sharp aquiline face, calm brown eyes, and shaggy black hair. He kept nodding his head to the music coming from his iPad. While physically challenged, he was very comfortable in his body and very clear with his words.

"I've had lots of miracles. But maybe you're right, right now. Miracles don't always do much good," Nariah confessed thinking what a flawed person she still was. The glittering water of the Pacific Ocean was starting to look even more beautiful than she remembered.

"Are you a student at UCSC?" he asked, shifting the topic away from the supernatural.

"I used to be a prostitute," she replied. "Then I mostly helped out with a few Jews in Judea trying to start a spiritual revolution."

Nariah found her mind was slowing down. This boy sitting at her side reminded her of a young fisherman she'd been enamored with as a young girl. That boy moved to Hebron when his parents married him off. Nariah didn't have many good prospects for marriage because her father was dead and her mother was barely around, already a prostitute herself.

Old thoughts were coming up in Nariah's mind and other thoughts weren't sticking as much. She forgot that she was two thousand years in the future. She forgot that Jesus had been crucified. She forgot how sore her body was after the horrible night of sleep. Then she remembered. And forgot again. And remembered her sweet strong younger brother's laugh before the Romans took him away to make him a slave for being part of a politically subversive coalition.

"You were a prostitute? Then you mostly helped out with some Jews trying to start a spiritual revolution?" The boy repeated most of Nariah's answer with a laugh. He played along with what he thought was a joke. "I used to be a bullfighter. Then I got involved in this animal rights movement and jumped on a ship to sail around the world with Mickey Mouse."

"You can't sail around the world," she laughed. "You'd fall off the edges of it."

"We did fall off the edges of it. I grew wings."

"Is that why you have this muscular dystrophy?" she asked in a somber tone.

"Very funny." Once again he welcomed her insensitive comment without taking much offense.

Then the weed kicked in strongly. To Nariah, it seemed like a burst of light was pulsing in every direction. Her body shivered a little. "What's happening to me?" she asked. "I am feeling very strange."

"You've smoked pot before, right?"

"Is pot that smoke?" she asked and squirmed uncomfortably. She looked back-and-forth nervously. "I've never inhaled smoke before."

"Oy vey. Just relax. My car's right over there. I'll give you a ride to where I live and you can just chill out."

"Am I cursed?"

"No!" the boy exclaimed. "The first time I smoked pot I felt pretty freaked out too. It's all good. It can just make you a little paranoid."

"Paranoid?"

"Well, you just might not want to be out in public places. You'll get the munchies too!"

"The Munchies will get me?" Nariah asked, even more terrified.

"Please tell me you understand that munchies means you're going to get very hungry."

Over the months before arriving at the shoreline of Haifa and then walking to the sea of Galilee with the other Greeks, Kle and the other men from his boat had gone many places. They went to what is now Turkey and exchanged some of their textiles for copper ore. They'd been to Ethiopia, where they traded a few swords for a crate of shiny wonderful gold. And, in what is now Hungary, they gave nine jars of sweet wine for a humble stock of oriental silk. Kle thought Judea would be their last stop before returning to Greece. Instead, he stumbled into Santa Cruz.

In many ways, Kle landed in this new world the ineffective rookie his Greek peers saw him as. He'd always been more lost in the clouds of making up songs and bumbling along than being a serious trader. The other men on his crews methodically worked to find anything of value in the lands they visited. They had a whole system of blending in, making allies, identifying the local resources, and negotiating. Again, Kle mostly just made up songs. Staying this ineffective course, Kle walked around town until stumbling into a Food Not Bombs setup, a program that redistributes unused food from local groceries and restaurants to those in need. Kle ate leftover bagels, four bananas, and a can of Fresca. As he shoveled the bananas into his mouth, a grungy bearded kid told everyone, "They're giving away new sleeping bags for free at the camp."

"What is this camp," Kle asked earnestly.

The bearded kid scratched the tattoos on his face saying, "the homeless camp," and pointed up the street.

Kle sought out this free sleeping bag. At Santa Cruz's homeless encampment next to San Lorenzo River, as hoped, he was given a free new sleeping bag. Not only that, a local city councilman was handing out a few new tents (and Kle was lucky enough to get one!)

While gratefully holding these gifts, Kle saw a beautiful black-haired woman walking through the park. The beauty of this woman zung through him with a rush of electricity. Thinking he had gathered treasures, he proudly clung to the sleeping bag and tent and ran towards this lady hollering "fair vision of Aphrodite, might I be of service to you in any way?"

The woman looked scared, "are you okay? Are you on drugs?" She was dialing numbers on her cell phone. "I'm calling the cops. Please stay back."

"I scare you, please tell me why and I will leave you?" Kle pleaded.

Instead of fear, the woman jumped over to anger, "you homeless people. How dare you take up some of our parks, running at me like that!! The cops will be here in a few minutes and then you'll have a home.... In jail!."

Kle had already been threatened by police officers. He took the hint and left her alone. He turned around and headed back to the homeless camp. Talking to some of the others there, he realized his sleeping bag and tent were basic necessities, not the rare sought after treasures he'd assumed. He felt dejected. Surrounded by the tough luck and discouraged talk in the camp, he saw himself like his crew had seen him. He saw himself as a bottom feeding sloucher in this world. He built his tent and crawled inside his sleeping bag. He felt paralyzed by dejection. The unconscious nothingness of sleep seemed the only oasis in sight.

In the morning, Kle overheard someone say, "if you want things to get better, you have to try doing something different." Hearing that, a light went on in Kle. He resolved him to become worthy of the fairest of maidens in this land, he had to become a better person. And, to do that, he decided to use the strategies the other Greeks used when they arrived in new lands (which he always lazily relied on them to do). What were those strategies? Wherever his boat full of Greek traders arrived, whatever the culture or geography they landed in, all of them except Kle quickly adopted local fashion trends (the colors worn, the way robes were tied or headgear adorned). Next, they observed the many systems of each place - how the locals get their food and what they eat, how and why they laugh, and who propels business! To this end, they looked out for desirable resources and allies. They immersed themselves in these foreign worlds and, from that vantage, could find the treasures there.

"I will do what my crewmates did in those lands. I will imitate them in this world. I will change myself so that Aphrodite herself would be enchanted by me!"

Still, it didn't happen right away!

Kle tumbled around downtown noticing as much as he could. He Kle climbed into a dozen dirty dumpsters trying on countless thrown out clothes before settling with an old pair of decent jeans and a Red Hot Chili Peppers T-shirt that didn't have any stains. He kept his sandals on as he believed they fit in with the Santa Cruz fashion anyway.

Then, over the next two days, Kle went back to noticing what he could… staying mainly downtown, he paid attention to what people said to each other (and what they weren't saying to each other.) Clothes, food, gadgets, memorabilia, he did his best to take in modern commerce (and fumbled with talking to people along the way). He saw himself as analytical as Aristotle and as one-pointed as any warrior from the Iliad.

Kle heard about Amazon and Facebook and other "giants of the web." He asked everyone to show him where the web was. Nobody gave him the time of day... that is, until a friendly librarian got him set up on a library computer and got him started. By the grace of the magic Enkida unleashed, of course, he could not only understand modern English but he could read and write it too! The people lounging around the Santa Cruz public main library reminded him of the thoughtful but dirty unkempt bedraggled philosophers scurrying around Athens, the ever-questioning hobos in the Athenian main square.

Online, still thinking of Athens and its philosophers, he typed in "Athens." From there, he found himself at a wiki article about Greece. The ancient Greek transplant to the modern world read about what happened to the society of Greece (he didn't cry when he found out that civilization was now little more than a tourist destination, its ancient days of supreme glory long gone).

Then Kle typed in Aphrodite. Instead of a goddess, Kle found himself confronted by glaring spread eagled pornography. Wanting to quickly change the screen, Kle typed in where am I… Kle learned about the geography and history of Santa Cruz (with its counterculture 60's being the closest thing to a glorious past.) He learned Santa Cruz had a school (university) for older children (he later talked with students on Pacific Avenue from the University of California at Santa Cruz. It seemed this was a place for people to get deep rest for four years before committing to a type of indentured servitude called mortgage.) In addition to this university, there were companies in Santa Cruz that made clever gadgets and medicines Kle couldn't really understand; there were a lot of organic farmers, and there was a harbor with surprisingly no trade. Overwhelmed by information, Kle pulled himself back to Food Not Bombs and then the homeless camp at the end of the day.

The next morning, Kle was lured into bumming around downtown. He begged a bit, talked with some junkies, and thought his quest to "figure out" his challenge might be hopeless. Things felt heavy, too foreign, undoable. Still, later that afternoon, he pushed himself back the web and surfed cyber-reality until realizing a profound insight about two significant local sources of industry-recreational tourism (something nearly unheard of in ancient Greece) and "natural" wellness (nutritional magic vitamin potions, masseuses, chiropractors, yoga teachers and acupuncturists and psychotherapists, along with workshops on shaman totems and feminine empowerment and mindfulness... self-development stuff.) These two components – tourism and hippy style wellness – glowed like treasures to Kle.

The modern world of traveling for fun and health remedies glowed like treasures to Kle. He knew they were his key. While he had always relied on his crewmates to find the valuables in the foreign cultures they visited, he believed he had come to pinpoint an interesting market gap, a business realm which could possibly be much more tapped. He was as scientific as he could be with the whole thing, applied his limited mental might with as much creative ferocity as he could muster to figure out how he could inject himself into these markets- tourism and wellness. What talents or knowledge did he possess which could leverage himself in these niches? He wondered and wondered and wondered until his answer unfolded…

At the end of his third day in Santa Cruz, the idea to leverage himself in this foreign land emerged: "Zeus's Holotropic Spatial Seminar!"

Kle visualized Zues's Holotropic Spatial Seminar as fitting right in with the yoga classes, nutritional seminars, herbal wisdom certification programs, and tai-chi workshops of this land. He saw it as starting as an afternoon workshop but evolving into a massive program- a series of classes and multi-phase training certificated programs.

He envisioned life coaching meets physical prowess and maritime (boat-oriented) magic. It was the occult teaching of the Greek gods, the power of Zeus, the freedom of Dionysius, and the sexual prowess of Aphrodite. Talk about empowerment on so many levels. And, in taking this task, he could revise/ retell the narrative of his travels through the Mediterranean portraying himself as the ultimate hero! Kle fantasized about franchises and marketing it to big money like Google, Apple, universities, or prisons.

On that fateful day that "Eureka" visited Kle, Kle was downtown and he saw a man was forging balloons into the shapes of hats, animals, and airplanes. The balloon guy was dressed up as a clown. Kle also saw the most beautiful red-haired woman on that cool early evening.

"What do you think of the balloon guy?" Kle jubilantly asked the woman with red hair as she passed by him along downtown Santa Cruz. Kle assumed she would scoff at him as the black-haired woman had done a few days before.

Truth is, the woman hadn't initially seen the balloon guy and his colorful balloon animals. She didn't see his face paint or the wild and wacky clown outfit balloon guy wore. She'd walked by the balloon guy without thinking so many times, he and his balloons had become invisible to her. She now looked at the balloon guy with his dozens of balloons blown up and twisted into the shapes of cars and giraffes and spaceships. The balloons were red and yellow and orange and green and blue and purple. Zaera laughed out loud and said, "I feel like I haven't even noticed the wildness that was right in front of me."

Kle nodded like a diligent student. He was wearing a somewhat scruffy Modest Mouse T-shirt, but the hairs from his chest came over the collar. The big blond ball of curly hair on his head seemed electrified with life, and his eyes were as bright and curious as the fourth grade children the woman worked with every day.

While she had a fiery blaze on her head, the woman felt like life was bland, colorless, right then. She was a schoolteacher and worked hard trying to inspire fourth graders who were trucked to her classroom day after day. But the educational standards and scripted lessons had slowly suffocated her, left her little creative room to enjoy educating. When she first started teaching, she'd done a lot of painting and games and songs and jokes and field trips with the kids. She invited guest speakers and brought in animals and musicians. But, as everyone around her repeatedly insisted on the value of improving testing scores, the majority of these enrichment activities were largely replaced by worksheets, supplementary curriculum programs on the computers in the back of the classroom, and stricter classroom management.

It had been a particularly bleak workday when she went downtown late that evening to pick up some vegetables at New Leaf natural foods market. By the time she heard Kle point out the bizarre balloon guy on Pacific Avenue, her world seemed to have become a gray glue factory.

"What do you think of the balloons?" she retorted back to Kle, afraid this moment of color would end far too quickly.

Kle looked pensively at the balloon man before dropping his gaze back on this red-head, "they're bright but you're even brighter."

"I'm Zaera," she told him.

Within an hour, Kle was in Zaera's townhouse and they were both disrobed and he was slowly licking every centimeter of her body. He was so patient, stoking her burning passion until her pleasure sensors were celebrating her personal Fourth of July. She was sweating and her breasts pulsing and his thrusts were so gentle she experienced oneness like all the Tantra books she'd read from. It just went on and on as she hungrily ate it all up.

At the end of the night, Zaera said to herself in front of the bathroom mirror, "ecstasy is not just a legend." Her eyes were glowing and her hair was more red than it had ever been. For the first time in a long time, she liked who was looking back at her in the mirror. Then she climbed back into her bed and lay her head to sleep on her strange new lover's muscular chest.

When Kle woke up, she confided to him, "a couple days before I met you, I had the weirdest experience. I was washing dishes, not feeling exceptionally spectacular. Then my kitchen floor just seemed to not be there. I don't know for how long it was like that. I was floating on an island where everything around me suddenly didn't exist. I never did hard drugs, but I was totally tripped out and it seemed like anything could happen. I wondered whether I was having some psychic breakdown, but then the floor filled in again, I felt like I dropped three inches, and the only difference was that I wasn't in my kitchen anymore. I was in my living room. When I saw you and you asked me about the balloon guy, I felt like you were part of that somehow. I read about people falling into parallel universes that were almost exactly like their own, but slightly different. I thought that was just a bunch of pseudo-science New Age bullshit but…"

"No!" Kle said. "It sounds like you fell through the same portal as me!" Then she listened as he countered her confession by claiming to her that he was from ancient Greece. She thought he was playing a game with her, but she didn't care. She thought it was fun, sort of a sexy role-play. By the time he finished his explanation, she trusted and desired him enough to give him keys to her house and delighted in expecting him again that next night. And she decided to do everything she could to help him succeed with the crazy workshop idea he went on to rant enthusiastically about.

Even that first day Zaera's students noticed her renewed joy in the classroom. One of the children even mentioned, "It's like you're a light bulb and someone turned you on!"

After another day, Zaera dropped her overwhelming preoccupation with the standards and laughed heartily again with the children. She had nobody go on the computer or do worksheets and didn't need to send anyone to the principal. She joked and told stories and led games and sang and felt herself as the mischievous child-teacher of the school.

"You're silly and fun. My dad was like that when he first got out of jail," another student said to her at the end of the day.

"Exactly," she agreed, feeling like she just got out of the jail of selling her soul to blah standards and tests.

Arito

In the tree, the man had said the people in this house were all part of his tribe. As Enkida followed Santiago inside to sit down on some high white stools in front of a blue tile counter, Enkida smelled food and none of it reeked of human flesh.

"May I have some food?" she asked Santiago after he led her there.

Enkida's loose fitting leather dress and dreadlocked hair didn't strike the people in the room of that big community house as unusual. They were hipster millennials. Furthermore, she was with a young man who lived there. Dropping through the portal had left her intensely hungry. Someone heard her request for food and handed her a big plastic plate with an ample helping of coconut curry tofu over basmati rice. Enkida ate with her hands, but, after noticing everyone else was using tiny shovels to eat, she switched to a fork too.

There were always between five and eight people eating and talking in the mix at any one time. Aside from a huge pile of stained glass on one side of the living room, it was an exceptionally clean living dining space for a co-op of young semi-professional hipster artists and students.

"What is all that?" Enkida pointed to a pile of stained glass in a corner of the room. She'd never seen colored glass before. It reminded her of the astral world of dreams.

"David uses those to make mosaics," someone said and gestured around the room. The walls were lined with large pieces of rectangular wood covered with colorful pieces of stained glass. One of them had a picture of Osiris, another had the Taoist yin yang symbol, another was a lightning bolt, and another had a big Om symbol. While Enkida looked around at these religious symbols from around the world, a discussion bubbled up around current politics.

"I'd let Trump win before voting for Hilary," one of them said.

"You're voting for World War III, congratulations!" someone snapped.

"Donald will bulldoze his way to the presidency. He'll crush Hillary."

"Hilary's a sellout."

"Democracy doesn't work because of Citizens United."

"Bernie won't be able to get anything done."

'"Except tell the truth."

"That he doesn't know how to cut his hair."

"Socialism doesn't work."

"Neither does having 20 of the richest people in the US own as much as the poorest 130 million."

"That's such bullshit."

"Socialism works a lot better than whatever Trump would do in office. He'll help the rich get richer and the poor get poorer. Same old shit."

"Bernie's giving a speech tonight."

"He's going to tell us to vote for Hilary, probably."

"He's going to say the movement's been started, now it's up to us to keep the momentum going and all that inspire-the-young-people stuff but the reality is nobody wants much change and..."

It went on like that, typical liberal college town talk, theoretical utopias versus the establishment status quo. Enkida took it all in, learning about these yahoos battling for power – Hilary Clinton and Donald Trump and Bernie Sanders. As she took more and more bites of the coconut curry tofu, her smile grew wider and wider, the coconut curry tofu's rich sweet flavor was like nothing she'd tasted before. She smiled because she found herself attracted to playing a role in power struggles they talked about and because the food tasted good. The coconut curry tofu reminded her of the harp music that she listened to as a young child. Every night, before going to sleep, her father sent in a harpist to lull her to the world of sweet dreams.

The music was good magic for the angel of sleep. And this food was good magic for calling her to wake up.

The conversation continued and this Donald Trump they talked about reminded her of Maka, her brother. She remembered what a power hungry brute he was, stopping at anything to solidify his position. She felt pain remembering how Maka twisted logic and principles so that he was now a social infection more than a real man. Hilary and Bernie sounded like the soothsaying ministers who'd betrayed her.

She couldn't take a stand back in Uruq. She hadn't been ready then, but the gods had brought her here and maybe she could still take a stand. She would do it in honor of her son. She would do it with her whole heart. She would do it, calling up all the strength the gods had hidden in her.

"Who are the servants of Donald Trump?" Enkida asked.

The conversation stopped, and, for the first time, a computer programmer, some college students, a coffee barista, an electrician, and a teacher turned to really look at this stranger among them. They noticed that she was strikingly beautiful, that her dark eyes were hawk-like and piercing. One of them responded, "People who are worried that immigrants are taking our jobs and bringing crime follow Donald Trump."

"Come on. Plenty of people are voting for him simply because Hillary's such a shitty alternative," a young computer programmer suggested.

"Or because they just want cheaper taxes so they can pay for their kids to go to college," a girl who studied economics at UCSC offered.

"And who follows Bernie Sanders?" Enkida asked.

There was nervous laughter but somebody answered, "privileged white people who think body paint and marching protests will save the world. People who hate religion and authority and capitalism. Hippies and yuppies."

"Then I want an army of these hippies and yuppies who are ready to paint their bodies and march," Enkida announced resolutely.

"But what about Hillary?" the computer programmer chimed.

"It sounds like nobody follows her," Enkida responded.

"Are you a political science major?" an aspiring economics major asked Enkida.

"I am a priestess and I know only two things – magic to heal and magic to destroy," Enkida answered powerfully. Her strength was her credential, her PHD.

They didn't laugh. Their eyes refocused on this slightly older, infinitely decisive woman. They delighted in the thought that a real leader was in their midst, not just a participant in opinion sharing, but an actual piece of history, that these dreadlocks weren't just a rebellion against somebody's parents.

Enkida had already been empress-general of an army. She had battled the camel-riding Trifurdians to the south when they tried to steal away a hundred farmers from her kingdom to be their slaves. And she led the warriors of Ur against Mabomites to the east. The Mabomites were as fast as cheetahs running when they stole crops from one of Enkida's royal storehouses. Every time Enkida fell into battle, she threw her heart into it and almost always won. It was true that killing made her feel sick; she was haunted by the faces of those she slaughtered. But she hated being violated by invaders even more.

While she avoided decisions that might end in violence, Enkida actually relished something about the fight for what she believed was right. In this she was a good military leader. While her brother was a master at driving people by their fear, she harnessed people by the fury of the righteousness in their anger.

Enkida knew why the army came to lose all their trust in her... When her father was dying, she commanded all the leaders in the army to dedicate their soldiers' energy into searching for an herb or potion or incantation that might make him live much longer. She wanted to save her father. This sounded ridiculous and unfair to the other military leaders. Stopping death was not something that made sense. Even gods died. Death was part of life. In her frenzied yearning for her father's physical longevity, she left her servants feeling discarded and irrelevant.

"Arito!" almost everyone hollered together in triumph.

Enkida came back from her memories of war and turned around to see a boy coming through the door. He was using a cane to walk. This boy had feeble legs that wobbled along strangely, almost like a spider. He wore a big proud grin on his face that would have made him intimidating if not for his legs. And his eyes reminded her of something. But the person behind him did much more than remind her of something – it was Nariah from the lake town.

Enkida's mind went into a spin. Seeing Nariah reminded her of the yellow gem that she dropped from the top of the redwood tree. "I have lost the key out of here," she gasped. "I have lost my chance to save my son."

Enkida wasn't sure what she should do with this Nariah who, apparently unapologetically, derailed her magic and kept her from using the mantra to find her son back in Ur. While Enkida was trying to figure out what to say to this buffoon of a woman, Nariah grabbed a plate and started eating the coconut curry tofu ravenously. She looked up at Enkida, smiling relaxedly, "Hi Enkida. This food is delicious."

"How did you find me?" Enkida asked angrily.

"I found you?" Nariah laughed. And then laughed more and more until she confessed, "I'm peeing onto my leg."

"Are you okay?" Arito asked Nariah with sincere concern.

"Yes. Arito, your smoke is fun. Now everything is a bit bouncy."

"What is this world you've taken us to, Nariah?" Enkida asked unsure why Nariah was acting even more strangely than she had before they fell through the portal. What smoke?

"Me!" Nariah responded. "I reached out to take your hand only to ask you why you left my home without even saying thank you. Then I fell into this god-forsaken place. And this place is in the future, Enkida. What magic have you done to have brought us here when devil-possessed people claim they know what Jesus was all about?"

"People here know about your Jesus, the man in the meadow?" Enkida asked.

"Everyone knows about him. And they claim he said horrible hateful things about everybody!" Nariah answered Enkida and then got back to work eating more.

While Enkida and Nariah whispered to each other, the larger conversation was: a young lady with blonde hair was bragging to everyone about a "conscious hip hop" concert she went to the night before at a place called the Catalyst. "Talib Kweli and Mos Def did a rap battle and..." Nariah maintained rare silence as she burned through two plates of food.

Nariah was very stoned. Enkida wondered how she could build an army. Enkida wanted to find all of these hippies and yuppies and privileged liberals and topple this Donald Trump. She wanted to usurp all the dictators, redeem all that she'd lost because of her brother; create a seat for the throne of Gilgamesh in this land that didn't know the names of the gods.

Arito flopped himself down on an old brown couch next to the kitchen and asked, "Do you guys want to hear a new poem?"

Instead of anybody answering, a chubby boy wearing purple overalls started beat-boxing. Enkida did not understand how so many strange noises came from this boy's mouth. Chubby-in-overalls was a beat-boxing maestro. And Arito spit out the verse, "I got a fire within me that cannot breathe, it's gasping for air, but being pushed down by the weight of the leaves, changing seasons, feeding stuckness in the seed..." And he kicked out a long rhyme through the beats.

At first, Enkida stared judgmentally at the poet's sickly boney legs. She didn't understand why the young man wore shorts, not even trying to hide these legs, which would be a pathetic deadweight in battle. Still, she liked the strength of the boy's voice in the verses. Arito deliberately spoke his poems rhythmically like they were a mantra creating flowing presence.

Then, perhaps responding to her glare, Arito turned to Enkida and free-style rapped:

"You look like a hawk but where are you landing?

I see an idea in your heart

but not sure what you're planning

Is it with wisdom that scheming

or with hatred your damning

To grow your own wings you got to decide

Are you going to fester in your wounds

or Lift us up to fly

I'm an ancient soul, can you use your third eye..."

He tapped his legs to the pulse of the words he spat out. He didn't shy away from looking hard into her face. He even pointed at her and stood up and walked towards her. And, as he was spitting, Enkida saw a leather strap around one of his freakishly thin ankles. It had three black beads on it, each bead had an orange dot. The strap and beads looked impossibly similar to the leather strap of blessing and protection she'd put on her son before they took him away from her.

"Where did you get that thing on your ankle?" Enkida whispered.

"When I was adopted, it was there," Arito answered confidently.

Business

Kle's muscular physique, naïve enthusiasm, and emotional buoyancy made Zaera totally smitten with love. And because of that, she did everything she could to help him. She trusted him with the keys to her house, bought him new clothes (and even some shoes), she helped him shave, and she threw herself into helping him with the bizarre business idea, Zeus's Holo-tropic Spatial Seminar.

She started to laugh when he first told her what would be taught in this workshop. But it was an idea and, just like she knew to support the enthusiasm of the children she worked with (no matter how crazy their ideas!), she naturally supported the idea of this stranger she'd taken into her house and her heart.

Trying to support Kle, Zaera paid for Facebook postings about his workshop; she made fliers; she spent hundreds on Google ads, and she called all her friends, encouraging them to bite.

"What do they teach at this thing?" her friends would ask.

She responded with a pitch, which she taught to Kle, "You learn how to wrestle and throw a javelin like the ancient Olympians. You'll learn stories from the golden age of Greece about the gods and the ancient maritime magic Greeks used to encourage good weather and..." she whispered, "sexual techniques that have been forgotten for two thousand years!"

"What's his credentials?" they'd ask trying to sort through what box they should put this workshop in.

That one initially stumped her. She couldn't say, "Well, he's amazing in the sack," or, "He thinks he just teleported here from ancient Greece." She couldn't even say what schools he'd gone to as he only told her, "Like the other boys of Athens, we learned from our elders." But many people in Santa Cruz love cults, and the more ancient the better. Considering the situation, she thought that was the ultimate marketing hook. So, she responded to people's questions about Kle's credentials with, "He studied with masters of a Greek cult that's been around for thousands of years."

Anyway, after quickly investing a lot of her money and training Kle on the pitch, only a few days after he first arrived, Zaera told Kle, "It's time to go on your odyssey."

Kle lit up, eager for an actionable task, for this opportunity to be a hero. "What do you mean?"

She handed Kle a backpack. In it was a pile of fliers, a staple gun, and a cell phone she bought for him from Verizon.

"This cell phone's yours," she said. "Don't waste the minutes, they come out of my plan. Put these fliers up around Santa Cruz, hand them out, and tell everyone who will listen to you about your workshop."

"Thank you so much, but where do I start?" Kle asked, taking the cell phone, the pile of fliers, and the staple gun. He found himself suddenly overwhelmed with the task of self-delegation.

Zaera already understood her lover well. She knew he'd be overwhelmed with the task she was setting before him and she prepared accordingly. Red-headed Zaera gave Kle a small piece of paper from her notebook, something she'd written out the night before. It read: "This is your Holy Grail. It is a list for you. You can use my bike. I got an app that tracks the bike so I'm not afraid of you stealing it." The rest of it was a list:

"Start at the university-put up fliers at every bus stop

-Put up fliers at New Leaf Market on the westside

-Go to Herb Room and put up flier

-Go to the Abbey coffee shop and put up a flier

-Downtown- put up a flier at Santa Cruz Bookshop. Tell at least 6 people there about course

-Go to the Mystery Spot and take a tour (there's often tourists there from over the hill in San Jose looking for peculiarities only found in Santa Cruz. You and your workshop fit the bill. Hand out your fliers to them).

-Finish the day by putting up a flier at Charlie Hong Kong's noodle cafe. And that's just Day 1, my Gorgeous Greek God. Until tonight!"

Kle stared down at this list somberly. "Okay."

"And when I get home from work, if there's enough Hercules in you to finish every dang thing on this list, we're going to get sushi, soak, and have sex. Don't come home without conquering these tasks, lover boy."

Zaera didn't totally realize how much Kle took her command to heart, how literal he was. He elevated completing this list to the holiest of duties.

A part of Kle still burned bright with shame, feeling himself an outcast. What he remembered too often was returning from his last expedition. Like this last trip with Euty and Alos, he hadn't been successful then and Kle's dad told him disparagingly, "You just don't have the talent to transform an expedition so it's profitable. Maybe you should just work on the farms like our servants."

This list, to him, represented a final chance to prove himself to the world and extinguish that intolerable feeling of being disgraced. This list was the key to a new life where the world would honor him. So he looked up to the heavens, proclaiming to himself and Zaera, "Hermes will let me prove myself to you and to all the gods today."

Zaera had taught Kle how to ride a bike in the middle of the night when they went outside to get some fresh air after a very full night.

So Kle took the list, gave Zaera a kiss that electrified her whole body, and awkwardly rode off on that sleek purple street bike away from her Seabright townhouse.

For Kle, that morning was bright with purpose. He chanted prayers to Zues, Apollo and Athena with utmost zeal as he rode away.

Zaera laughed at herself for using a big chunk of her savings to springboard this foolhardy workshop idea on this seemingly delusional man. Then she locked up her house before getting in her leased Honda Civic and pressed the gas for another day of spirited efforts with the kids.

Infused with purpose and drive, Kle started with the first item on the list. He biked the strenuous uphill climb to the plateau overlooking Santa Cruz from a University of California at Santa Cruz meadow. There, he covered dozens of bus stops with stapled fliers. Then went to the New Leaf grocery market on the Westside and put his flier on their board. He did the same at Herb Room and the Abbey Coffee house and Santa Cruz Bookshop, going full throttle with his amateur marketing campaign.

All along the way, Kle talked to people about his program. His first and most repeated mistake was opting not to use the pitch Zaera had taught him. He went from his gut, telling young men, "It will transform you so you're not such a scrawny weakling." Or "It will show you how to be powerful and face the gods with pride instead of cowering over like such a pathetic hunchbacked goof." He even told men over thirty, "While Hades and the bringer of death cannot be far from your lot, I'll teach you how to reclaim some of your vitality so that you shine with life again." That's about as far as he got before any men over thirty hustled away from Kle. To Kle and ancient Greeks, thirty was fairly old.

And he told women, "You will learn about Athena, the goddess of war. And Artemis, the goddess of hunters. Unlike you, they were both pure virgins. Still, come to my seminar and you will learn the wisdom of these great warrior women."

Most people walked away from him, bewildered and unsure what he was trying to sell, but many took the flier. A few men considered telling him to "fuck off," but the size of this strange Greek's muscles convinced them to do otherwise.

A few women considered telling him to "fuck off," but found themselves being tempted to get dreamy, gawking at those same muscles and staring into his eyes.

While they didn't impulsively say, "Fuck off," everyone clearly walked away before the end of his advertised proposal. All this rejection was tiring, discouraging for eager Kle. His steam fizzled but he kept on. After going through the majority of the list, to take a break from the flow of pushback, he sat on a bench next to a sculpture outside of O'Neil's Surfwear Shop in downtown Santa Cruz. It was a weekday, with people busily walking along to work or en route to purchase something. O'Neil's shop was largely empty, the warm calm day having beckoned many of its potential non-working customers to the beach.

Kle watched everyone strutting by him, self-assured women and men in suits marching along like loyal soldiers, homeless teens donning old black denim and leather clothes sulking by with malnourished dogs, and an out of place fancy woman in red dress and high heels falling over her shoes. Right after seeing the red dress stumble, a young man, with legs that wobbled sideways like tentacles, used a cane to lower himself to the ground not far from Kle's bench.

Then this tentacle-legged kid started tapping his measly half-formed legs and bust out with some accompanying rhymes.

The kid rapped with a playful, surprisingly deep, voice,

"There's an ocean breeze blowing into my knees/

some call it a disease/

I just say it actually frees/

me to believe/

in what Arito conceives").

Kle liked it, pulled out his flute, and weaved some melodies through the kid's rhymes. Arito rapped on:

"Glory of the redwood trails/

Santa Cruz harbor's sails/

telepathically communicating with the whales."

Kle smiled and weaved on with his melodious flute through the verses. Then Arito:

"Kundalini yoga matters/

vegan gluten free platters/

sensitive new age white guy rappers."

Until Kle threw in a verse of his own,

"I'm like Hercules, born for a task/

If you ask where I'm from, I can only say since I was born two thousand years have passed/

but it went by very fast/

I feel like I'm wearing a mask/

to fit in with this time zone to earn me some cash."

Arito stopped.

"Did I mess it up?" Kle asked sincerely, apologetic. Kle had been thrilled to slip into the soul-medicine of music.

"No. I'm sorry. Your rhymes were killer." Arito looked at Kle strangely. "It's just that these two women came to my house last night, claiming to be from two thousand years ago. I'm more than a little creeped out that you jumped in rapping about being from two thousand years ago too."

Kle was thrilled and jumped up. "Who were these two women? I think I know them. I think we somehow fell through the same portal to get here."

"Please say you're joking."

"I only speak the truth. I am Kle of Athens, descended from Odysseus, and I shall be counted among the greatest of men."

Arito was exasperated, "Are you a whack job. Santa Cruz is full of too many crazies." Arito propped his cane to help himself back up and stood to go.

"Wait, please," Kle begged. "I know it sounds insane, but we are mortals and the way of the gods can be confusing. Please tell me where these ladies are."

Arito stared back hard at Kle, "the Jesus freak is staying in my loft. But the other one is only a couple years older than me and she's pretending to be an empress from Mesopotamia and my mom. She's totally nuts. She stayed with someone else at the Tannery. Anyway, I don't know where they are right now, or if they're coming back tonight."

"Please take me to the one who is totally nuts. the one pretending to be an empress."

"Please leave me alone."

Kle's ego, already deeply pricked, wanted to grab this feeble-legged boy and punch him in the face before forcing him to show the way to the Tannery. Then he remembered grabbing Nariah at the beach. He remembered the humiliation of being scolded by a mob of gentle elderly people in this world. Physical force would not yield results like it did in the old times.

"Then may we meet again," Kle said, watching the boy go his own way. Kle felt dazed, wondering why the gods had led him to this boy. It seems I am entwined with others by the magic that brought him to this world.

It had been a settled windless day, but, right then, a wild gust rushed through downtown, blowing a cowboy hat off an old man heading into Pizza My Heart. It threw up the red dress of a woman going into a store that sold ``ecologically conscious clothing," and it ripped Zaera's list from Kle's pocket.

Kle saw his list swim down the street and he took off after it. As he ran, he was so anxious about possibly losing his list, he almost knocked over an old woman getting tickets for a movie at Del Mar theater. He leapt over a Siberian Husky tied up outside of Pizza My Heart. The distraction derailed his run. He fell to the ground and skidded painfully on his knees and hands along the busy sidewalk. The physical pain was nothing next to the panic he felt about losing that list.

A Santa Cruz couple in their sixties bustled quickly over to Kle. "Are you okay, fella?" they asked sweetly.

He picked himself up, knees and hands dripping with thick blood. "I didn't do anything. Leave me alone."

He thought they were going to "call the cops" like the elderly people playing ukulele at the beach had done. He thought he had lost the list. He was pissed and couldn't hide it. He didn't see the list anywhere. He felt failure, failure, failure, and remembered his dad saying, "You just don't have the talent to make an expedition profitable."

"Sorry," the couple said and harrumphed away.

Having seen how he growled at them, nobody else approached Kle to help.

"I have let Zeus and Athena and the line of my ancestors down again," Kle confessed to the world and hit his fist violently on the ground, scaring those passing by.

They'd been across the street, but now cops did approach. "What's going on, sir? Why the temper?"

They were used to dealing with all sorts of loco people in Santa Cruz, but the intimidating size of this guy's muscles inspired them to already have their guns out and ready. Kle knew how guns worked. He'd watched the movie Matrix at Zaera's.

"I fell."

"Please show us your ID," they ordered. "Then put your hands over your head."

"You're going to shoot me?" Kle asked, scared.

"Please, sir. We're not interested in shooting you. We'd prefer to just take you in for questioning."

Kle dropped into the depth of the moment's turmoil. Jail, the ultimate disgrace. Only the grimiest grime of Athens would go to jail. He felt his heart and his breath thicken with pressure. Like a bow that's been pulled back for too long, he felt himself snapping. The world of Kle enclosed him like a dark cold hateful cave sucking him out of the voices and faces of downtown. He was drifting galaxies away, morphing into the constellation of a broken warrior.

But before he swung, before he grabbed for the neck of one of these officers, before he went berserk, though he was about to, Kle saw the paper list Zaera had given him. All was not lost!

The paper list had drifted onto a piece of pizza held by an old bearded man not far away. Zaera's list of places was getting soaked with the pizza's grease. This old man was wearing a cowboy hat and had the paper plate with the pizza and the list.

"There it is!" Kle smiled at the extraordinary sight of something that was lost but was now found.

"Damned, that's an unusual wind," an officer noted as a huge gust flushed down Pacific Avenue. And Kle saw another extraordinary sight. There was a long bluish, barely perceptible, tiny tornado just above the heads of the police officers. The tornado couldn't have been more than five feet tall. The tornado made the police officer's shirts ripple with life. And then the tornado above the cops dissolved into nothing, leaving downtown again miraculously windless.

Instead of asking for Kle's ID again, the police officers stared dumbfounded at Kle. Then they looked at each other. The one wearing big sunglasses asked, "What are we doing in front of this guy?"

"Ya," the other sounded scared. "I can't remember how we got here."

"Let's go see what's going on over there," the one with sunglasses pointed at a homeless couple arguing with each other.

"Have a nice day, sir," they told Kle. The policemen looked embarrassed and walked away more than a bit disoriented. Kle didn't know why the cops left him like that. Anyway, his eyes, again, were drawn to the man with a cowboy hat. Kle leapt up.

"That's my list on your piece of pizza," Kle declared after stopping in front of the bearded man.

"Who are you?"

"I am Kle." Then, perhaps to add authority to his request, he instinctively added, "From the line of Odysseus."

The man with the cowboy hat grumbled through his beard. Then he took another bite, chomping stubbornly through the list that had blown onto his pizza.

"Can I please have it?" Kle stayed cool. He didn't want to attract the attention of the policemen again.

The man took another bite.

"Please, no..." Kle started to speak but then just watched the list, which represented all his hopes, get eaten by this cowboy enjoying the taste of his pizza and his paper list. The man gulped his last bite and the list was gone.

"I just wanted that piece of paper," Kle said.

"All eaten. Sorry," the old man whispered.

"Why did you eat my list?"

"Because you don't know who you are."

"I told you my name is Kle."

"Names aren't who you are," the old man replied. "Tasks aren't who you are. Your lineage is not who you are."

"Okay," Kle conceded. "I was arrogant for referring to myself as someone from the line of Odysseus. I just wanted to show you I am."

"You can only show me who you are, if you are who you are. Anyway, why would you pride yourself on being descended from such a man as Odysseus?"

"Odysseus was a great man."

"No. He wasn't. Odysseus was a war-broken distant asshole," this man insulted Kle's family line.

Still, Kle tried having sympathy, "You've had hard times?"

"Yes," the old man agreed. "But something better for me is on horizon." His words were a little broken but he didn't really seem dumb.

"Definitely. My misfortune may have been my greatest blessing," Kle said, thinking of Zaera. She had warmed not only a bed, but his heart. In a brief time, she gave Kle a sense of home he never knew back in harsh Greece or anywhere.

"Never think you are less than Odysseus again. I made that mistake far too many times," the old man grieved.

"Ya, right." Kle was confused by the old man suggesting a connection to Odysseus. To change the subject, he said, "did you see the small tornado above the heads of those police officers?"

"You saw?" The man looked very hopeful. Kle, having seen that tornado, gave the old man some inexplicable delight. The old man had the most weather beaten face Kle had ever seen. He'd clearly spent most of his days out in the sun and wind.

"Ya, the tornado wobbled over the heads of the police officers I was talking to. Then the police officers forgot why they were talking to me. And they let me go! They were about to arrest me or something, but then they just ditched me."

"Wind of forgetting. There's many types of winds," the old man said and pulled a zip lock bag from his pocket and handed it to Kle. The bag was sealed but empty.

Kle took the bag and, again thinking the old man was crazy, asked, "What is this?"

The old man mumbled, "A few winds escaped. Winds of forgetting, winds of change, winds of discord, a few gusts of passion."

Not particularly inspired by this gift of an empty zip lock bag, Kle thanked the old man and walked away, pushing the bag into his pocket. He couldn't remember everything on the list, but he remembered the next item there was the Mystery Spot. He still intended to do as much of Zaera's tasks as he could.

He was starting to realize all this devotion to that list meant he was in love with Zaera.

Revolt

When she was eleven, Enkida's father explained to her, "The gods have given your brother the nectar of my fear and you the nectar of my anger. Because of this, your brother will know how to lead people by drawing from their fear. And you, to lead, will know how to master others' wills through understanding their anger. That is your gift as a ruler."

Her father had become a monarch when he was only thirteen. And Uruk at that time was enmeshed in a power struggle of more than a dozen clans vying for control from the line of Gilgamesh. Her father had united them all in only two years, crushed any remnants of opposition, and doubled the size of their kingdom. He clearly had some gifts as a ruler. Thousands of years later, this same Enkida called on her gift as a ruler, but not in Uruk – she emerged in Santa Cruz. She attended a rally for environmental justice and climate change awareness. Only a day before the event she met its organizers and told them she was an avid environmental justice advocate and a refugee from a Middle Eastern country. She also suggested, "I would love to talk at your gathering."

"What will you talk about?" the main organizer asked after somebody from the Tannery introduced her to this guy. He wore a patchouli dosed organic certified fair trade button shirt.

"I will insist people take some action to care more earnestly for this earth," she said simply. Her voice was resolute, strong and clear.

"How much would you charge to speak?" Something in this young dreadlocked immigrant impressed the forward-thinking organizer of the conference.

"I will charge nothing. I will just demand change." Unlike every other person who was speaking that day, Enkida asked for no compensation to present.

The organizer thought this woman was aligned with the conference's values- a passionate refugee, an empowered woman, the perfect symbols for what this conference considered progress. "You really want to make a difference! Not only will I let you speak at our event but I think you should be an unplanned keynote speaker!"

On the day of the event there were five speeches before Enkida went up. The speeches embedded catch phrases like "Don't be mean, be green," "A good planet is hard to find," "Modern technology owes ecology an apology," and "Green is sexy."

Then Enkida took the microphone and stood in front of thousands of people. She started practically in a whisper, "you have all waited long enough." She got louder. "You've patiently sat on the sidelines hoping for some minuscule change, some inkling that the powers-that-be care for the rivers and trees, care for the air, care for you." Some people harrumphed in agreement, others scratched their heads wondering if the talk on solar panels was next on the lineup, and others judged the ferocity in this dark-skinned woman's voice overkill for the ecology conference they were at.

Now Enkida practically roared and pushed aside the podium, "well, maybe it's time to stop waiting, people! They've already destroyed enough – our lands, our hopes, our rights, our bodies, all that is sacred to us. We have the answers, but we've stayed safe far too long. We have the vision, but have never been fully willing to step in and claim that vision. We've groveled and tried to convince them with science, but they out-advertised us, continuing to aggressively cut down every tree, pollute every river, and start every war without care about our pathetic little protests." The organizer of the event was already rushing towards the security guards to stop this train wreck of a speaker.

Enkida yelled like a crazed person, "follow me and we will no longer be ignored, no longer be discarded as dreamy unicorns, no longer be stomped. Those who try to stop us must be crushed."

"Huh?" A wave of confusion rolled through the audience. The big group of people in the Kaiser Permanente Center were there for a conference with a long list of speakers on the "eco-revolution." There had already been an expert on compost toilets, a representative from Greenpeace, Julia Butterfly Hill, and nine others speaking insightfully on sustainability and the "new" economy. The organizers and the attendees did not expect or want to hear this woman call for a full-blown revolution.

Enkida did not let up, "they prefer us to remain slaves to their buying and selling; but they will feel pain when we break out of our shackles. It is time to rise up, for the uprising, for them to hear our power, or suffer far beyond what they think a few hippies can do. You know, that's how they see you, as a sheepish band of impotent hippies-singing about sustainability and driving our SUV's,!" Enkida was fearless of the uncomfortable squirming in the large crowd, undeterred by the murmurings about the "crazy lady on the mic" The organizers had been thrilled to have a dark-skinned immigrant willing to speak at their event. They thought she would look good but now they regretted not vetting her.

Enkida was unfazed when her microphone was turned off and security guards told her, "follow me." The black and yellow uniformed security guard didn't wait for an answer;

they grabbed her. Surprised and actually happy their services were needed, the security guards escorted her out of the large auditorium. As the auditorium door shut behind her, Enkida was told, "don't dare come back in here or we will have you arrested."

But her words and presence left behind a curious magic. Ripe with purpose, many felt inspired to follow this dragon lady out of the desert of hellish consumerism. As Enkida walked up Pacific Avenue and past Saturn Café, a few dozen brave souls followed alongside her. By the time she got to the Catalyst, it was at least a hundred. And, by the time she arrived at the clock tower, where she stopped and spoke again, journalists guessed there were at least four hundred and thirty riled up followers ready to obey this self-appointed general.

At the clock tower, Enkida's speech referred to things she heard discussed over dinner during her first night at the Tannery. She called up waves of anger at the politicians for being so controlled by money's power; anger at schools for being so focused on factory style learning and tests; anger at the medical industry for being outrageously expensive and ignoring holistic sensibilities; anger at capitalism for destroying the environment and propagating such a dramatic income gap between the rich and poor; anger at religious institutions for the way they pitted people against each other and fed off guilt; anger at the mega-farming industry for harvesting crops dripping with pesticides; and fury at men who refused to recognize women, like her, as equals.

She did not ask them to write emails to their local congressman or make signs protesting Monsanto. Her verse was no gentle poem. It was an arrow dipped in poison and flame. It was nearly the same thing that had filled hippy-dippy messages for decades with one significant twist: an elimination of the non-violent piece of that equation. She never encouraged killing but she didn't exclude that option. She was explicit about insisting on results.

"It's time to use not only our speech or even our punch," she said, "but to use whatever means we have to wipe away the institutions that heartlessly oppress us."

The fire began! Within hours of Enkida's clock tower speech, a group of ten college students went into Wells Fargo, wearing Donald Trump masks, and pulled down their pants to take a shit (they all drank powerful diuretics not long before). Then they bolted, leaving piles of brown stinky crap all over the bank. Then nine of the nicest yachts at the harbor were flipped on their sides by young people dressed head to toe in black. Spray paint reading "fuck the man" was left on the capsized luxury items. And dozens of individuals wearing the mask from "V for Vendetta" movie invaded Santa Cruz High School, scaring the teachers off the campus, and telling the kids, "leave here. Be free. And never come back unless this school becomes a beacon of the arts and innovation instead of a machine serving the overlords of industrialization."

Enkida knew about these escapades. She was part of some of them, even proud of them, but then her message evolved into something more vicious than what she honestly expected, offshoots emerging completely without her awareness that very afternoon. The McDonald's on Ocean Ave. was burned to the ground. Reports say seven lithe individuals showed up painted with very elaborate face paint, and yelled "Everyone get out."

After it was cleared, they set a few sticks of dynamite in the kitchen before making a break for it. Almost exactly at the same time, something similar happened at a Burger King, a Taco Bell, and even a Panda Express. It was too much for the authorities; the fire trucks were overburdened and always too late. The fast food industry – being corporate chains that exploited minimum wage workers and promoted eating questionable food, inspired no mercy from the Pandora's box Enkida opened. Two CVS's, one on 41st and one on Front Street, were ransacked like a tidal wave hit them. Pharmaceuticals were smashed and spray paint again displayed the ultimate message: "fuck the man" across the walls. Windows were unsparingly smashed. Nobody was killed but there was plenty of terror.

Too much was going on – the police didn't catch a single person. People just dispersed and blended in too quickly into what is Santa Cruz. People already look weird in Santa Cruz.

An online article in the Santa Cruz Sentinel about that night headlined: "Vicious Rhetoric of General Dreadlocks Results in Chaos across Santa Cruz." Enkida's whole speech was printed out in this same article. While the intention of the article was to scandalize her, or anyone who might consider her leadership benign, it garnered at least as much support as antipathy.

Whispers of what was happening in Santa Cruz began popping up all across the country, making a lot of people nervous. The overwhelmed local forces called the Feds. "This is terrorism," they said pleading for help. But the evening came and things quieted down. The powers that be wanted to do more research before acting at all.

Without even going to Santa Cruz, twenty FBI operatives linked the whole mess back to Enkida. Round table discussions in Washington considered an appropriate response to this woman who started an uproar at an environmental awareness rally.

After resting for a night back in the woods above Santa Cruz, Enkida saw the helicopters buzzing over town. She saw the coast guard active along the coast. She saw sleek black cars full of FBI agents zipping along the roads. She was proud of her work, stating out loud to the trees around her, "The people here are sleepy and need a fart in the face to wake them up (a common expression in ancient Mesopotamia). They're treating their lives like they're zombie sheep. I'm here for the people who are ready to live again."

Still, she did consider the potential danger of starting such kindling in people's lives. She felt a growing sense of panic about the backlash and even got to wondering if Arito might somehow be linked to her, and what that could mean to his life. It's amazing how quickly we can recognize the good in the bad and the bad in the good. She remembered the grim warning of the man who taught her the mantra that brought her here – "It takes skill to control and should only be used if you are ready for everything in your life to be destroyed." Enkida was starting to acknowledge to herself that she couldn't contain this.

The Mystery Spot

Kle biked as hard as he could towards the Mystery Spot, the last location on Zaera's list as he could remember. The Mystery Spot is famed for having an actual gravity vortex, making trees grow in unexpected ways, balls roll uphill, and birds avoid the area.

Kle pedaled up a hill on Branciforte Avenue. The road left the city and faded into the trees. The cars became fewer (though the ones that drove by zoomed along like maniacs, almost hitting Kle three times).

He was tired and wanted to go home to Zaera, but he wanted to return to her as victorious. He wanted to tell her about the old man with the cowboy hat.

Kle exerted himself to the maximum, pedaling up the hills and into the woods towards the Mystery Spot. Everyone he'd asked in town knew where the Mystery Spot was, but they discouraged him from biking there saying, "It's just a tourist trap," or "It's a stupid optical illusion." Sounded dangerous and foolish, two things he was willing to be for Zaera.

He passed DeLaVeaga Park and then the giant sign for The Mystery Spot. When he passed a deer eating grass just off the road, he stopped to gaze into the deer's peaceful eyes for a few moments. The deer wasn't so interested. It bolted, jumping along like it weighed nothing. Standing there by himself, Kle wondered whether any task would give him the pride he so yearned for. He wondered if his workshop idea would work in this world (or any other!). He wondered whether there was just something the matter with him that made it so he could only come up with dud ideas.

There were at least eight helicopters roving overhead when he muttered, "There is a lot of crazy magic in this world." He didn't know some of the helicopters were news crews and others were FBI choppers and Swat teams scoping out Santa Cruz to figure out how such a wildfire of mobs erupted here. And he hopped back on his bike for the final mile to the Mystery Spot.

Just before wheeling into the parking lot, Kle saw a monstrously huge cat not far off the road. It was yellow. Kle stopped again. This beast didn't flee as readily as the deer had. This animal locked eyes with Kle and even walked steadily towards him. It moved with clear intent. Kle broke from his reverie and kicked away on his bike to get away from what looked like a ferocious and majestic cat approaching him. "I'm a coward," he confessed to himself out loud.

There were only two cars at Mystery Spot's huge parking lot. Kle poked around the area and even knocked on the door of the souvenir shop. "Sorry. We're already closed. We just had our last tour," a heavily freckled smiling kid hollered while he was walking down some steps from the Mystery Spot.

"And he did that last tour just for me," a man in a light gray business suit laughed unnervingly.

"There's no other tourists here?" Kle grieved, asking the freckled kid.

"There's always tomorrow," the man in the business suit offered. "And even sometimes a few yesterdays."

"Would you at least take this flier?" Kle asked the man in the business suit.

"What is it?"

"It's a workshop I'm trying to sell," Kle said.

"Do you teach it?" the businessman asked.

"Yes."

The man took the flier.

"Huh. It says I'll learn how to throw a javelin and wrestle like an Olympian. And I'll learn about the ancient gods of Greece. Interesting. I'm not sure if this is something Mark would be interested in."

"Mark who?"

"My boss," the man replied succinctly, uninterested in talking further. Then he skipped over to his fancy red Audi and turned on some gnarly punk rock before speeding away. The freckled tour guide turned to Kle saying, "He was talking about Mark Zuckerberg, the founder of Facebook. That dude's like one of his personal assistants or something."

"I was supposed to check out the Mystery Spot today," Kle said. "It was on my list."

The kid with freckles stopped smiling.

"On your list? Okay. Well. Hey, if you go into the hills around here, you'll be in the vortex and won't have to pay for an entrance fee. You'll get how gravity really is pretty weird in the Mystery Spot is."

"What's gravity?"

"Very funny. I'm leaving and we've locked up the gate to the tour path but I won't stop you from walking up the trail that starts at the far side of the parking lot." Freckles pointed to a trailhead adjacent to the Mystery Spot.

"Thanks," Kle nodded. "How do I check gravity's weirdness?"

"I overheard you teach javelin throwing. Why don't you throw a stick or something?"

"Okay."

As usual, Kle followed the advice he heard. Kle's sandaled feet were weary, worn down from the many miles they kicked the bike through. His mind was just as fatigued, traumatized even (by his interaction with the cops and losing his list and meeting that wild old man). It had been little more than a week since he landed in this frighteningly odd world and he'd already dropped into the high stress life of a salesman, a task he was proving to be exceptionally poor at. Still, the redwood forest was sweet to him. The trees, clearly hundreds of years old, exuded a feeling of steadiness that had been all too inaccessible lately. As he walked up into the hills of the Mystery Spot, perhaps tuning into the vortex he suddenly thought he heard his mother's voice. Being that was impossible, he remembered her long blonde hair and dark olive skin. She was always talking, either with him or the philosophers or business people or slaves or herself. She laughed easily, grimaced rarely, and shied away from no one. But, in her brashness, she made enemies – people who thought she was immodest and set a bad example for other women.

When Kle was eight years old, she had told him, "The trees are wiser than the gods. The gods fight for their power. The gods are jealous and stupid and short-tempered. The trees are just there… wise."

Two weeks later, his mother disappeared. It was assumed that someone she offended had her killed. And, as he recalled his melancholy over losing her, Kle again thought he heard his mother singing a lullaby. He turned around and didn't see anything. He saw nothing, but followed the singing further up the hill.

It seemed the voice was coming from just up the hill. He sprinted in that direction, forcing his tired muscles to burn. Then a stick dropped from above him and the music stopped. "Does Poseidon or Athena possess me with some madness?" he screamed at the stick. "Why do I hear my mother's voice?"

Then, furious, and perhaps inspired by the freckled tour guide, he picked up the stick that fell and hurled it with all the skill of an average ancient Greek warrior trained in throwing a javelin. To start the throw, he flicked the javelin off the edge of his pointer finger. Then he again heard his mother's voice; it was coming from the stick he had hurled into the sky. Kle watched his perfect throw begin with an expected arc up into the sky but, then, as it came down, it seemed to be pulled diagonally in a whole other direction, until it landed not far away, but in a place Kle'd never have expected.

And her voice rang again from the place where the stick landed. "Athena, have mercy on me with this madness?" Kle yelled again at the sky and ran towards the voice. Remembering his mother ran painfully through his heart. He tripped over the roots of a tree. And a big tree branch jabbed him painfully in the side. But he followed the singing. He expected his mother to be there – young and beautiful and loving – waiting to embrace her frightened child. But all he found was the quiet branch that he had thrown.

Realizing there had to be some twisted magic in this place, he fell to his knees, not just with tears but full-blown sobbing. He shook and held back nothing. He'd never openly grieved losing his mother but now it coursed through and out of him.

A good cry can cleanse one's vision, literally lubricate and cool the eyes, purge the mind of small thinking. In that clarity of sight, he saw a small yellow glittering thing with nine dots on it, next to the stick he had thrown. This small gem was familiar. He picked it up and examined it.

Yes, it was the thing he'd touched just before falling into this world. As he held the enchanted object, Kle closed his eyes passively and fell into another vision – it was something he never even imagined before... he was eight and his mother was putting some jewels and coins from their house into a big sack. Then she excitedly ran out of their home to live out her life with a bohemian foreigner who'd met her while traveling through Athens.

Kle assumed this vision came from some magic within the nine dotted talisman and wanted to disconnect from it. Kle pulled the zip lock bag that the old man downtown had given him. He opened the bag, put the gem thing in, and stuffed it back into his pocket. Then he curled up into the fetal position on the ground and remained there as if frozen.

"She left me behind," Kle said out loud. "My mother left me behind to run off with some wandering hobo."

A vicious wind cut through what had been a calm day. Where there had been a clear sky only minutes before, it seemed the heavens above were suddenly full of dark clouds ripe with rain. But he remained on the ground immobilized by emotion. And it did rain. Poured hard. Saturating the ground and his clothes. And he'd have stayed there all night, but kind warm arms wrapped around him, "What are you doing out here, you idiot!"

"Mom?"

"What? It's me Zaera. You didn't come back. I didn't really know what to think. But I tracked my bike to the parking lot of the Mystery Spot! Some kid smoking a joint told me that you went up the trail. And then, while I was looking for you, I totally tripped out. I thought I saw a fucking lion. Not just a holy shit mountain lion. But I thought I saw a saber-tooth-sized giant lion. And it chased me this direction. But, after I saw you curled up like a baby, I looked back and the fucking thing was gone. And this fucking rain's come out of nowhere and, shit, we got to get you home. You're freezing!"

She helped Kle up and they walked down the hill together to her car. They stuffed the bike in so it hung out of the Honda's trunk. The freckled joint smoker wasn't there. "What happened to you, Kle?" she asked again gently.

"I found out the people who brought me to this world are staying at the Tannery. And I think I realized my mother wasn't killed. She left me behind. And it's all too much."

"We're going to the Tannery," Zaera said. She wanted to be clearer about who this Kle, this strange man she'd taken in, was. She loved him and was trying to go down the rabbit hole to follow that love.

A Loft in the Santa Cruz Tannery Artist Live/Work Center

"Where am I?" Nariah rubbed her eyes as she woke up. She was lying on a couch in a dark room. Because of Arito's pot, her head was fuzzy.

"The Tannery," a voice answered Nariah from across the barely lit room. Nariah could only see the silhouette of the person who spoke. Her heart leapt. The deep gentle effeminate voice, the long hair, the flowing robe. She thought it had to be John the Apostle. Somehow, Jesus had sent John across time and space, perhaps to rescue her from this despairing dystopia.

"Oh, John, why did Jesus send me to this horrid place?" she asked. "Why are we here?"

"John?" The voice objected and lifted a large window's blinds so that the room flooded with the light of a clear blue late morning sky. The person looked mostly male, but wearing a yellow blouse, a long skirt, some bright red lipstick, and had what appeared to be breasts.

Nariah fell back on the couch. "Who are you?"

"Who am I? I am Arito's roommate and you are taking space in our apartment. I am in this same place every morning but today I have tried to be quiet and not open the blinds so I don't awaken this little pumpkin sleeping on our couch. No, my princess, the question is who are you?"

"I'm sorry. I was just confused and thought you were someone else, someone here to rescue me."

"Rescue you! Nobody's here to save you, sweetie."

"Jesus is," she disagreed.

"If you say so," the man dressed as a woman allowed, rolling his eyes.

"So, what's the tannery?"

"A tannery is a place that makes things out of leather. This place used to be a tannery. Now it is only called that. Now it is a theater, with art galleries, and a bunch of spacious lofts set aside so that mightily progressive Santa Cruz can have lofty minded artists to bless this city with their creative brilliance."

"Huh?"

"And I'll tell you how you got here. Arito said you got too stoned off of three drags from his joint and he couldn't figure out where to take you home. You were just eating and giggling until you passed out in the community room. Then, as an act of goodwill, Arito lugged you here and plopped your holy personage on our couch."

Nariah bit her lip to keep from crying. "I'm sorry I got stoned and giggled until I passed out."

"I am not sorry about anything. If I get stoned and pass out somewhere, I would be just as proud of myself as though I'd won a Miss America contest, god forbid. By the way, I am Rafael, darling."

"Good to meet you, Rafael. I am Nariah."

"It is not yet good to meet you, but I can only hope." Rafael smiled dramatically. "And back to wondering why you're here, I'll give you a piece of advice, honey. If I was always complaining about the place I was in and wondering why, why, why it's so horrid! I couldn't wake up in the morning. Why was I born a woman in a man's body? Why have the bigots of this world been taken so seriously for so long? Why do all the good handsome guys die in Game of Thrones? Oh, the drama of life! Got it?"

Nariah nodded timidly.

"The second thing." Rafael held up two fingers. Nariah still wasn't sure what the first thing was. "Decide why you're here. If you don't, somebody will decide for you and that makes you only a shadow of whatever you could have been in the first place."

"Decide why I'm here? What if my conclusion is wrong?"

"That's beside the point," Rafael waved his arms in the air as if he was exaggerating his frustration. "Nobody's here for any reason, so there's no way to know if you're wrong. And no matter the reason you choose, somebody will say ugh, that a stupid reason."

"Okay," Nariah agreed.

"I'm waiting, my plump little honey."

"What? What are you waiting for?"

"For you to tell me why you're here. I have stopped talking and shown interest in your answer; still, you haven't shared anything except a demure agreement to every little proposition I've made. I'm waiting to talk to somebody. Stop being nobody. If you happened to become somebody, who would that person be? What is that one thing that makes you roar?"

Nariah pulled herself up off the couch. "It's time for me to decide?"

"Exactly."

Nariah felt a surge of energy about being in a crucial moment for her life in this new world. From what she could tell, this very exacting man was asking her to establish what her greater underlying purpose in life was. Nariah, unable to spit out an instant answer, searched back through her memories for something that might inform her now. She went back thousands of years to a key moment… when she and Mary first met Jesus.

Everyone was raving about the well-traveled Jesus, who had a superstar mystique after just returning from India. He'd been gone from Nazareth and the rest of Judea for ten years. Nariah didn't know him, but heard that Jesus left Judea as a skittish arrogant crass teenager, and hitched a ride along with a colorful merchant's caravan. He had returned, supposedly humble, somber, and alone.

Since Jesus's return, dozens of people claimed that they slept better after meeting with this carpenter turned healer. Furthermore, their aches and pains went away or their hatred ceased or they simply found some greater sense of peace. Some rabbis were inspired by these healings and said his teachings could build on the teachings the ancient sages had established. Other Jewish religious authorities, particularly the Pharisees, thought he disrespected the tradition and was poisoning young people's minds with hopes of rebellion against Rome and spiritual aspirations completely alien to Jewish scripture.

One rabbi even said, "Any Jew who spends time with this heretic should be ashamed of himself. Spending time with this Jesus is crapping on the wisdom of our patriarchs' authority."

Mary and Nariah were 'women of the night.' Their whole lives were darkened by some degree of shame about this. And, in that vein, as they passed by through the outdoor market of Nazareth, the town's most well-dressed man spit a big loogie on them, grimacing and shouting "Get out of here, whores!"

Most everyone who thought they had class considered Mary and Nariah to be less than dogs. It was not really secret what the girls did to survive. "You here looking for business. No Roman soldiers around to fuck," a young daughter at the man's side crassly scorned Mary and Nariah. The man also had five strong looking sons following resolutely behind him. They just grunted.

"Leave us alone," Mary commanded more assertively than most women in her profession would dare.

Then Nariah led them both in starting to walk away. The shopkeepers at that corner of the market looked on, and, whether they sympathized with the girls or not, they were unwilling to stand up to the well-to-do man and his sons for harassing a whore. They just stood behind the shelves with their wares – sandals and fruits and knives and cloth and spices.

Nariah, clumsy as usual, tripped on a rock as they scurried away. Her hands and face fell directly onto a pile of fresh pony shit. The man spoke up again, laughing brashly, "Shit for the shit. Perfect."

While she was scared of the wealthy merchant and his sons, Mary didn't leave Nariah behind. She went back, helped her up, and wiped her face with the one item she treasured, the shawl she used to cover her hair. Then Mary scooped up a piece of shit with her left hand, and, feeling the dark weight of her years as a prostitute, turned daringly to the man who scorned them.

"Yes, shit for shit," she said and threw it unsuccessfully towards the man. Still mostly unconcerned for these girls, the shopkeepers suddenly grew anxious. If things got violent, Roman soldiers might be compelled to make their way over to stop the beating of these ladies by the wealthy man and his sons. What they really feared was that Roman soldiers always took the liberty of swiping a chunk of their wares as a sort of commission for responding to any trouble that happened near them; it would not be good for business.

But just as the sons got to Mary, thirty other young Judean men bustled into that section of the market. They were following a man with a serene, even noble, demeanor. The man's sons ignored the arrival of this atypical leader and his troupe.

Wealthy, the family was used to the privilege of immunity from any crime. They threw Mary to the ground, yelling, "You fucking cunt. Prepare to get the beating of your life. The people who come to fuck you are going to be scared off by the mess of sores you'll be bleeding from tonight, you loose bitch."

But before they hit her even once, the leader of the newcomers said calmly and slowly, but with a ferocious authority, "Get off her now." His voice was so clear and strong, it was impossible for the boys to ignore it and they stopped.

"Who commands my sons but me?" the businessman blurted out furiously.

"My name is Jesus. You are not worthy of commanding your sons."

"Ah, the Prodigal Son. Well, welcome home, bastard boy. I'm not interested in what you learned from the pagans. Carry on so I can beat these whores as I please. If you still like, you can hire them afterwards. I'll make sure they'll be so ugly that they're cheap enough for even you to afford."

Jesus turned to the man's sons and said, "Turn away from your father's lead, friends."

"Don't listen to that apostate. Teach that bitch a lesson," the businessman hissed back.

Jesus moved with the levity of a cloud, but the weight of a planet, to an inch away from the man saying, "You and your family will leave this blessed woman alone."

"You speak up for a prostitute," the man replied, "calling her blessed. Then you order me to leave! Hah!"

Jesus locked eyes with the man. Perhaps trusting that their father could deal with this heathen himself, or out of fear of this heathen's rough looking entourage, his sons did stay back. The way Jesus looked into this man's eyes cannot be described. There was anger and kindness but, much more, a vast openness that contained something of a space exposing a reflection of any man to himself.

To those watching, it was a flash. To this man, it was an eternity through hell, purgatory, and a glimpse of heaven's light. He fell to his knees and threw his face into his hands. He cried and cried and shook and put his hands over his eyes as if to protect himself from what he just saw.

Then the boys fell to their father asking, "What is the matter?"

"I am wretched. Wretched. Please forgive me," the man looked shamefully at Mary and then Jesus. "Please rid me of the demons that make me like this."

To the man's relief, Jesus placed a hand on his forehead saying, "Begone demons. May God bring you and your family to the crossroads of new life, a life that sees everyone as children of God."

Jesus said no more to them, his words lingering in the air like a choice that could be taken or ignored.

Jesus walked back to Mary, lovingly took her hands into his, and said, "I am here for the gentle souls in this world. And you are the gentlest. I am so glad to see you."

That day both Nariah and Mary joined Jesus, though Mary clearly emerged as Jesus's closest companion. With Jesus, both of them were supported to live without prostitution and realized a vibrant sense of wholeness and purity they never knew existed.

"I am here for the gentle souls," Nariah proudly announced to Rafael then at the Tannery. That was the turning point of her life and the moment she would hold onto as a guide for the rest of her days. Rafael leapt up dancing around the room like a preteen ballerina.

"Perfect! Too perfect! Really. Wow. I'm a gentle soul."

"Why's it perfect?" Nariah asked.

"You really didn't know? The whole Tannery's having a party here tonight. We've been planning it for months. And look." Rafael handed Nariah a flier. It read "Party for Gentle Souls at the Tannery. Come celebrate the Winter Solstice and the returning of the light. The night will be full of ecstatic chanting, mystical dancing, rhymes by McMega Samadhi, and beats by DJ Aftertaste. All gentle souls will ride the waves of music." Along the flier's edge were the logos of business sponsors who were selling their products at the Tannery's festival/party – Brew Cruz, Kombucha Botanica, Roots Kava Bar, and Staff of Life Natural Foods Market.

"Baruch Hashem," Nariah praised God in Hebrew.

"You said what you are you here for and the universe was ready!" Rafael exalted. "I'm going to pee in my pants. I'm so excited!"

"What are you here for?" Nariah asked Rafael.

"Fashion domination," Rafael purred back without hesitation. Then something rumbled outside.

"What's that, Rafael?" Nariah pointed outside. They both saw a full-fledged tornado at least a hundred feet tall, spewing up red dust as it moved along Highway 9. It was coming from San Lorenzo Valley and heading towards downtown.

"Twisters don't happen in Santa Cruz! Holy mother of Jesus!"

Cat

Police officers, FBI agents, and most other authority figures scurrying Santa Cruz found themselves mysteriously incapable of finding Enkida. It wasn't because she was particularly clever in her efforts to hide. She had cast a spell of protection on herself and her closest vigilante comrades.

Enkida was in Crepe Place trying to celebrate some sense of victory. Crepe Place is a fantastic restaurant with old creaky uneven wooden floors. It feels more like the hull of an old ship than the classy restaurant/ music venue it is for Santa Cruz. The band playing that night was a heavy bass funk band with a reggae-influenced pro-technology lyricist telling all about his "irie rasta i-pad Jah Love."

Enkida danced alongside her tribe of eager young revolutionaries relishing in having leadership in their midst. There were mostly college students – English Literature/ Molecular Biology/ Community Studies majors all equally did their best to brush up against Enkida or, at least, touch her ancient dreadlocks. They yearned to absorb some small bit of her greatness into themselves.

Semi-oblivious as to what had really brewed that day, they didn't ask themselves why police officers hadn't picked up Enkida or any of them yet. They were intoxicated on the potency of the moment. Enkida's Mesopotamian bouncy-down moves, all the way to her bottom, further induced a sort of hysteria, so unique and yet so appropriate to the music. And while many adored and got close to her briefly, only one among the crowd dared to really face Enkida as a dance partner. He looked like he was from the same country as Surya, the Ayurvedic shaman who'd given her the talisman for opening up the portal here. But, instead of self-controlled selfless Surya, the young Indian man dancing before her impulsively took Enkida's hands and bumped bottoms with her and yelped like a wild animal next to her.

And Enkida liked it. As they danced, juicy energy from her groin swirled up. Wanting more, she yelled above the music, "What is your name?"

"Paul." Their hips bumped.

"Do you know about Ayurveda?" Thinking of Surya reminded Enkida of what he shared about Ayurveda.

Paul laughed. "Dude, I've never even been to India. My grandma taught me to pour salt water through my nose when I'm sick. That's about as much Ayurveda as I know. You know you're gorgeous?"

Enkida blushed for the second time in her life. It was not customary for a woman to be praised for her beauty in Mesopotamia, unless it was husband to wife or an illicit affair. She felt very unaware of what her body could do to men (and some women).

The only other time someone had appreciated her beauty was in the wheat fields near her palace. One afternoon she escaped her royal duties alone and unescorted when a lone peasant boldly told her she was a delight. It was a simple flattery but it so moved Enkida she offered him her virginity right there in the fields. She was perfectly inexperienced. The peasant wasn't much more of an adept. Neither of them thought it might result in a baby.

And, even months later, after she grew ripe with child, she never considered returning to those fields to seek the man out. Of course, everyone assumed the child was a gift from a visit by Enlil, king of the Gods, with Enkida. She didn't correct this rumor, knowing this would only help her child be revered in the days to come as a God-man.

Now, dancing with Paul in the Crepe Place, Enkida felt ten times as much electrical desire as she had with that peasant. The pull for physical contact was unstoppable. With each beat of the drums, it seemed to become more. This free-spirited Paul invoked feelings that no magic spell could conjure. He looked a small bit younger than her, so green in years he had little more than peach fuzz on his face. But she didn't have to hold out for a monarch to rule at her side anymore. She was free to have fun with this young morsel.

"I could really get used to this," Enkida told Paul.

Paul wasn't sure what she meant by this, the empress really coming down from her pedestal. And he didn't question it. He just happily kept dancing with her. Paul jumped higher and higher, enjoying this new friend who was clearly on the verge of becoming something more with him, serious chemistry fermenting. Enkida let Paul skim his hands against her neck under her dreadlocks and along her tanned back and ass and thighs and... then they were rudely interrupted.

Enkida's spell of protection had not repelled everyone outside of her piously enamored circle. Arito slipped into the Crepe Place and pushed through the rowdy tribe swirling around Enkida. He hissed at a woman who fell against him.

Arito's arms, more erratic and spider-like than usual, were holding a newspaper which he promptly shoved up into Enkida's face, saying, "What do you think of this, oh wise leader of imbeciles?"

Enkida stopped dancing and took the newspaper from his hand. Arito didn't wait for her to read it and respond. He growled, "Whoever you really are, you opened up the gates of hell for us. Read what your leadership awakened. Read it and then ask yourself if what you're doing is right at all? I'm glad at least I know you're not my mother."

Arito stomped out of the Crepe Place without trying to dance, without drinking a single beer or eating a single crepe.

"Who was that?" Paul asked.

"I'm not sure," Enkida said honestly, unsure whether Arito was her son or not.

While he wore the anklet and looked similar to the peasant she'd had sex with, Enkida knew she really couldn't sure be who Arito was. Or if it should matter to her.

"Really," Paul asked doubtfully, unsure of what secret she was holding back.

"I'll be right back," she said. "I need to look at this." Enkida slipped away from Paul and the lustful arousal that was exploding in her on the dance floor. She went to the Crepe Place's back patio, where a few couples were calmly eating crepes. She wanted to figure out why Arito shoved a newspaper into her hands. What did the Santa Cruz Sentinel say?

What Enkida read described a weird day in Santa Cruz, much exceeding any usual weirdness of the status quo, which was already very high here. There was an article called "Blowing in the Wind" on a wild plethora of tornadoes/ glacier cold winds/ whirlpools/ and hot winds surging across the hills and coastline. The explanation for this was "the semi-expected results of too many tons of Carbon Dioxide emissions pumped into the air."

She read the next article: "Giant Mutant Cat Spotted by Mushroom Hunter," an article about a fungi connoisseur looking for chanterelle mushrooms who claimed to see an eight foot tall mountain lion leaping from the top of his car in a parking lot back into the veil of redwood trees. Then she flipped back to the front page and the biggest headline:

"Environmental Machiavelli." There were photos of military choppers bringing in SWAT teams to control this relatively small California coastal town. And the accompanying article described a young lady derailing an environmental justice rally, and how she inspired mutinous uprisings across the county. It detailed the fast food fires and bank shit-ins. Its conclusion was: "This is terrorism, an excess of university town liberal extremism…We wish it was a mass-hallucination we could wake up from. This level of destruction only breeds more violence and fear."

Enkida cried and wasn't sure why. Of course, there was something about being unsure where her leadership was taking all these people. This news was such a jarring contrast from the delight she'd felt dancing with Paul. But mostly she cried because the boy whom she thought was her son had just told her off with not only disgust, but hatred in his eyes.

"I have to find the gem I lost in the forest when I first fell into this world," she said to the Crepe Place's back patio. "I have to go now."

Enkida knew if she saw Paul back in the dance hall of the Crepe Place, she'd be lured into enjoying this world more and get more entrenched in letting go of all the problems she'd caused. So she invoked an invisibility cloak spell and jumped over the fence behind the back patio. She ran from joy. She ran past the Rio Theater, up Water Street past a tattoo shop, a tire store, and Divinitree Yoga. She just kept running and running, not turning right until she got to River Street.

And, heaving, she shot up into the mountains of San Lorenzo Valley, hoping to find her way back to the tree where she'd first fallen into this world.

Enkida ran up the road alongside trees and hills. She ran so that her legs and lungs burned. She wasn't really sure where she was going but she ran for hours. She ran past boulders and leaped over creeks, promising out loud, "I will find that gem and do the incantation again. Maybe I can undo everything. Maybe I can fix this. Maybe I can leap back in time to when my son was born and maybe…"

Then she saw the cat standing a hundred feet away from her. It was her cat. They sprinted towards each other and she wrapped her arms around it. She hadn't seen it since she was in Judea. "What happened to you," Enkida asked looking at a two-foot long gash in its side. This nasty wound was sizzling with the infection of dark magic, dark magic. Because of this poisoned cut, the cat's breathing was strained.

"Who did this done to you?" Enkida asked her as she, again, wrapped her arms around him. She felt both elated at finding him, but grieved to see him so hurt. "How is it that you managed to follow me into this world and that such evil has found you?"

Enkida didn't even want to say the name of her brother's loyal sorcerer, Efaau. To her it seemed obvious that blasted sorcerer's magic was fermenting in her feline friend. Knowing what she had to do, Enkida leaped upon the back of her giant loyal friend and told it to run towards the greatest nexus of magic it could sense nearby in this world. She would do whatever she thought she had to do to free the cat from the dark zombie magic.

She held onto the cat as it raced up the hillside, frequently looking back over her shoulder. A few times, Enkida thought she saw a multi-tentacled demon slithering following along behind them and she shivered coldly.

Kle got out of Zaera's Honda and right away began asking around for "the two ladies from another time." He got a few blank looks, some laughs, and a very stoned looking artist who replied smartly, "No artists are from this time."

Then Kle described Enkida's leather dress to a young artist with a Seventies-style ponytail. Mr. Ponytail responded, "You mean the one starting the revolution?"

"Oh shit," Zaera groaned, freaked out that Kle might somehow be connected to that lady she heard was cajoling mutiny from within the environmental justice community. Zaera had been very active with promoting awareness of ocean pollution. She'd taken her young students numerous times to beach clean-up days; was a member of Surfrider Foundation; and she almost got arrested protesting frackers in Monterey County. But she was disgusted how violence was used by these followers of Enkida.

"What revolution?" Kle asked.

An arctic cold wind whisked across the plaza area outside the Tannery. Zaera, Kle, and the kid with the ponytail got goosebumps. The kid shrugged his shoulders and walked away, anxious to get out of the cold and away from these people giving him a bad trip. Zaera pulled up an image of Enkida on her iphone, of Enkida speaking in Kaiser arena at the Environmental Justice convention. Zaera asked Kle, "is this who we're looking for?"

"Yes," Kle smiled widely. "Have you seen her?"

Zaera shook her head. "I don't know what the fuck I've been thinking, letting you stay at my house, putting my money into your workshop. Listen, I need some time to myself. I have to figure this out."

"Why are you saying all this?" Kle asked, confused.

"If you're connected with that crazy lady, I realize I may have been betting on the wrong horse. I'm so pissed at myself." Zaera's hair was always red but now her face was just as red. "I'm so pissed at myself. Pissed away money. Pissed away my time. Pissed away my heart. Argh. I need a real man right now. Not another Santa Cruz Peter Pan piece of shit."

Zaera walked away, leaving Kle standing there alone. Before he hollered for Zaera to stop, the pony tailed kid he'd been talking to ran back saying, "I just heard from someone that the chick you're looking for – Enkida – was seen riding a big cat up the hill behind the Tannery. It wasn't long ago, maybe she's still somewhere back there. That is, if the person who saw this was sober." At the same time, Zaera burned rubber speeding from the Tannery parking lot and back onto Highway 9.

Because of the gem's original pulse of magic, Kle, Enkida, and Nariah were all drawn within a hundred feet of each other right around the same time. Enkida was raceing up the hills behind the Tannery on her cat, Kle watched Zaera walk away from him. And Nariah was in a Medieval Culinary Class (taught in a studio at the Tannery.)

Kle didn't move to stop Zaera. Instead, shocked, he shook in a cold sweat. It had only been a couple hours since he discovered that his mom had left him when he was a child. This, on top of Zaera rushing off without much of an explanation, left him feeling flat, a half person, unlovable, broken. Not knowing what else to do, Kle went back behind the Tannery (where the kid said Enkida had been seen riding a cat.)

As Kle approached the shadowy side of the Tannery, he thought he saw something lurking in the forested ravine below there. In the cover of the trees, for a half a second, there was a slithering mess of tentacles and slime sucking blood from some small animal. But he blinked and then he just heard a person groaning next to the creek down there.

"You okay?" Kle asked the moaning person.

Whoever it was didn't answer. Thinking the person was hurt, Kle climbed down rocks to make sure the person was okay. He saw what he thought was a very skinny man contorted in strange ways groaning.

"You okay?" Kle asked again.

Instead of a skinny man, he now saw a young lady, disheveled but with beautiful blonde hair. And she answered, "me? Never been better! Please join me."

Realizing a hero was unnecessary, Kle didn't race back up the hill. There was no one and nowhere drawing him out of this shadow lair. He just put his hand to his forehead and felt an overwhelming feeling of abandonment.

"Can you be my hero, good looking?" the girl asked. On closer look, Kle wasn't sure if she was in her twenties or seventies. Her hair had a vital sheen and her body inspired a flush of attraction, but something in her eyes or face looked sucked dry. But it was hard to see clearly in the shadows.

"I'd love to feel like a hero," Kle grunted. Kle didn't know the term hero was junkie code for smoking heroin, a drug that gives the euphoric feeling of being victorious. She held up a sheet of aluminum foil, clicked her lighter under it, and said, "Then go ahead and breathe some of this, buddy. We'll be heroes together."

Again, Kle didn't understand. He thought it was some incense that the girl/woman burned to honor her gods, perhaps a fragrance that might inspire him to return more courageously to Zaera. He inhaled deeply, very deeply, and then coughed.

"Easy," the girl laughed and took a hit herself before offering Kle another shot at freebasing. Kle did feel like a hero! After four puffs of her magic dust he was soaring, his whole body buzzed higher than the sun. He suddenly didn't care at all about the lingering humiliation from Alos, Euty, and the others. He suddenly didn't crave acknowledgement from his father or the return of his mother. He felt completely relieved of the heartache of watching Zaera discard him only minutes before. He didn't care that his Greek arts workshop business seemed a pathetic failure. Even being suddenly homeless seemed an insignificant part of some glorious ride.

In the flow of his trip, Kle had somehow pulled down his pants and was having sex with this woman in the forest. After a while, the woman put some more of the dust on the sheet of aluminum and they burned some more. It was getting darker. After they finished it, she told him, "fuck me again."

But he started wondering if his mind was getting a little twisted. Time seemed uncomfortably warped. Sometimes he thought he saw tentacles instead of arms on the woman. And he wondered why he was having sex with her.

The pinch of missing Zaera returned, making him feel like he was punched in the stomach.

"I must stop all this," Kle told the woman. She turned her face around just as a flashlight shined down on them. Instead of a woman, her face looked like a mess of worms eating away a brain, and, for a flash it seemed like she hissed at the light. Again, he blinked and she was a woman at least three times his age, a sickly looking person.

"Don't move!" Kle saw police officers above them, shining their lights down.

"I'm like a cop magnet," Kle groaned and ran off into the woods. "What is it with me and those guys?" In the darkness, and still partially intoxicated from the heroin, Kle fell over branches, fell onto rocks, and got completely scratched up stumbling along. He already wanted more of that heroin. Lights flashed everywhere around him. The face of the wench he'd found himself having sex with seemed to be hissing all around him. His nose smashed against a branch and gushed with blood. He wanted to get back to Zaera even more, but all that seemed like an underwater thought he couldn't fully hear. He thought he heard Zaera calling him a piece of shit over and over again. He heard people yelling at him to stop. He fell hard onto his face and lost consciousness.

Solstice Party

Nariah followed Rafael down stairs at the Tannery to his art studio on the ground floor of the complex. Rafael's studio was full of tailoring tools, rolls of fabric, and stylish dresses/ skirts/ pants he'd designed. Rafael's work was all made with organic earth toned cloth and peculiarly cut angled edges.

Rafael really lit up with full gusto when showing off one of the clothing's most hidden and unique features, "watch this," Rafael said and turned off the light in the art studio. All the clothing lit up with complex geometric patterns imprinted into them with bright black ink thread. Nariah was totally in awe, gazing around wide-eyed. It was like a galaxy of glow worms, "Jesus would have loved these," she said.

Rafael thought her comment about Jesus was a joke, but he got the sincerity in her appreciation. He clarified insecurely, "Do you really think it's nice?"

"This is what they must wear in heaven," Nariah said without hesitation or the forced emphasis of flattery.

Rafael happily blinked his long fake eyelashes, ran to the other side of his studio and checked for something there.

Then he handed Nariah a skirt. "I want you to have this. It will fit you. And it will move with you when you're dancing your butt off at the Solstice party. It will shine like the moon for you if the lighting is dark enough. It will be the perfect fashion domination move for stepping up your game with all the gentle souls."

Nariah took it and started crying.

"What?" Rafael asked, confused.

"I've never been given clothes before." She'd worn little more than rags her whole life. Even among the apostles, there was little gift giving; with them there was little more than wisdom to give.

After graciously putting on her gift, and surprising Rafael with her immodesty, Rafael led her out of the studio to do a catwalk, showing off her stuff in the common area between galleries.

Nariah loved how the material of the skirt softly caressed her legs. She enjoyed the slight ventilation from the thigh slivers. And, feeling proud of how she looked, she stood up taller than she had since before her father died. While strutting around the Tannery, they passed by a window and saw a dance class happening inside. Nariah asked Rafael, "What are they doing?"

There were drummers pounding on their big drums as a dozen women slowly gyrated with bellies exposed.

"They're dancing."

"Hmm."

"I think you should join them, girl! You've got to go dance in your new skirt. Go shake it. This dress will move with you. Just roll up your shirt and show your belly. Don't worry that you got a little more meat on your bones than those ghostly waifs."

Nariah shook her head modestly.

"But listen girl, if you don't throw yourself out there and take a risk, I mean really start saying yes a little more, you cannot be there for the gentle souls. You cannot do anything big if you're not brave."

"Okay. I'll do it," Nariah said nervously. She hesitantly went into the class as Rafael went back to do some things in his studio. The Middle-Eastern belly dancing class was already fifteen minutes in. The slim teacher rolled her eyes at the plump, seemingly out of shape Nariah, but she said, "come on in, dear. Just do what you can."

The other ladies in the class had lean hard bodies, muscle mass percentages suggesting ninja-regimented exercise routines. Still, after Nariah started moving her belly, the whole class lost interest in the teacher. The subtle movements of Nariah's belly aroused a powerful pulse of confident sexual energy. She gestated and shifted the muscles in between her ribs so sensually that both the women dancing, and the men attentively drumming, lost their tempo. They became increasingly absorbed by Nariah's erotic graces. Nariah had no idea she was wowing anyone until the whole class gathered around her and someone asked, "How did you learn to do that?"

"Where I used to live, in the Middle East."

"Oh, she's an Arab."

"I thought so."

"I'm Jewish," Nariah said.

"You're a prophetess," one lady wearing a *Drink Goat Milk* T-shirt added. The whole group, including the teacher, just watched Nariah for the remainder of class. Nariah loved moving her body in that skirt. And she loved that people were interested in watching her.

Afterwards, one of the other dance students said, "come with us to a cooking class. It's here at the Tannery too and we'll pay for it." They were very interested in this demure Jewish sexpot priestess. Nariah was agreeable and followed many of the dance students to a medieval culinary class also taking place in one of the Tannery's art studios.

The teacher of medieval culinary delights was a roundish red-haired man who warmly welcomed each of his students with a friendly handshake and brief greeting at the door.

"I'm Arthur. What's your name, new friend?"

"Nariah."

A lady pointed out a giant bookshelf to Nariah. "That's all of Arthur's recipe books!" she said.

And they gathered around a long table full of all sorts of strange cooking equipment – the sharpest knives Nariah had ever seen, a vitamix, a fire oven, a fridge – and barrels of ingredients – along with so many grains and spices and cheeses. It was a cooking paradise.

Nariah instantly loved this boisterous heavyset medieval culinary maestro, who peppered his cooking lessons with fun tales and bizarre facts about the "so-called Dark Ages." He sounded nostalgic about the days of knights, feudal kingdoms, peasants, jesters and minstrels.

At one point, Arthur shared jokingly, "You know, one day I expect to wake up in some castle from the Middle Ages and feel completely at home."

"And they'll call you King Arthur," one of his students chimed in. Arthur smirked.

Nariah not only learned intricate details of what life was like in the Dark Ages, a thousand years after Jesus, but they worked through a recipe for gruel and meat pudding. She ate plenty of the ingredients as she prepared her bit. After everything was done, they all sat together with a full plate of their medieval cuisines. While most groaned in antipathy for what they were about to taste (the allure of the class was not so much the end product as much as the process of preparing something with Arthur), Nariah sincerely responded to the simple food, "This is the best thing I've ever eaten since I've been here."

"To be honest, dear Nariah, I intentionally chose a recipe that is fairly tasteless. I thought that would make for a more memorable gruel making class experience." He was not shooting for delicious food.

Still, for fun, this Arthur tasted a spoonful of what Nariah prepared. She used the same ingredients as everyone else. She followed the same instructions, but, while everyone else's portion tasted mediocre, bordering on appropriately gross, Nariah's portion made him laugh in surprise. "Your gruel is actually good! How did you do that?"

As they went on to prepare medieval desert out of liver, Nariah grew to see two things around this Arthur. First, there was a dark cruel hex-curse in the aura above this man. Nariah knew this type of hex likely bound him to a premature death. She didn't always see hexes, preferred to tune out that level of things, but this one was too obvious to ignore. It was so intense, which meant even today could be Arthur's unfortunate time.

Second, this Arthur also had a glowing sphere above him, a sign of somebody who had developed unusually advanced kindness. It glowed brightly in a way that reminded her of Thomas the Apostle. The glow sang of holiness. Nariah really liked Arthur. He told stories about the tribulations of serfs and kings with endearing fervor. He was full of gravitas. In both his humor and his care for others, there was such humanness in him. She felt a natural affection for him.

After eating gruel, meat pudding, and sweet liver biscuits, Arthur finished class with a brief retelling of how William the Conqueror lost his virginity on a small mythical island off of Scotland, an island full of fair skinned beautiful maiden-warriors.

After an hour and a half, Arthur proclaimed, "That's it for tonight. I hope to see you all at the Party for Gentle Souls Solstice party." Nariah didn't want to leave the cooking class.

That night's gathering was more than a party. Tannery residents and the Santa Cruz arts community really pulled together. DF Aftertaste's Afro-Indian Enya-meets-Kanye West beats were thread together by McMega Samadhi's wicked rhymes about how conscious he was, how meditative he feels drinking microbrews, and how he'd mastered allowing the flow of kundalini out of his lingam.

People were slurping biodegradable plastic cups filled from kegs of kombucha and kava tea. Sweating so hard from dancing, people threw off layers and showed off their tattoos, piercings, and lots of skin. McMega Samadhi chanted with less than divine arrogance, "I am the most transcendent. I am the most transcendent. I am..." McMega Samadhi wore battery powered shoes that emanate neon blue and sharp yellow from their soles.

The walls were decorated with watercolors of nude bodies and oil paintings of people's auras. People chatted, "Did you see that woman speak at Kaiser? Did you see one of the tornados? Did you see that giant cat? Did you see the choppers? Did you see the kids run out of the bank after their shit-in?" Santa Cruz had been weird but things had definitely gotten weirder.

The people breaking it down on the dance floor were: artists who lived at the Tannery, dishwashers, lawyers, acupuncturists, teachers, psychotherapists, computer engineers, unemployed visionaries, and trustafarians. No matter their socio-economic classification, they mingled in egalitarian celebration of their Santa Cruziness. Then seven women from the Conscious Mama Collective marched in like the mafia. With them, the vibe of the party quickly shifted. The Conscious Mama Collective was a tight knit band of New Age born-again goddesses, well versed in dedication to buying the most eco-conscious make-up, subscribing to the best hypo-allergenic cloth diaper changing service, and knowing which political activist online petitions to sign. They claimed their children were "indigo" and used that fact to assert themselves as the next step in human evolution. Their babies were competing to become the next Maitreya/Messiah.

This Conscious Mama Collective filled the room with an aire of judgments and self-consciousness. The dancing got stiffer and more contrived. And the conversation shifted away from the macro to micro – from the big things going on towards more gossip-oriented, "who is making how much money/who inherited what/what positions on the Grange and PTA and local charter school boards have been recently filled?" They were non-hierarchically minded in theory, recalling classless matriarchal societies that may or may not have ever existed. In actuality, they were social climbers, each playing up their qualifications to eventually nab the role of alpha blue star female.

Nariah quietly watched from the periphery of the party. Having never gone to a secular, non-prostitute related party, she felt as awkward as a thirteen year old girl, with both an onslaught of acne and the emergence of little hills on her chest. She tried to be invisible and started off successfully. Then, despite being winter solstice, a hot wind suddenly shot across the hall that night. As if in response to this misplaced rainforest breeze blew, a pregnant lady from the Conscious Mama Collective writhed to the ground groaning. She was apparently on her way into labor. Simultaneously, Arthur started to spasm violently against a wall in an epileptic fit.

An off duty EMT had been whirling round and round like a Sufi dervish. The two incidents brought him to attention – his eyes darted from Arthur to the pregnant woman. Trying to calculate the most imminent need, this hero-to-be jumped on Arthur to do his best to keep the jovial bloke from hurting himself. Arthur was a big guy. Keeping him still was not an easy feat. And the EMT was not big enough to be successful; he was hurled across the room onto his back. After moaning weakly, the EMT just lay there scared and unwilling to try helping Arthur again.

Nariah was among the apostles when their messiah taught them incantations and other secret healing techniques Jesus had learned from the sages and physicians of the Far East. While she usually opted out of intellectual learning, Jesus had insisted Nariah join them in repeating some of the incantations and instructions. Nariah didn't think of herself as a healer; she brought the apostles and other students of Jesus food and water. She cleaned when it was necessary. She aspired to be little more than a mascot for the team. But Jesus said almost with a roar, "You are so much more than you think, Nariah."

And, right then, leaning against the dance hall's wall below a large painting of a dog and his aura, Nariah recalled this training and chanted a prayer for peace in the environment. The hot wind receded immediately. Nariah then calmly walked towards Arthur, whose face was being thrown bloodily by himself to the floor over and over again. Rafael screeched, "Leave Arthur alone! You'll get yourself killed, Nariah."

Such a weighted man without any control could literally crush most normal-sized mortals as easily as small fruit. Nariah ignored Rafael's warning and placed her hand on the back of Arthur's neck. She held it in a subtle way, just as Jesus had shown her. Arthur's shaking slowed so that he gently rocked back and forth. It looked freakishly miraculous to everyone there, Nariah confidently placing her hand on this giant of a man who'd been shaking uncontrollably. And then he instantly slowed to little more than a gentle rocking.

Nariah saw the dark hateful cursed sphere again, the hex of death, above Arthur's head. She could almost hear this sphere growl as it inched down towards Arthur to fulfill its darkness. But Nariah chanted an ancient healing mantra Jesus had long ago taught just her Thomas, Bartholomew, and John. She said it again and again until Arthur stopped his spasms altogether. Then the dark hex looked weak, only a shadow of what it had been.

Nariah was not sure if he'd be okay, but she felt she could do no more. Arthur lay on his side snoring. Nariah, remembering she was there for all the gentle souls, then rushed over to the pregnant woman. She knelt down by the large bellied lady, who was taking only quick tiny breaths, hyperventilating. Her skin was turning a deep purple bordering on gray. Burdened by her fear and what felt like poison coursing through her body, she yelled at Nariah, "who the hell are you, you stupid fat whore?"

"I am here for your children," Nariah said, ignoring the woman's insults.

"Stupid fat whore," the woman said again. Nobody from the Conscious Mama Collective was trying to help their friend. One of them was a doula, but she was afraid of getting involved because of the liability issue. She called 911.

Nariah pushed on the woman's shoulders, tapped the valley between the woman's breasts, and then placed one hand on her forehead and the other on her big belly, while making a buzzing sound very much like a bee. Nariah knew right away an evil wind had seeped into the woman. The wind was agitating labor and cajoling a premature birth. And, with her inner vision, she saw there were two beautiful children inside the woman's belly having to struggle to stay there because of the unnatural wind.

Nariah talked to the twins growing in the mother's womb, "it's not quite time to be born for you two. Wait some time. Enjoy your place in your mother's love for now. And blessings to you when you're ready to show up in this world."

Then she shot kindness-lightning straight from the center of her heart, filling this woman's womb with all the light and care in her soul. Nariah felt herself become depleted, but she kept showering more of this light towards this woman. Jesus had said, "Love until there is nothing left of you. That's the only way."

She kept on even as she heard Rafael say at her side, "the paramedics are here, honey."

Again with inner-sight, Nariah saw the wind alongside the twins wriggle viciously. It was a determined piece of evil. Nariah had seen Jesus obliterate countless such wisps of darkness. She hadn't dealt with so many herself.

Then, as if gathering its final strength, the dark wind flew from the woman's belly and hurled itself in between Nariah's eyes. The evil latched itself into Nariah's mind with all the force it had left. Those watching saw an unfamiliar object fall from the ceiling onto Nariah's head. They saw her nose bleed freely all over her shirt and even onto the skirt Rafael had given her. They saw her lurch forward and puke onto the floor.

After being hit on the head (or zapped by an evil wind depending on perspective), Nariah became nauseous and her head filled with a scream. She stood up and groaned in the worst pain she'd ever known. She didn't remember. She didn't remember living in Tiberias, or knowing Mary Magdalene, or falling through a portal. All she had left were bits and pieces of things – arguing with a man while ukulele players played around her. She remembered someone suggesting the man was her husband. She remembered sleeping in the homeless shelter and talking with Rafael. She screamed out, "Where am I?" Even scarier than not knowing where she was, she suddenly didn't know who she was.

Moon Rocks

Despite its wound, Enkida's large muscular lion friend raced up the mountain. Enkida held fast to its back, wondering if she was ruthless enough to kill the cat and free it from the rancid evil fizzing in the wound at its side. Enkida's cheeks were wet with her tears. She'd been in this situation before. And she remembered it all as her cat furiously struggled to ascend the mountainside. She remembered a horrible situation which, she suspected, was most instrumental in tainting her relationship with her brother...

Long before Enkida arrived in Santa Cruz, Parthians invaded her kingdom. It is hard to imagine how they had scaled the massive walls around Uruk but Parthian invaders did and they got their hands on gold, emeralds, rubies, and piles of silk cloth. Parthians, known for their stealth, seemed to have free access. And, far worse than anything else they plundered, the Parthians opened the palace room of Enkida's brother's most beloved wife, Elin.

As when Surya was caught among Maka's harem, Enkida's brother was not there. This time he was away in a hilltop village praying within an ancient ziggurat, a temple devoted to Ishtar, a temple meant to help with fertility. Maka was making offerings to the goddess and wishing for the blessings of a child through his beloved wife, Elin. He already had many children but none from Elin.

As the theft of treasures and abduction of Elin occurred, Enkida heard her brother's wife make a shrill scream of terror. It was hours before Enkida usually took her morning ritual bath, long before she oiled her body with almond oil. That dark early morning smelled of terror. It was only Enkida who recognized the scream wasn't a shriek from a bad dream. Enkida shook herself up, immediately raced to the lookouts along the walls of her palace room. Outside, indeed, she saw the abductees racing off, with her brother's wife roped over one of their shoulders. The thieves rode horses, the kind of horse only Parthians used, and moved as quickly as the wind. Enkida didn't hesitate. She blew a conch from her tower calling hundreds of warriors to respond.

As quickly as she could, Enkida leapt upon one of her snorting camels and chased the assailant. Above all, Enkida yearned to bring her brother's wife home. She felt sick thinking of the danger her brother's beloved was in. Spitting out chants faster than gangster raps, she called all the spirits of nature she knew to stop the men on horses fleeing north. To be sure of his sorcery, she repeated each chant twice. Clearly in response to her powers, a sandstorm hundreds of feet high thundered along over the horizon. And Enkida led her camel towards this tidal wave of dust, fearlessly trailing the devilish band of Parthians.

As she plowed into the sandstorm, Enkida's magic opened up a path for herself to catch the Parthians. Those who took her brother's wife were coughing and struggling to breathe. The horses they rode stumbled.

And Enkida found Enil. Enil was held by a man dressed all in black. He smiled, "you shall bring your brother's wife back worse than dead."

Enkida threw a blade right into the abductor's throat, not willing to let a moment's hesitation allow the murder of her sister-in-law. For a second, the man looked unaffected, even as blood coursed from his throat he smiled grimly. Then he fell over, a sack of hell.

Enkida ran to her sister-in-law. "Are you okay, sister?"

Enil's response was not someone happy to be saved. "You're too late, sister. Thank you for trying, but now you must kill me."

"What? Why?" Enkida shook her head. "I would never." The woman showed her shoulder. There was a clean incision. "He put the poison here. I know what this poison is. It will turn me into a zombie, hungry only for human flesh. I will wither like dried fruit within days if I don't feed on living human flesh. There's no cure for this. Kill me now. Save me from the shame and horror that will come back with me if I live on in such a way." Enkida refused, insisting they find some antidote to this fate. Enkida returned to Uruk with her brother's wife.

Early that afternoon, her brother returned. He was overwhelmed to hear that his wife had been taken and then returned but, as soon as he saw her, he was horrified. Not only was her whole face and body withered and full of puss-laden infections, but she was snapping like a hungry dog. Her eyes looked twice their normal size and they had a blank vacuous look to them. Her hair had already turned green and strange bugs were flying from it. Even the color of her skin had changed from a warm brown to purplish black.

Half conscious of her state, she growled, pointing at Enkida. "She let this happen to me. She wouldn't kill me. That bitch. I pleaded with her to kill me. Now, you will all pay. I will feed on your flesh."

Her brother, suddenly cold to his core, pulled his sword from its sheath, closed his eyes, and put it into his wife's gut. The woman's withered remains crumpled to the floor.

Enkida's brother turned to her, furious, "Why did you not do as my wife asked?"

"I am sorry, brother."

"We both have been told of this dark Parthian magic. Did you bring her to me like this out of spite, so I will be destroyed, haunted for the rest of my life?"

"Brother, I hoped we could find an antidote. Please, forgive me."

"This will never be forgiven. You forced me to see something I shouldn't have seen. You forced me to do something you should have done yourself," her brother said and walked away. While they had smoothly shared the crown as equals beforehand, from then on Enkida's brother was increasingly brutish, uncaring, a sinister dictator.

Now, in the mountains above Santa Cruz, after nearly an hour of riding the cat and listening to its pained breathing get worse, the feline stopped high atop a mountain. She had asked it to take her to the greatest nexus of energy that could be sensed. This was clearly the place. She felt it. Now she only had to kill her dear lion friend, who she'd only just been reunited with.

The infection on the cat glowed, fermenting in the same way as Elin's wound. Even the cat's eyes were bulging spastically from their sockets, a frantic hunger growing. It looked tortured, scared, and small insects were now buzzing from its mouth. There was a full moon overhead, whose light reflected brightly upon the large rocks all around her. It was cool but not cold. Still, Enkida shivered knowing she would end the life of an animal that had worked so hard protecting hers on the way from Ur to Tiberias.

"I'm sorry, friend," she grieved to the cat. It laid itself unnaturally on its back below her, seemingly aware that she planned to sacrifice it. "I want you to live more than anything but I will not let you be turned into a monster. I will free you and maybe we'll find each other again in the world beyond." She didn't want to overthink it, to hesitate as she had with Enil. Not only did the infection look exactly the same, but the texture of the cat's skin was, without a doubt, doing the same thing as her brother's wife before she turned into a grotesque zombie.

Enkida picked up a long sharp rock she believed could pierce through to the cat's heart. She lifted the long rock over her head with both hands and closed her eyes. She whispered, "I'm sorry, Maka. I wish I'd done this for your Enil. I wish you hadn't been forced to kill her yourself." She blamed her unwise mercy for so much of what her brother had become. Enkida tightened her muscles to resolutely swing the blade downward towards the cat, hoping to not only free the cat but redeem herself.

"Enkida," a voice yelled angrily.

Enkida flashed her eyes open. On the other side of this summit filled with moonlit rocks, a shadowy shape moved like a giant spider steadily towards her. Below her, the cat was no longer there.

"Who are you?" Enkida growled. "What type of demon?!"

"What the—?"

"What are you?" Enkida repeated.

"You again?!"

Recognizing the voice, Enkida asked, "Arito?"

"Are you following me because you think I'm your son?!"

"No. I was not following you. I came here with a friend but my friend is gone."

"You are not my mother."

"I agree. You may not be my son." Enkida sighed coldly, wondering where the cat went, feeling bad about failing her duty again. Where did the cat go? This time I was willing but I've failed the greatest of allies. How did it get away so quickly?"

"You really set off hellfire today." Arito growled, referring to the buildings that burned, the boats damaged, and the pharmacies decimated by looting from the hyper-liberal vigilantes.

Enkida was unapologetic, "sometimes we need to be vicious to do what is right." She was still thinking about the cat.

"Why did you pretend to be my mom?" Arito asked.

"I made a mistake. Why does it bother you so much? Like I said, I put an anklet like yours on my son just after he was born. Then he was taken away from me. But you are not my son. My son would not hate me so. Let it be."

The milky dreaminess of the full moon's light was amplified by Bonny Doon's rocky landscape. The moonlight left everything awash in a mix of dark and light grays. A Zoroastrian shaman had once told Enkida, "the moon's light both opens and closes subtle doors."

"Just because I wear a similar anklet, it doesn't make me your son."

"I'm not arguing with you. Yes, you have made that clear. It is just a strange coincidence. Nothing more," Enkida frowned. "Anyway, before I had a child, an oracle confounded me by telling me my son would grow up in a land of giant fish and giant walls of ice. This is not a land of giant fish and giant walls of ice. Like I said, you're not my son. You are nothing to me but a weak-legged boy who finds me insufferably irritating."

Arito coughed and stuttered, "E-e-even if you were my mother, which is totally impossible with you being just a few years older than me, it's a pretty shitty way to reunite...with you on your way to a life of either r-run-ning from the law as a refugee or on your way to j-j-jail."

Arito didn't mention that he grew up in Seward, an Alaskan fishing town. He rarely told anyone that he'd lived in Alaska for much of his childhood. He didn't talk about his childhood much. The couple that raised him were good and kind but they were killed in a car accident when he was fourteen, after which he was shipped off to Oregon to be raised by an uninterested uncle. Anyway, Enkida's words shook him as Alaska was a place famous for its giant fish and giant walls of ice-glaciers. Who was this strange lady he was so triggered by?

A clanging and booming mess of noise disturbed their dialogue. Enkida tensed up and lifted the rock high again ready for battle. She thought some other magical mischief was at play.

"At ease soldier," Arito scoffed harshly at her alert posture. "It's my friends. We're meeting just down the trail to play music together here like we do every full moon. Now, if you don't mind, please don't kill yourself."

"That's not what I was about to do," Enkida clarified, realizing the boy was concerned about what she'd planned to do with the long sharp rockin her hand.

"Whatever," he hesitated, "maybe you're my mother and maybe not but, anyway, just come listen to music with us..." Arito walked away to meet with a rowdy bunch gathering nearby. Three of them were lugging didgeridoos, seven of them had djembe drums, two hada mandolins, one was pulling out a native American style flute, and three had guitars. They were putting everything down on the south side of Moon Rocks to jam and smoke pot until dawn.

"He thought I was going to kill myself, and he hollered out to save me," Enkida thought out loud. "And, for some reason, he suggested I may be his mother. Maybe, if I can find my way through the fires I've started here, maybe..." Startled from her hopeful reverie, through the night breeze, Enkida didn't just hear Arito and his friends' playful music. She heard the ferocious blood chilling roar of a lion. Instead of homecoming fantasies, she started worrying about being somehow responsible for a giant zombie lion ravaging the odd town of Santa Cruz.

Hero

Kle's curly blond hair covered head lay face down on the dirt. He was completely covered with grime, arm layered with bloody little gashes he got while running through the trees the night before. His head felt empty of any goodness – eyes felt like they were caving in, ears ringing, forehead feeling bruised and filled with smoke on the inside. Everything seemed raw and overexposed. Still, he craved that smoke again, the poison she'd told him would, "make you feel like a hero."

"I give up. I don't want to be a hero anymore," Kle told a rock jutting into his stomach. He remembered what the old man downtown said about Odysseus, that he was an asshole. "I'm sick of it, sick of trying to be Odysseus. Fuck Odysseus. He hasn't helped me. Fuck facing the Cyclops and twenty-eyed monsters, and whatever else that piece of shit Odysseus did. I am good enough without him." And remembering Euty, Alos, and the other men he'd gone across the Mediterranean with, he concluded– *like Odysseus, they're not smarter than me.* They're dead and forgotten except in my memory. And the wealth they brought home is now worth even less than nothing or stuffed into a museum they know nothing about.

"I have journeyed across space and time. My life is already more of an epic than any of my ancestors. I don't need to be more of a hero than what I already am. I have escaped a wild mob of ukulele players, faced my fears of Poseidon, met with the oracle, done my best to take on the tasks given to me by the fairest of goddesses, Zaera, and survived the vicious poison of a demon-woman."

Kle willed himself up, found everything was spinning, and then crumbled back to the ground dry heaving. When his body stopped its convulsions, he looked up through the branches of redwood trees to the cloudy heavens. He hollered, "did you hear me, Athena? Fuck Odysseus. I don't want to have anything to do with that cunt of a man." And he stood up again, endured the spinning sensation but this time remaining as solid as a rock.

Kle heard running water and pushed himself to go in that direction. He pulled himself over boulders, ducked under branches and arrived at a stream. There he removed the ripped and tattered T-shirt he wore. He threw water on his face. He scrubbed the thick chunks of dirt that had filled the wound in his shoulder. He rinsed blood and grime from his whole body. And the sun lifted, warming him. The craving for smoke returned, but Kle recognized these impulses as demons urging a return to the miserable depths of Hades Underworld. He resolved on his one thing – to find his way back to Zaera's heart.

Kle walked shirtless down River Street and south on Water Street. He passed other homeless shirtless men (and one woman) along the way, each nodding to him as a brother. He walked past Costanoa High School, Akira Sushi House, and Rio Theater. Along the way, while having given up on being a hero, he felt himself as more hero than he'd ever been. From the grimiest pits of disgrace, he had reemerged without the burden of trying to be someone he was not. He was a phoenix climbing from the ashes to fly. And Zaera was the fiery nest that he flew to. The burden of Kle's meaningless intercourse with the woman in the woods, however, still remained. He twitched, recalling it, barfed up into his mouth, felt his spirits drop. But stayed resolute, as buoyant as he could be.

Zaera's car was in its carport. He rang the doorbell. Nobody answered. He rang the doorbell again. Still nothing. "I have a key," he considered out loud and dug the key from his pant's pocket. He put the key in the door and… it didn't work.

The key Zaera had given him was not a fit. He twisted and jammed the key every which way to open the door until an old lady neighbor approached Kle asking with all the authority of her many years, "can I help you with something, young man?"

"My key doesn't seem to work."

"Maybe you lost your way. A young lady lives here so if your key doesn't work, it means it's because you're not allowed in. You don't belong there. It's not your house. So, it would be best if you skipped along or I can just say a magical word and my cell phone will automatically call the cops and send them here to help you along."

"A magical word?" Kle was trying to figure out if she was a sorceress.

"I programmed my damned phone, boy. Now skat." She was tough even though she wore a dress with blue and yellow flower prints.

Kle still felt inwardly optimistic but conceded he would have to back off for now. This lady was not to be challenged. Kle turned around and headed back down the sidewalk, away from the oasis of Zaera's townhouse.

Overhead, Kle could see a wild storm coming in, "I will be wet and cold tonight. I will be alone."

"Kle," a voice called him.

Turning around, Kle was disappointed with what he saw. It was not Zaera. It was Nariah. Confused, but grateful to at least be recognized by somebody, Kle ran back. The old woman was still nearby. She snorted but didn't say anything.

"Hi Nariah," Kle said. "What are you doing here?"

"We saw you last night."

"What? Who?"

"Zaera and I saw you…"

"Okay. You don't look so good, Nariah."

"Something hit my head. I'm not good. Arthur's cousin, Zaera, took me here last night after the party. Arthur would have taken me himself, but I was very disoriented and he thought I should go with a woman to feel safe."

"I don't know who Arthur is. What party?"

"The Solstice party for Gentle Souls."

"Sounds like a blast," Kle said sarcastically.

"They said at the party I helped a pregnant woman somehow from going into preterm labor and I helped my friend Arthur while he was having an epileptic fit. I was a hero but then I got hit in the head. Zaera picked me up and while we drove to her house, we saw you running along River Street. You looked like a ghost. Your eyes were all buggy. We called your name from the car and you didn't hear anything. Then you dashed down into the forest away from us. We got out of the car and called after you, but you were gone. We were worried about you. Zaera said she knew you very well and she cared about you and she regretted sending you away earlier.

I told Zaera you're my husband. And she told me you were her lover. It was very hard for both of us, Kle. I can't remember everything right now."

"What?" Kle asked, unsure if he'd heard correctly.

"To be honest, I don't recall much more than you carrying me to a beach and the ukulele players telling you to leave me alone and… I guess I'm too confused to feel hurt by you but Zaera's completely crushed to find out you're married. She even said you had keys to her house and she's already changed the lock."

Kle looked at her blankly. "I'm not your husband. I followed you into this world through a magical portal. That's everything between us. Those people at the beach just assumed we were married."

"I don't know what drugs you do but stop. They are destroying you. And to make light of this with a joke about magic portals. Now go away and leave both Zaera and me alone. We need time to recover."

Kle didn't know what to say. From his recently found buoyancy, he collapsed. He turned around and walked away, eyes glazed, no direction in mind. Every once in a while, he growled, "fuck Odysseus."

He walked and walked and, eventually, with mind completely numb, he stopped outside a big red and yellow sign, "Charlie Hong Kong's." There was food there. He smelled savory noodle dishes inside. He hadn't eaten for a long time. He followed his nose in and begged for a plate. The lady taking orders at the cash register looked at him and cringed. He looked bad. But then she pulled a little cash from her tip jar and put it into her cash registry to buy him a dish, "just wait a few minutes. I'll get you something."

Kle curled up on a chair in a corner of the noodle café, ragtime music coming from the kitchen.

"Fuck Odysseus," Kle kept saying - whispering it as to not to draw any attention to himself and get kicked out of Charlie Hong Kong's (before getting his savory smelling plate of food). While he was huddled there waiting for his food, Kle watched a large bellied Indian wearing an orange Indian kurta, order a dish, and sit to wait. Then another man came in. This one had unnaturally sharp features – a sharp nose, sharp ears, sharp teeth, sharp cheekbones. Even his clothes looked sharply angled – the high collars, the belt. It almost didn't look real.

"Here," the girl taking orders said and held out a bowl to Kle from behind her cash register. "Enjoy. I've been where you are, friend."

Kle got up and took it. "Thank you so much. Thank you so much." He couldn't remember receiving such generosity – without any strings attached – back in Greece. The man with sharp features was staring intently at Kle. Kle noticed the man's eyes – appropriately sharp – they looked purplish green.

"You need something?" Kle asked him while gratefully taking his first bite.

"Do you eat here much?" the man asked. His voice wasn't as sharp as his visual features, making him seem even more mismatched.

Kle decided to play with this man, to be ridiculously honest about who he was, enjoying the levity of having fun amidst his helplessness.

"I only came to this world a week ago. Before that I was in a small fairly useless town called Tiberias two thousand years ago. I followed some woman who belonged to a cult, which a good chunk of the world has since taken to – she followed a man named Jesus. Anyway, thinking she was leading me to some good fortune, with which I could impress my sailing mates, I followed her. I followed her and reached for a small golden speckle while this witch chanted some devilish spell. And I ended up here. And since then…"

"She was a witch?" the strange angulr man asked, as if offended.

Kle stood up. While he had a rough night, he still had an impressively strong physique – and he knew it. As if something suddenly possessed, him, he walked towards the angular man answering, "yes. A wicked horrible Hades worshiping crone."

"Are you sure?" The man was very interested in Enkida. This man actually creeped Kle out, but Kle kept going, "yes, by no fault of my own, she dropped me headfirst into this world. I crashed right into the water. Only by Zeus's grace do I know how to swim. Yes, she is a wicked warthog of a sorceress full of vileness." And Kle started shoveling the rest of the food into his mouth for his eager belly.

The sharp-faced man stood there more blank than such a sharp-faced man could be. Then he put his hand on his face and spoke in an incomprehensible language. Kle felt nervous, realizing this man had some mischief about him. When the man took his hand away from his face, there was a dark-skinned woman with thick dreadlocks standing there. She had melancholic eyes, beautiful elegance, and an angry grimace on her face.

"Infantile idiot of man," she said, "how dare you call me vile?"

"Can I help you sir, I mean ma'am?" the girl at the register asked, baffled by Enkida. "Wait, uh, you're the one they're looking for?" the girl said.

"You brought me to this world without my understanding." Kle surprised even himself with his courage as he spoke up.

"You leapt into my magic without an invitation," Enkida corrected.

"I found a home here. I found love in a woman named Zaera. And when Zaera discovered I was somehow connected with you, she wanted nothing more to do with me."

"Your problem, not mine."

"That's what you like to say to everyone around you! Earlier I found a boy who said you claimed to be his mother. However powerful you are, even he said you are a lunatic and I agree."

"Please don't hurt us. We use all organic food and I like working here," the girl at the register pleaded with a look of terror on her face. She'd heard about the fast food restaurants that had been set afire.

Enkida remembered fighting alongside her father as they conquered surrounding clans. Diplomacy worked differently in those days. It was more brutal. Enkida's father took control of the desert as far as one could see from their palace. Initially, Enkida just followed this momentum, being cutthroat with anyone who threatened her father's law. Yes, she had killed. Now, looking at Kle hungrily bad talk her and stuff his face at Charlie Hong Kong's, Enkida fell back into the memory of why she had chosen a less brutal path…

She remembered when her father, the monarch, got sick. Even in the oppressive heat of the desert, in a warm bed laden with blankets, the monarch shivered as if cold. He sweat through lesions all over his body. Physicians and shamans came and tried their arts with him. Some packed the king away in his palace room, closed the windows tightly to "protect him from impure airs." Other healers used herbal concoctions, chants or root baths, but these did nothing for the king. They just took their pinch of gold and left.

Then Mugida arrived. She had gray hair, suggesting age, but radiated the vitality of youth. Mugida boldly told the king, "you will die soon, old man. I will make you more comfortable along the way. I will give you all the care I can to prepare your journey over the threshold."

At first the king yelled meekly (as he was weak): "How dare you suggest I will die? You are no healer. Leave at once and be forever banished from my kingdom."

Mugida nodded timidly, "As you wish, my Lord."

But Enkida objected, "The others promised what they could not deliver. Perhaps this one alone is honest, father. Perhaps you are being hasty. Do not banish her. Maybe she offers all that she can. We have exhausted all our resources to save you. Maybe it is your time."

The king groaned humbly, "yes, my child. Maybe it is time to stop fighting… If I am to die, come back and help me along the way, healer."

"Then I am not banished?"

"No. I think you are right that it is I who will soon be banished from this land."

"Death need not be a banishment," Mugida, the healer, corrected. "You may find yourself facing the wounds you've inflicted on others. You may wish you looked more to give than take. You may find that which you are ashamed of now gives joy and that which gives you joy now is a miserable burden."

"You speak in riddles."

"I speak as clearly as I can," Mugida said and sat with the king. At first, she just held his wrist, saying she was "listening to his body." Her first instruction was for him to go outside to breath fresh air, to be in the sun. Then she prepared teas and herbs for him. She placed special rocks on various parts of his body. And she said a few simple words of prayer. More than any of the others, the king felt cared for with Mugida.

Enkida saw Mugida patiently tend to her father and bring some peace into his heart. She saw Mugida tell the king, "this kingdom is nothing. Your wealth is nothing. All the killing you did for your kingdom served only your pride."

"Do you tell me this only to pain me now?"

"No. I tell you this so you consciously take the opportunity to choose to stop serving your pride before you die. So you are ready to die as real royalty." In Mugida's company, Enkida reexamined her life. And, inspired by Mugida's counsel to her father, Enkida vowed at that moment, "I will never kill another to serve my pride again."

And the thread of that vow is what kept Enkida now from calling on a spell of obliteration against this man insulting her to no end. In Charlie Hong Kong's pasta shop, Enkida stopped herself, ignoring the rush of electricity pushing her to inflict wrath on this shirtless blonde thorn in her side.

Instead of casting a spell, turning him into a rat, or even simply shooting a fireball at him, she conceded, "yes, that boy who may be my son thinks I am a lunatic."

Kle grunted.

"And maybe your fate here has been burdened by me. This may be so. I am sorry and do not know what I can do for you now. I would return you to your home – to that far away long ago. But I lost the gem, which is the key to such magic. And I am not sure the magic I used to get here could promise your return."

"Do we only need that gem? The one with nine dots on it?" Kle asked, feeling his insides warm and not just from the noodles. He had that gem in a bag in his pocket.

"Yes, we need that gem. You have to be touching it while you say the mantra. The position of the stars and your thoughts affect it. And you need to focus your mind on what you want, but it may be more complicated than that. I think it draws our fears and fantasies towards everyone touching it…I really don't know how it works. Somehow, it even pulls along people and beings who weren't even touching it."

Neither of them noticed the swat team surrounding Charlie Hong Kong's pasta shop until they heard a chopper buzzing down not far outside. And a megaphone announced loud and clear, "come out with your hands up. We have this area completely contained."

Enkida looked at Kle, sadly accepting. "I'm stuck, finished, destroyed."

"Yes, maybe you are," Kle said, putting his hand in his pocket and feeling for the gem hidden inside the ziplock bag. As he relished his sense of power, the window in front of Charlie Hong Kong's exploded and seven ninja-like soldiers smashed in and threw Enkida to the ground and put her in handcuffs. They were not concerned whether or not they hurt her as they frisked her and locked up her wrists.

Kle was ignored by the special forces that crashed into the noodle house. There was no reason to consider him a suspect. The cashier hadn't mentioned that they seemed to know each other when she called 911. She'd said, "that girl who inspired the shit-ins is here."

The swat team had been ready and acted fast. CIA had concluded Enkida was from Iran and here to encourage domestic terrorism.

At the end of this really bad day for Kle (he'd endured opioid withdrawal after unknowingly stumbling into an experience with heroin, faced a break-up with Zaera for reasons beyond his comprehension, got scolded by Nariah for being an abusive husband), and now he was surrounded by the most fearsome cops in this world.

But they left him alone, leaving him feeling only pity, remembering the defeated look on Enkida's face. And, as she was pushed outside towards the chopper, she didn't resist. She just cried, "I'm sorry, Arito!" over and over again.

"Is she finished?" Kle asked while scooping up the last bite of his noodles. "Have I helped destroy her?"

Efaau

Efaau was not elated. So much had not gone according to his plan. Enkida was banished from Uruk but the desert did not kill her. Some inexplicably strange spirit kept popping up in her life and saving her, even making her stronger. Efaau had exhausted himself sending curse after curse, but she easily averted all of them until she somehow got far enough away from him so that his magic couldn't affect her at all.

And now, he was pulled through a portal, which sucked him out of his comforts and plopped him down in a smelly pile of beer bottles, rotten vegetables, and notebooks covered with incomprehensible doodles. Only moments before a lovely servant in the palace was feeding him grapes while another luscious lady was patiently fanning him with a giant palm leaf, and a third diligently massaged his feet with her breasts. Then he fell through the magical trapdoor portal out of that plush palace to land in a heap of refuse.

Efaau lifted himself up, shook off his long robe, and walked proudly towards what looked like a temple. The magic of the portal somehow enabled him to read the local language. Above this temple was a giant sign that read, Costco.

Following a stream of people, Efaau headed towards the entrance of this enchanted place. Maybe some powerful priest there would graciously help him get back to his comfortable palace in Uruk. From just outside the gateway into this Costco, Efaau saw flat screen televisions, ceilings higher than any ziggurat in Ur, lights that required no fire, and the fever of consumerism that made him smile so widely he got goosebumps. "I am supposed to be here," Efaau announced to nobody in particular.

Unfortunately, not everybody agreed with his statement. A large frowning man tapped Efaau on his shoulder and said grimly, "where's your card, buddy?"

"Don't you dare touch my shoulder again, you miserable ogre," Efaau threatened.

The man pulled back his head and lifted his eyebrows as if amused by this belligerent customer wearing what looked like a Batman cape, a tall green hat, and the widest mustache he'd ever seen.

"Okay. No shoulder. Won't touch it. Got it. But please show me your card."

"What card?"

"Your Costco card," the greeter restated.

"Costco card?" Efaau repeated. He deduced this card was proof of having completed an initiatory rite into all the magic and technologies luring him inside.

"Is everything okay here?" a polite manager who'd seen what looked like a dispute between a greeter and a very strangely dressed customer, approached. This manager was skinnier and taller than anyone Efaau had ever seen.

The greeter said, "yes sir. Except I haven't seen this customer's Costco card."

Inwardly, the manager called on his power of patience and looked expectantly at Efaau. "Do you have your card, sir?"

Efaau gathered his energy, drew back his hands with all the might he could muster, and chanted a spell to ward off both of these obstacles. But nothing happened.

"Do you need help?" the manager asked Efaau with a concerned voice. Unlike some Santa Cruz locals, the manager was sensitive to mentally ill people who waved their arms and muttered incomprehensible garble.

Efaau figured he hadn't done something right in his incantation. It was rare with him but it happened. He pulled in his energy again, drew back his hands, and shazam, said the words. Again. Nothing. Instead of turning into frogs, these two men didn't even turn green.

"What has happened to me?" Efaau bemoaned. "My magic is impotent here. I have no card with me. I have no hope."

"Listen, to buy something you have to have your card. But you clearly want to go inside. How about today you just look around, decide what you want to buy and come back another day. Perhaps with a helpful friend of yours. Okay? We're fine. Just relax. You are valued and we want you to have a good customer experience here."

"I can go in?" Efaau almost felt tears come, confused why this stranger was being nice in the name of customer experience.

"Next time, just bring your card," the manager said with a firmness in his voice that was slightly intimidating. The manager felt sympathy for this crazy person. There were so many of them and so few services for them. The manager motioned for the greeter to get back to checking the ID of other people rushing in.

Efaau nodded gratefully and continued in. Only a few steps in, he was given a tiny paper plate with a taster of a single ravioli on it. Cautiously tasting it, Effau spit it out. To him, it did not taste like real food. With all its preservatives and processed meat, Efaau thought the ravioli was a poison being sold to people wanting to destroy enemies.

"How much of this poison does one need to kill an enemy?" Efaau asked the person giving samples.

"What? Poison?"

"Never mind." Efaau walked further into the store, lured on by the screens and sights.

Efaau wanted control in his life. He'd already been kicked out of two kingdoms before being dropped from Ur into this land. To have control, he always strived to have power over others or tap into what has power over them. He looked around at the people hurriedly rushing by to put giant jars of peanut butter, a five-pack of frozen pizzas, or giant cartons of liquid detergent in their shopping carts. He wondered, "how do these items control these people so completely? It's like they're asleep, totally unconscious of what they're doing."

Efaau tapped into this yearning to buy. It was an overwhelming compulsion and it gave him a sense of how powerful Costco was.

Feeling like he was facing his match, Efaau let himself get sucked towards the buying mentality – so many boxes of cereal and paper towels and chemicals. They all had uses and increased convenience. Behind all these products, Efaau saw, peeked his third eye, a deep hypnotic hum promising contentment to his soul. All he had to do was buy. Knowing he, too, was being hypnotized, he put his fingers over his eyes and ears and would have prayed to one of the gods if he thought they gave a damn about him. He knew he had lost control.

"Are you okay?" asked a woman pushing a shopping cart with tons of food and two fighting toddler twins in it.

"How can I have some of this?" Efaau frantically gestured to everything stockpiled in Costco. He felt the onslaught of greed for so many things he'd never even known could exist.

The mom thought this oddball was making a joke, another nut in Santa Cruz criticizing the material bounty capitalism created. Still, she answered "you just need enough money. Let me know when you get it. We need some too."

"And how can I get enough money?"

"Get a job!" she laughed.

"How do I do that?"

"Go to stores and tell them you're looking for one. Everyone's understaffed right now."

"Where are the stores?"

Before continuing nervously along her way towards the frozen section, she felt her patience getting depleted but answered one last time honestly enough, "try downtown."

Outside of Costco, Efaau tried a hundred spells. None of his basic transmutation skills worked, which meant he couldn't turn others into rats, frogs, bears or anything. He couldn't make his trademark terrifying fireballs. He couldn't do so many very simple things he had come to take for granted.

Only six of his primary spells still worked. He still had some sway over the weather (a few clouds popped up when he beckoned a storm but it didn't even rain). He could still fly (but it was exhausting and he only lasted about thirty seconds). He could make another's clothes disappear (but he had a hard time directing this spell accurately and accidentally made an old man embarrassed, instead of getting to perv on the young lady trying to help the old man move boxes from his shopping cart into his car). Efaau could still make someone think they were ugly. Even he hated doing that. And he easily changed someone's eye color. He undid his magic quickly so as not to attract undue attention to himself.

And Efaau sensed he still had some power to unlock other's memory to draw out their secrets (but he didn't play with this one as it was an exhausting spell).

After assessing his powers, Efaau walked down River Street away from Costco. He accepted the mother's counsel and went into shops along the way – PetSmart, Ross, Pro Build Hardware Store, and Outdoor World camping gear – telling whoever would listen, "I am looking for a job."

Each time he heard, "We're not hiring right now." In Ross, he was given advice on his presentation, "we wouldn't consider hiring someone wearing a hat like yours." At PetSmart, another person indicated, "your robe does not give a good impression as a potential employee here." And at Outdoor World, someone grimaced saying, "interesting mustache." Along the way, Efaau noticed he got smirks, eye rolls and people pointing at him without any admiration. He grew reflective and considered all the advice he had picked up directly or otherwise.

In the CVS on Front Street, Efaau found some scissors and tearfully trimmed his mustache and long hair right in aisle sixteen before being escorted out of the store by a security guard. His mustache became barely a shadow of what it had been. He gave his green hat to be the house for a squirrel in San Lorenzo Park. Because of some curious markings on the squirrel, Efaau suspected it was once a great mage, but had somehow been cursed to take the form of that small critter. And, at a vintage boutique downtown, he exchanged his robe for retro brown suede slacks and a purple button shirt.

The manager said, "yes. I won't make you pay a cent more than your robe and this is undoubtedly a generous upgrade for you."

Efaau was not happy about his new look. He saw his reflection in the glass on a storefront and did not like it. First, the hat was gone. That hat had been carefully lacquered by thirteen types of feces – rats, camel, vulture, fox, hyena, jackal, lizard, porcupine, cobra, scorpion, chameleon, viper, and human. The combination of all these types of shit, along with the right spells, of course, made his hat extraordinarily powerful.

The robe had been very special to him too. He'd stolen that robe from a three hundred year old sage in what is now Turkey, a sage who'd accumulated incomparable power by meditating for decades in the depths of the serpent Oshik Makoz's cave.

But it was the loss of his mustache that made Efaau feel castrated. He wondered whether he could truly be of any importance without such a dignified display of facial hair. He'd started growing that mustache the day he devoted himself to becoming a sorcerer in the Nordic lands. He just sat on a bench downtown, too demoralized by what he saw now as his own pathetic reflection. He closed his eyes and fermented with the feeling of losing the identity of whom he thought he was.

He'd have continued grieving the loss for hours, or even days, upon that bench if he'd not heard a lot of excitement bustling around him. He opened his eyes to people whispering, "there he is." and "should I poke him?" or "he owns three adjoining houses in Palo Alto but he could own a thousand more."

"Who is that?" Efaau asked someone passing by.

"Just one of the richest guys in the world, Mark Zuckerberg."

"Who?"

"The founder of Facebook, King Zuckerberg." someone jokingly said, but Efaau didn't get it.

This King Zuckerberg, as Efaau heard him called, was walking with an Asian woman pushing a stroller. While very clearly an attention-inspiring young man, he did not look exceptionally fearsome. But Efaau knew appearances were often misleading. He also knew there was always limited time with such people.

Efaau ran through the crowd that was meandering along near Mark and introduced himself to this King of Facebook.

"I am Efaau. I know some magic that I think you may be very interested in, Mr. Zuckerberg."

"You got fifteen seconds," Mark said calmly, earning an approving smile from his wife. He was apparently giving Efaau a chance to make a pitch.

"I know a secret from long ago. It is magic as old as the days of giant lizards. It was one of the Creator's Fantastic Accidents. By the power of this Fantastic Accident, one can know all of someone's most hidden secrets."

"Sorry, friend. But, while Facebook might not be ancient, it's already got everyone's most cherished secrets nice and packaged, free of charge for me!"

"But I can levitate and…"

"Listen. buddy, what's your name?"

"Efaau."

Mark smiled kindly.

"Efaau, you got spunk. You got chutzpah. I think you will put yourself out there and something amazing will happen."

"I need a favor," Efaau innocently confessed.

He was going to ask for a job, but before he did, Mark interrupted him as he pulled out a card and handed it to Efaau and said, "call this number next week. I can't promise you but you remind me of somebody who helped me out once. Depending on what it is that you want, I may be willing to grant you a favor."

"You speak with the light of a thousand suns. You are a true king. I am a worm next to you."

Mark assumed Efaau's comment was just born of a quirky sense of humor. He laughed and said, "we're all worms here, Efaau."

Efaau was refreshing to Mark, made him giggle, that comment about how his business idea was "as old as the days of giant lizards." Most people were too self-conscious and filtered to make a joke with him. Their pitches were too polished. But, even more, Efaau reminded Mark so very completely of a mysterious man who showed up at his Harvard dorm one night and gave him the idea for Facebook.

Mark patted Efaau on the shoulder. "I look forward to hearing from you."

Mark and the small entourage around him continued on, but Efaau was left behind lingering in the aroma of hope. Sometimes a few words of encouragement can play a role in transforming one's world. With Efaau, that was the case.

Meeting Mark helped Efaau shake off whatever grief was trying to drown him (about shedding his robe, hat and mustache after being dropped in this foreign land he knew nothing about).

Efaau went back to trying to find a job – Café Gratitude, the movie theater, O'Neil's, Santa Cruz Bookshop, and Pleasure Pizza. They all told him they weren't hiring or he wasn't qualified. Then, at the end of Pacific Avenue, he came to Jamba Juice. It was across from the clock tower, a place full of small crates of wheatgrass, and the smell of citrus, with walls painted in bright oranges and yellows. With all the optimism he could muster, Efaau addressed a peppy young girl at the cash register.

"Hi. I'm looking for a job."

"You're looking for a job?"

"I'm looking for a job," he repeated.

"You like our smoothies?"

"I've never had one."

"Well, you're honest. Here's a sample."

She handed a glassful to Efaau and he drank it. "It's painfully cold," he said. "But it's very nice."

Efaau had never tasted something quite like that smoothie. The cold reminded him of being a small child in northern Europe. He grinned.

"Alright. You want to join our team, tell me a joke."

Efaau was not familiar with the idea of a joke. His brain translated the word joke in his head to something closer to a riddle. His response was, "if I had a hundred camels and offered them to your father as a bride-price..."

The Jamba Juice girl started laughing before he even finished asking the question, before he said the stuff that would have truly offended her. She liked what she thought was this applicant pretending to be completely out of touch. She asked, "are you good with money?"

"Very good."

"Good customer service... customer's always right and all that stuff?" She eyed him carefully.

"I would change a customer's eye color if they wanted me to," he responded more honestly than she could have known.

"I think you're a winner. Moriah didn't show up today. This is her third flake. So she's out and you're in. Could you start tomorrow?"

"Yes. Yes!"

"Awesome. I'm giving you a green light now but you can fill out the application tomorrow. I'm very tired right now. Anyway, welcome to the Jamba Juice Team."

He looked at her with thankful eyes. He didn't even have to perform a ferocious magic spell to attain this position. He just had to say the first line of a riddle.

"I'm most pleased."

"If you flake on your first day, you'll be out of luck. Be here at seven-thirty sharp tomorrow morning."

Castle

Santa Cruz itself attracts many people who may have been more comfortable living in other worlds, people who seem like they're from other planets, or are tuned in to mystical dimensions but tuned out of this one. Because of that, Santa Cruz's Dominican hospital psych ward is very active and rarely has a dull moment. The ward was not generally violent but, by the time a patient arrived there, the unpredictability factor of its clientele necessitated that the ward's caregivers be ever on the alert.

Due to Nariah's symptoms, the busy M.D. 's quickly assumed she had taken L.S.D. or mushrooms or she'd been roofied at a brain damage level high dose. There was no significant bruise on her head and, still, her memory was disturbingly fragmented.

Nariah was given a mild sedative, as she was hyper-ventilating and freaking out about not remembering much of anything. She shared scattered recollections of violent sexual encounters (impressions sustained from her time working as a prostitute in ancient Tiberias), a dream-like sandy landscape (that of the desert landscape she traveled many times between Tiberias and Nazareth), and excitement about seeing some guy in a meadow (whom she couldn't identify) with the name Jesus.

Other than that, there was only the memory of who she guessed was her husband at the beach (they'd been fighting), talking with Rafael about being "here for the gentle souls," belly dancing in a class at the Tannery, and then zap! That was it.

She cried and screamed, reaching for the rest of herself initially, but the medication helped her relax and look at this conundrum with more patience. The medication helped her accept the disorientation of not being able to access a huge majority of her memories.

How did she get to the psych ward? The morning after Kle banged on the door, Nariah woke up in Zaera's townhouse and started panicking, screaming to Zaera, "I thought I was just having a temporary case of forgetting everything. But it's really not coming back. All of this is worse than any bad dream."

"You are very much awake, my dear. This is more than a bad dream. But it'll all. come back," Zaera tried to console her. Nariah was in a very discombobulated inconsolable state.

"No matter what you say, maybe I am dreaming." To determine whether she was awake or not, Nariah intentionally picked up one of Zaera's treasured ceramic vases and dropped it crashing to the floor.

"My grandmother gave that to me," Zaera whispered, shocked.

"Sorry. I guess I am awake. What should I do?" Zaera had already spent two days feeding and doing whatever she could for this stranger. Nariah couldn't sleep. She was a wreck. The vase incident pushed Zaera over the edge. She had to take Nariah to get professional help. After checking her into Santa Cruz's Dominican Hospital, Zaera went home to really sleep.

Within hours, Rafael and Arthur arrived and waited in the lobby to be allowed in. Rafael and Arthur were not friends but they recognized each other from their respective obligations at the Tannery, the fashion designer and medieval cooking instructor.

"You two are here to see Nariah?" a nurse asked them.

"Yes, Ma'am," Arthur replied.

"I'm sorry, but since you're not family, and you have no legal guardian-ship over her, you can't be let in."

"But she's scared and nobody else has come and only…" Rafael argued with dramatic indignation, arms swinging around, emphasizing the depth of feeling.

"Yes, yes. It's the law but I will talk to the doctor."

"Thank you."

A few minutes later, a doctor came out and didn't even look up from his clipboard. He seemed lost in his own thoughts.

"I'm sorry buddies. Since you're not family and all that jazz, you can't see Nariah today. I know your friend Zaera brought Nariah in, but, since I cannot say Nariah is fully capable of taking care of herself, until her family arrives she is a warden of the state. But I promise you that your friend Nariah is being well taken care of."

"Jack?" Arthur asked the doctor.

Then the doctor did look up and excitedly offered his handshake. "Holy shit, Arthur O'Toole!"

"I thought you moved to Iowa. To that meditation city in Fairfield," Arthur said.

"Ya. I've been back for almost a year now. Iowa's winters are pretty brutal. I didn't last there. Anyway, I love the redwoods and the ocean and… uh, what are you up to?"

"I do little more than teach Medieval cooking classes at the Tannery. And work on my stories of course."

"Medieval cooking classes! Wow. Sign me up. And I loved your last book, great plot – Knights Templars infiltrating Columbus's mission. Very cool," Jack grunted with a mind that seemed perpetually conflicted. "So is Nariah one of your students?"

"Yes."

"Well, if anyone asks, you are now that young lady's uncle." The doctor motioned for them to follow him into the facility.

"I appreciate it, Jack," Arthur said. Both he and Rafael jumped up and followed this doctor, Jack, through the high security door.

"I'm Dr. Shanahan in the hospital," Jack clarified, not wholly devoid of ego.

"Well, Dr. Shanahan, I am very concerned about Nariah. She helped me in a major way when I was having an epileptic fit a few days ago." The rooms along the hallway were all locked down. Some patients were screaming or singing loudly or howling as Rafael and Arthur followed the doctor down a long hallway full of small windows to Nariah's room.

"How did Nariah help you, Arthur?" the doctor asked.

"You're gonna say I'm the crazy one. But, because of one of my epileptic fits, I was really throwing myself around. It hadn't happened in years. Without concern for herself, Nariah just fearlessly put her hands on me. And I'm sure there was something special in her touch. Anyway, it calmed me down so much that I didn't break any ribs or bloody up my face like the last time."

A long-haired man with impeccably upright posture passed by them. He was escorted by a very muscular psych-ward nurse. The long-haired guy's eyes were so radiant it was even disorienting. Jack whispered into Arthur's ear. "We call him Fabio, a pretty sad case. The guy claims he is Phillip, one of Jesus's twelve apostles. He has a whole life story he spilled out to us, very dedicated to the tale. He describes what it's like to see Jesus and Mary Magdalene and then claims he fell through some trapdoor in time and space. Thing is, he fell into a UCSC dorm girl's shower. Perv. But he seems to have some trick for unlocking our doors so the nurse has to bring him back to his room over and over again."

"I wouldn't mind getting perved on by him," Rafael looked dreamily at Phillip. "That apostle could save my soul any day of the week."

"He fell into a girls' dorm shower?" Arthur added. "I guess if you're going to try to explain that away, you might as well claim to be an apostle."

Jack didn't comment more about "Fabio." He unlocked Nariah's door and said, "We can only give you guys twenty minutes. We have an MRI and some other diagnostics scheduled soon to help us figure out what's going on in her brain."

Rafael ran into the room and threw his arms lovingly around Nariah. Arthur asked, unsure whether his tone sounded too fatherly, "How ya holding up, dear?"

"A nurse comes by every three minutes. He'll let you know when it's time to go," Jack said and locked the door behind him.

Nariah looked up blankly. "Lots of sand. And sex. That's all I really remember. I'm really messed up."

"And you're drugged up, sweetie," Rafael grieved. He was wearing orange lipstick and a long conservative gray dress

"I know the doctor," Arthur announced. "If anyone can help you, he will. He's a good man," Then, thinking maybe he could help draw out some memory, Arthur asked, "Can you describe the sand you remember so much?"

"It's brown," Nariah responded innocently.

"Sounds about right." Rafael rolled his eyes at Arthur's question.

"You're going to be okay," Arthur encouraged Nariah.

"You just have to remember. At least you don't think you're an apostle of Jesus."

"Interesting that you say that, at Zaera's house I dreamt I was surrounded by sand but it wasn't so bad. I was with Jesus and some of his apostles. It was such a realistic dream. And when Zaera first brought me here, I thought I saw one of the people who was a disciple in that dream."

"I think he's got more problems than you," Arthur said.

"I don't even know if he was real or a hallucination," Nariah confessed.

"The doctor pointed out a patient here who thinks he's one of the twelve apostles," Arthur said.

Rafael asked, "She had the dream of that guy as an apostle before getting here?"

Nariah just looked at them blankly.

"Maybe remembering all the sand is past life stuff. I did a past life regression once and that's how I got into my whole medieval fetish. It's how I got a lot of the ideas for my books."

"But if she dreamt about the guy who is here now, the guy who thinks he is an apostle, and he was an apostle in her dream, that is pretty odd," Rafael pointed out.

"Hundreds of people have come to this hospital thinking they're Jesus. That may be odd, but that's how it is, Rafael. Let's stay grounded here."

"No. This is more odd than a bunch of messiahs. Or do I say odder?"

"Rafael, no matter how strange it is, we have to help Nariah be in this world. And entertaining too many fantastic ideas might not be so helpful."

"I just want to remember," Nariah said. "But the scariest part is that I can't remember what I want to remember."

"It'll come," Rafael affirmed confidently and defiantly turned to Arthur. Even if Jesus himself has to come here to heal you."

Nariah had a flash of a memory of seeing Jesus telling Mary, You are the gentlest. "Jesus wouldn't come here for me. It's not like I'm Mary or something. I'm not so special."

"You're special to me," Arthur said. Then they sat talking about the weather and what a weird party it had been, trying not to work Nariah up too much…

The nurse came in. "Sorry," she said. "We have to do some tests now. How are you feeling, Nariah?"

"Just remembering a lot of brown sand with my friends. And my imagination's really busy, obsessed with things I must have read about Jesus."

Before Arthur and Rafael left, Fabio happened to pass by outside of Nariah's cell. Nariah looked up and seemed to tremble at the sight of him. She told him, "I had a dream about someone who looked just like you."

"Nariah, do you not remember me?"

The nurse, confused and irritated, yelled up the hall, "I need help in front of QC32. Fabio's free again. And our two guests need to leave. There are diagnostics we have to do with patient QC24."

Winds

Nariah was in the psych-ward, Enkida was being led away from Charlie Hong Kong's pasta shop by a SWAT team who had helicoptered in, and Kle was fondling the nine-dotted talisman he'd found. At the same time, a player in this story was getting ready to go to Burning Man.

Telemachus was the name of the crusty, skin-as-thick-as-leather, bearded old man who gave Kle the bag of winds, the one who ate Zaera's paper list. Telemachus had told Kle that, "Odysseus was an asshole." Kle had no idea that the old man spoke from such very direct experience. The old man named Telemachus was the son of Odysseus.

Telemachus still remembered seeing the many fleets of ships and legions of soldiers, including his own father, leaving after drawn into that stupid squabble over the painfully attractive Helen, a conflict later detailed in the epic known as the Iliad. The result of this legendary war was not a union full of great love. It was a superficial alliance heavily tainted by suspicion and possessiveness.

Anyway, during the war but largely outside the radar of the epic, Telemachus was left behind without a father. He was left to fend for himself, to go through puberty without a significant man there to tell him what was going on. He had to learn to run his father's estate without much counsel. And he was the one given the responsibility of warding off suitors coming to take possession of his mother's money and booty (not that she was a possession, but that's how it was perceived then).

Telemachus remembered being eight years old and being told a legend by a traveling minstrel about siblings raised by animals. These twins were left in the wild to die, but were found by a pack of wolves. An alpha male wolf licked them, picked them up gently with his teeth, and nurtured them until they were strong enough to take care of themselves.

The thing that most struck Telemachus about this story was his jealousy of these wolves for having a sibling and his envy that there was an animal as ferocious as a wolf there to protect them. His mother had never struck him as ferocious. And his father was never there; he had no one else, no wolf, no one.

Even when the suitors came by, his mother just gently suggested she wasn't interested in them. And she always added a "yet." There was no confirmation that daddy Odysseus was dead. Odysseus, the legendary hero of the Trojan War, always had a mystique around him. But, for his family, he was just never around, thus a legend to his own son.

As other warriors trickled back from the Trojan War, Telemachus learned about the Greek's tragic defeats and ultimate triumph. He learned about the trickery of the Trojan horse; the fate of Ajax, Agamemnon, and so many others. Still, his father didn't come home. As so many fatherless boys might do, Telemachus yearned to prove himself to the father he never knew. In the hopeful idea of meeting his father as a proud man eventually, Telemachus sailed farther and farther out to sea by himself. Upon returning, he always told his mother little more than, "I sailed today." She didn't bother to ask more. Telemachus had fantasies of finding his father Odysseus on a shipwrecked raft and saving him. Still, the boy never met his father in the open sea.

One day his father did return and, in the spirit of a loyal sidekick, Telemachus helped his father massacre the suitors who'd incessantly plagued his mother. And, gloriously, Odysseus settled back into his estate. But he never really returned in the way that Telemachus hoped. He remained lost in his memories of battlefield gore and desperate journeys. Usually, Odysseus was impeccably stoic, no more loving than a rock. On a few vulnerable days, Odysseus was shaky and painfully cautious, clearly traumatized. He occasionally recalled the treacherous tribulations during his great battle in the East. He shared with vivid detail the deaths he'd seen too closely to forget. The family remained as broken as before Odysseus had returned.

By habit, even after his father's long delayed return, Telemachus continued going out to sea regularly. Rowing away from his homeland was something of an act of worship, a way to release his anxieties and reconnect to a feeling of hope for wholeness within himself. Telemachus loved being out in the endless expanse of ocean. On one such excursion, he saw what he thought were dolphins, the delightful water-beasts that some said you could ride like a horse. Telemachus had no interest in riding anything. He just wanted to see them leap, flip and play freely and innocently.

But as he rode up and down in his boat through the choppy Mediterranean waters, he saw they were not dolphins at all. Mermaids were gathered together, wondering out loud about whether their father, Poseidon, had ever lived on solid land. They were so lost in reverie of what land life might be like that they didn't notice Telemachus take off his clothes and jump from his boat to swim up alongside them.

As he neared the mermaids, he saw their unusually bright green base fins. He saw their human well-formed bare chests. And he noticed one of the water women as particularly lovely. She was not more beautiful than the others, but she had a sweetness in her cheeks and eyes and mouth, arousing the fullest bounty in the heart of Telemachus to explode. Shy to speak among such noble ancient creatures, all Telemachus could think of was reciting a poem he conjured while swimming towards them through the waves:

"Maritime vision of goddesses rare.

Zeus himself would be jealous to find me here.

Near such beauty beyond any description…"

The mermaids interrupted his recitation by splashing him. Then one dove down and pulled at his legs. And another threw some seaweed on his head. He thought maybe they would drown him but then, as he sank a bit, the group let him go and scurried away.

He doggy-paddled up through the water and seaweed pushing himself back up to the surface, breathing deeply and then exalting, "My god! Mermaids!"

And then the face he'd seen so much sweetness in popped up in front of him.

"I'm sorry," this mermaid said, biting her lower lip demurely. "My sisters were trying to scare you and your beautiful poetry away."

"I am Telemachus," he told her proudly. In that long ago, he was handsome.

"We don't care so much about names. But we now know each other," she gazed into his eyes.

"You are much more beautiful than any poetry."

She blushed. He asked her about her underwater lifestyle, what and how she ate, how she danced, how she celebrated. And she asked about his world above the waters.

Very quickly, a mutually living love between this human and the mermaid emerged. They knew this despite the obvious and insurmountable obstacles between them. They hugged innocently but without clothes. Then, as the sun began to set, she told him anxiously, "you should go. I sense my father is near and he is far less playful with humans than my sisters."

"I am at home with you here in these waters."

"No. That is a whim I wish were fully true. My father has granted other humans their desire to become one of us. Most eventually grow weary of our ways, struggle for power against my father, and even try to wage wars against him. We are of two worlds. You are mortal. I am not. You live in a world bound to hard ground. My home is the fluid ocean."

"Without love for you, I am not at home anywhere," he argued.

"Embrace me one last time and go before you shrivel up, sweet man."

Telemachus felt far away from shriveling but, before they even got to passionately embrace one last time, the mermaid's father rose up from the sea. The giant monster Poseidon looked like a bearded sailor from one angle and in the next seemed to be a giant whale. His form was elusive, but his voice was not.

"Lover boy," he roared at Telemachus. "You dare flirt with one of my daughters?" Waves rolled up and away from this man-god-beast as if the sea itself feared his wraith.

"I want to be one of yours. Be my father, let me be a merman and swim ever at your daughter's side. I want to be her protector and confidante."

"You just want to flip around with my daughter's tail." Waves flew up, again submerging Telemachus under a dozen feet of water.

Telemachus kicked furiously through it all and, before he even took a deep breath, yelled, "Have mercy!"

"Fickle human."

"My love for your daughter will endure thousands of years. That is not fickle."

"And how could we know that your love would endure so long?"

"You're the god. You tell me."

"Hmm," he considered.

The waves settled. The mermaid, with all the sweetness of all the universe, looked to her daddy pleadingly to have mercy. And Telemachus teared up sincerely. "I'll tell you the truth," Telemachus said. "The home I was born into has nothing for me. Give me my true home and I will forever be in your debt."

"Alright, I, too, will tell you a truth. I will not always be Poseidon. My power will eventually be less potent in this ocean and then I will just be a nameless elemental spirit working subtly through the movement of the waters and the prayers of faithful sailors. But, even then, I will still be able to fulfill a few promises."

"Tell me more," Telemachus encouraged.

"Boy, you said you would be forever in my debt. Are you both willing to endure many years apart to prove that statement?"

They nodded.

"There's a few tasks I'll put on your plate," Poseidon told Telemachus.

The potential son of Odysseus nodded.

"Please remember this," Poseidon continued, "no matter how grand the tasks you achieve for me, they will likely not be sung far and wide for their greatness like your father's foolish bravery. Your acts will be anonymous and, at times, seemingly irrelevant. Still, you will find hidden heroism in them and good will come of them. And you will be granted near immortality to complete them. And, if you complete them, I will do what I can to make your wish of swimming as a merman alongside my daughter a long lasting reality."

From that was born an agreement between Telemachus, Poseidon, and one of Poseidon's daughters.

"That was so long ago," Telemachus said out loud, looking out to the sea from Natural Bridges beach. "Do you remember your promise, Poseidon?"

Telemachus wasn't even really sure if he remembered the God of the Sea accurately. Sometimes in the memory of Telemachus, Poseidon was transformed into a timid young man on a raft. Sometimes Poseidon was a face within a drifting piece of seaweed. But the mermaid's face was always the same.

Now, Telemachus was old, much older than most anyone in the world. Telemachus had lived so many lives across the world. He had served as a politician, an artist, a merchant, and a scientist. He was constantly being given clues by the God of the Sea as to what his next task was. Telemachus became more skilled than any Renaissance man.

Most recently, Telemachus gave a bag of winds he'd gathered to a man named Kle. Telemachus had already followed countless other bizarre and incomprehensibly unimportant tasks. After each task, he sat near the sea and listened for what the next task would be. It would be whispered to him. And, now, he was about to fulfill what he knew was nearing the final item from the sea's requests. This one even made sense.

The task – he drove away from Natural Bridges State Beach and dropped a pile of parcels in a blue mail drop box near Safeway on Morissey road. Each one of these parcels transferred some item to the Surfrider Foundation. There were quitclaim deeds to at least a hundred properties, donation checks closing out at least thirty bank accounts, and wills from various names Telemachus had used to blend in with local peoples around the world over the centuries. All these boons went to Surfrider Foundation, a non-profit organization devoted to the wellbeing of the world's marine habitats and coastline. This gift made sense as directly pleasing Poseidon and his lair.

Telemachus had some anxiety as to whether Poseidon still really had the power to fulfill his promise. Nobody talked anymore of Poseidon's greatness. He was a character, absorbed by the collective rational mind as a forgotten, laughable surf break in mythology. The superstitions around Poseidon were deemed unnecessary amidst modern knowledge of global currents, weather patterns, and GPS.

Still, Telemachus thought daily of that lovely nameless mermaid. He wondered what had become of her over these many years, whether she still ever thought of him. In the last three thousand years, she could have been married a couple hundred times. Did she know or care that the list her father gave him was almost completed?

Telemachus looked out at the sea from the parking lot at the last major possession he still retained, a big RV. He got back in it and started the engine to pick up some people who'd agreed to join him on the long drive away from his beloved sea to Burning Man's fateful Black Rock.

The Dragon

Burning Man's homebase of Black Rock is in the bleak Nevada desert wasteland, a solid ten hours from Santa Cruz. Most of the year nobody lives there except a few snakes and some coyotes. But, for a few weeks every year, a massive multitude exceeding sixty thousand people fill it with tents, cars and giant provocative artwork.

Burning Man attendees often wear costumes, barely any clothes, or walk on stilts. Fire-exhaling organs thump out flames and melodies in pyrotechnic performances. There is the sound of heavy bass and blustering sandstorms colliding with RV's along with people yelping in ecstatic decompression, feeling free of conventional society's engine.

People don't go there for the freedom to wave a flag, own a gun or refuse someone service. It is longing for one's soul to express itself more freely and fully. That longing is in the hundreds of cars that get approved by Burning Man's Department of Mutant Vehicles. That longing is in the elaborate costumes and hyper-fantastic sculptures and dancing. And it is very much in the giant wooden man that is set afire at the end of each year's festival. People transform Black Rock's sandy hell into an oasis of creativity; they submerge themselves in its chaos of sand, sensuality, and communal mayhem, for that longing.

Nariah was released into Rafael's care. She still couldn't remember her past but Jack the doctor knew that the few drugs available for her treatment weren't helping and she wasn't a menace to society and, of course, keeping her at the ward might even make her worse (by isolating). Rafael took responsibility for her because he felt a wondrous kinship with this woman who claimed to "be here for the gentle souls." From Rafael's perspective, he was sure they were soul sisters.

The only problem was Nariah wouldn't leave without Fabio, the impossibly handsome patient who thought he was Phillip the Apostle. The ward didn't want to keep Fabio there either but, legally, the hospital had to have somebody to release him to. The doctor let Rafael, who was very curious about this long haired mystery, sign him out as his brother.

Still, only a day after they left the hospital, Rafael had unalterable plans. He had tickets for Burning Man. He even miraculously had two extras (two queens who chickened out, sighting the "sandstorms this year.") Knowing they might be in too fragile of a condition for such an experience, Rafael sat Nariah and Fabio down in his Tannery studio, "You two may want to stay here with Arthur. Burning Man is totally unhinged, anything goes; it makes even the rocks a bit crazy. So I don't know what it would do to you two."

"I don't know who I am," Nariah said with strong conviction, "so I'm going to have to dig deeper into crazy to find out. I'm going. Bring on the crazy."

"I'm not crazy, but Nariah's the only one in this world I know. So, if she goes to Burning Man, I go to Burning Man too," Fabio/Phillip committed. They weren't staying behind in Santa Cruz with Arthur.

"Then the game's on. I'm scared for you two... but perhaps I am glad we're staying together," Rafael teared up. Like many Burners, Rafael wanted to share Burning Man with others as passionately as a born again Christian wants to share their Jesus.

The last item Telemachus heard whispered from the waves of the ocean were: "Transform an RV into a dragon and drive five people in it to the Burning Man Festival in Nevada. At this event, you will finally find your long awaited mermaid. Best wishes, Father Poseidon."

Telemachus, while looking like a homeless vagrant, was most recently involved in the world as a successful stock trader. Still, he remained a hermit and indulged in very little. He endured his long life as a non-social detached being. Thus, to follow through on the final items from the ocean's list, Telemachus had to advertise on Craigslist that he was "inviting five nudists to join me en route to Burning Man in my RV. Very comfortable RV/dragon. I pay for gas."

He included *nudist* because he hoped he would soon be a merman and wanted to get used to doing everything bare balls. For somebody willing to nude on the trip to Burning Man, his offer was a bargain.

Before giving away almost all of his tens of millions of dollars of assets, Telemachus had hired welders, electricians and painters to forge his RV into Smaug, a ferocious looking dragon sculpture vehicle. The wings were installed so they could move. The neck went up and down like a crane. At nighttime, the whole thing glowed like the Northern Lights.

Telemachus got really into this artistic task. It was his final project and, while his exterior suggested an uneducated simpleton, he was a classically trained brilliant man who'd accumulated knowledge over three thousand years. Thus, his brilliance was reflected in that dragon. The RV was unquestionably a fine piece of artistry. Nariah, Arito, Phillip, Zaera, and Rafael answered the Craigslist call to remain disrobed for the journey with Telemachus to burn. Arito had signed up randomly and didn't know who his co-passengers would be.

The first three quarters of the journey were mostly silent, everyone completely exhausted by their lives, by trying to fulfill some aspect of their life's trajectory that they didn't even fully understand. There were a few failed attempts at conversation but it had all fallen flat, until Arito fully broke the silence spell. He just announced, "There is a lot of sand out here."

"Does it seem familiar? Kindling any memories?" Rafael nudged Nariah. She had repeatedly said she remembered a lot of sand.

"This isn't that much like the deserts where Nariah's from," Phillip corrected. They all assumed and accepted that Phillip/Fabio was crazy. They had even decided privately not to contradict his claims to be one of Jesus's chosen.

"What is it like where you are from?" Rafael gently played along with what he thought was beautiful Phillip's fantasy.

"Some olive trees, a little grass, sheep and shepherds. Much less people. Many of us even lived in caves. But Jesus would make everything seem brighter."

"Dear Phillip," Nariah put her hand on his shoulder. "If I was really there with you, what was I there for? Was I a decoration or was I there to wash the clothes for all you men?"

"Nariah. Of course not. Jesus said you were a pillar of Knowledge, that you understood it better than any of us, that you had a very important role to play in making his Love come alive outside of Israel."

"Oh, Israel!" Zaera broke the agreement a bit, rolling her eyes. "What's up with all these people who think they're from the past. At least be from the future if you're coming from a different time zone. Give us a preview of some advanced remote control technology from the future, something that can give innumerable orgasms or make us levitate or make us live forever. Now that would be cooler than this legion of out-of-date clowns." She was still crotchety from what happened between her and Kle.

"It was plenty cool to be with Jesus," Phillip bragged. "All your giant flat screen TV's, microwaves, this crap from *my* future are nothing compared to the buzz of being around him."

"Wherever we all came from, it doesn't matter so much. Past or future, this is where we are now," Nariah said, something nobody wanted to argue with. They just looked straight ahead towards the endless desert of Nevada state.

"It's like being on a sailboat out in the middle of the sea here in the desert," Arito tried to change the subject.

"Because of all the waves," Rafael said, thinking Arito was joking.

"No, the vastness of it all. In every direction there's endless brown rock and dirt."

"I like being in the ocean," Telemachus's words made him sound like a caveman. But, as he had been so completely silent the whole trip, everyone turned to him after he spoke.

"What kind of boat do you like to go out into the sea in?" Arito asked, trying to encourage the old man to talk some more. In this situation, Arito preferred discussing maritime preferences.

"Prefer no boat. Just swimming. I had a giant yacht not too long ago. But I gave that away. But many years ago I had a small sailboat. And I jumped off it and found sweetness. Worth everything."

"Uh-huh?" Nobody really understood Telemachus.

"The ocean is where all sweetness is. Mermaid." Telemachus knew they didn't really understand him and didn't care.

"Ya," Arito agreed. "I'm sure after being out here in the dry desert for a few days, going back to the moist ocean in Santa Cruz is going to seem that much sweeter."

In a whisper, Nariah asked Zaera, "Are you doing okay?" Zaera shook her head no.

"Tell me what's up."

"Still messed up. Kle is a real piece of shit, a real wrong turn for me. I just feel so deceived I can't shake it. I gave him money. I let him stay at my house. I really thought I loved him. I thought he was god's gift to me after falling into life's mediocrity. And it turns out he's married and a con."

"I already told you, maybe my memory was wrong. Maybe we were never married. I just got fragments."

"Well, there's enough red flags with him that I know to stay away from him. That much I know."

Rafael overheard them and put in, "Zaera, I saw Kle downtown. He just wanted me to tell you that he loves..."

"Please shut up, Rafael," Zaera interrupted with a solidly confusing mixture of mean and nice in her voice. "I know you mean well, but I don't want to know what Kle feels for me. I'm going to Burning Man to move on, to burn it away, to remind myself that I don't become a boring old maid school teacher without him. I'm my own woman and I'm powerful and independent."

Even saying his name, Zaera couldn't help but remember all the orgasms she'd experienced with Kle. She also remembered sneaking into a swimming pool with Kle, in the middle of the night, and, because of their mischief, laughing until she saw her yellow pee in the water around her hips. And she remembered how gratefully Kle looked at her each night when they cuddled describing their days to one another. She'd felt at home with him.

The RV had a shower, sleeping spaces for everyone, a nice kitchenette, even a big TV. But they didn't put on any shows. They just sat around – naked and raw and hoping some important part of their lives would change for the better at the festival. Arito pulled out some chips and salsa and the dragon kept on driving silently again.

Villain

The night after getting his job at Jamba Juice, Efauu asked people downtown where a "visiting magician might sleep." He was directed to a homeless camp near San Lorenzo Park. He was welcomed warmly by a teenage homeless couple, who'd just hitchhiked to the coast (which they called "Cali" from Indiana.) The Indianians even shared some of the rice and beans they'd scoured from Tacqueria Vallarta's dumpster. And they gave Efaau an extra blanket of theirs. Efaau was shocked that they really wanted nothing in return, not the slightest request for him to put a curse on one of their enemies.

The next morning, Efaau showed up to his job at Jamba Juice. He'd asked the homeless couple to wake him up by six in the morning. While they'd have slept until ten, they set their alarm and made sure to get him up. Because of them, he was not late and could start his first job. Rachel, the nineteen year old manager, was friendly and showed him how to use the register, make the different types of smoothies and clean the machines. Then she gave him a green Jamba Juice shirt to replace his purple dress shirt.

The first day of work at Jamba Juice went on to be a winner for Efaau, miraculously smooth (ie). He was intimidated by everyone's niceness, their camaraderie, and that they instantly treated him with a playful goodwill. Disarmed, Efaau played the observer, mostly watching the joking around without reacting much.

During his second day, one of the other employees involved him in the teasing. Corey said, "what's up douchebag?"

Efaau quietly fermented in his familiar feeling of calculating vindictiveness. But, remembering the power of consumerism he felt in Costco, he took a deep breath and didn't show his wraith.

But Rachel lauged, "if you're going to survive in this job, you'll have to fight insults with insults, Efaau."

"What's up douchebag?" Efaau said back to Corey, trying his best to appease his superior.

"Hey, Efaau. Did one of those freak tornadoes mess your hair up on the way to work today?" Corey kept teasing.

"Did your face get eaten by a Siberian troll?" Efaau countered with all the hatred in his heart. He couldn't control himself anymore. The lure of consumerism loosened its grip and he was readying for war!

Thinking Efaau was making a joke, Efaau's workmate laughed with a generous smile and happily pat Efaau on the back.

"Hey guys, enough of your bromance. Make twenty Caribbean Passions ASAP. It's an online order for a new local account," Rachel commanded.

Once again, confused because his vitriol was returned with kindness, Efaau just followed Rachel's order. He made Caribbean Passion smoothies alongside his co-worker, who complained, "That's a lot of Caribbean Passions. Do they not know we have other flavors?"

Trying to fit in, Efaau sincerely said, "maybe somebody hexed their taste buds so they fell in love with the taste of Caribbean Passion. I know such a spell."

And, again confusing Efaau's comments as a joke, his co-worker, laughed and offered, "I used to know a magic spell that would transform my farts into perfumes."

Rachel said, "I wish you still knew that spell. We would all be much better off."

Corey kept going, "what did the Maxi-pad say to the fart?" The co-worker didn't wait for anyone's guess. "You are the wind beneath my wings.

Landing on the subject of farts, Efaau tried contributing, "I was once trying to escape from a dungeon. There was no way out but I infused my belly with magi, farted and..."

Efaau's quirky comments, misinterpreted as jokes, grew to make him quite popular among the Jamba Juice staff. He even realized their taunts were not malicious. He realized they actually liked him. And, because of being liked and appreciated so much, Efaau had a hard time clinging to his usual routine of hatefulness.

Efaau didn't really get these things called jokes, the stories he told were true but his co-worker/friends thought he was joking and someone always interrupted him before any punchline (especially since had never had a punchline). Furthermore, Efaau liked the smoothies, never missing out on his work perk of a daily free smoothie. He preferred the smoothie with peanut butter, Peanut Butter Moo'd. And he even got into taking shots of wheatgrass. His digestive system never felt so good. All that was good for him, but being around so much humor was what really cleared out his insides and turned Efaau into another person entirely. In the next few days, a dark cloud dissolved into the friendliness, laughing and casual playfulness alive at the Jamba Juice.

Rachel generated an abundance of team player attitude as a leader. Corey was a self-deprecating hilarious jackass. And there was Petra. She was sweet and treated Efaau with as much familiarity as a brother. It was an experience like none Efaau had ever never known in his life. Every day of work sucked out years of bitterness and rejection from Efaau's gut. Suspecting he needed a place to live, Petra mentioned to Efaau, "there's a room available in the vegetarian co-op where I live." And, with a solid pile of Rachel's personal cash fronted to him (without asking for interest or collateral), Efaau got to move into Petra's co-housing after his fifth day on the job. He moved in with a bunch of UCSC students, peace loving yogi and community studies major types. Corey helped too, hooking Efaau up with a free fairly clean mattress and sheets.

For years most of Efaau's thoughts circled around schemes to accumulate more power or solidify any power he already had. This obsession fizzled as he spent time in the Jamba. For the first time in many years, Efaau saw beyond his ego's thirst to climb up some power hierarchy. Efaau loved feeling like just a normal dude in Santa Cruz, a place where very non-normal people can feel normal.

Efaau liked Rachel, and didn't even want to usurp her power. With these people, sometimes he even thought about awful things he'd done and wondered if there'd been a better way.

Still, Efaau arrived at a particularly strange blip in Santa Cruz's history. There was a giant lion spotted in the hills, unusual tornadoes, whirlwinds and spastic hot/cold winds. And he heard about the militant eco-revolutionary who was being sought out by a swat team. But none of it touched him that deeply until he discovered the name and description of the eco-revolutionary- Enkida. Dreadlocks. And that she'd been caught.

"What will they do with her?" Rachel asked.

"I heard they're going to put her in a federal holding cell at a penitentiary in Salinas." Corey answered.

"In the kingdom I used to work for, there was a dungeon full of death venom spiders," Efaau said.

"What did you do before you worked here Efaau, seriously?"

"I worked for dictators, conjured up curses and messes; I was a villain."

"You! An evil villain, right!" Rachel laughed.

"If you only knew," Efaau looked down sadly.

Rachel mostly thought he was still joking, but she shivered. Since leaving his home in the Norse lands, nobody'd shown even a little curiosity about where he'd been previously. Efaau thought back about his life, and to how he'd become such a crushing person…

Efaau was born and grew up in a Norse village. His strange lisp and unusually gawky body made it so was not taken seriously as a warrior, a fisherman, a leader or much of anything, he was even mocked in his efforts. Not really given a chance to have a role in more orthodox professions, Efaau hid away and turned to studying magical texts which promised some power.

After a few months of studying incantations by himself in the woods, he grew a little more confident; he straightened his gawky posture and asked some fishermen, "ith it okay if I go fith with you all today?"

"You want go fith? Go fith. I don't know how to fith," a proud young fisherman, whom all the women in the village fawned over, mocked Efaau's lisp calling fish fith. Efaau's mocker had the biggest muscles, he always caught the biggest fish, and he walked with a swagger that would make Kanye West blush. This was far from the first time Effau had been teased by this proud nordic man's man. Effau had been knocked over by this proud fisherman and stung by his words countless times.

"Please, I just to fith with you," Efaau tried again.

The proud fisherman pulled a small bait fish from a bucket and hurled it at Efaau's head, "there you go. Go fith that."

Instead of flittering away to lick his wounds like he had countless times, Efaau pulled back his black hair and responded, "you are very unkind."

"Unless you want me to throw you off our boat, you're not going fithing with us. So fith off, skeleton boy," the proud fisherman snapped back.

Efaau waved around his thin arms and quietly chanted. It was a cooling spell. He thought this minor curse would make the proud fisherman shiver and help affirm his place as a tough man among this small tribe of nordic ruffians.

Still, instead of just feeling chilled, the young man who imitated Efaau's lisp made a long drawn out screeching sound that faded to a wisp of wind. He went quiet – having been turned into a solid piece of ice.

Efaau was more powerful than he thought. He had not meant to kill anyone. Nevertheless, the wide-eyed dirty haired chief, terrified of what he'd just seen, half-pleaded half-commanded Efaau, "leave here now and forever or every one of us will be forced to hunt you until either you are killed or we are." Effau considered using his curse on all of them but already felt sick from the shock of killing someone for the first time. He left and walked into the cold darkness of the forest alone.

Officially banished, Efaau learned to live off fruits, berries and magic in the wilderness. In isolation, he practiced every incantation in his spell book and intuited other darker spells. Such magical exploration was his only companion. Though masterless, he was a naturally talented explorer of incantation and intention, discovering impressively unruly spells. Away from the nordic lands, Effau meandered farther south every day until he arrived in a small kingdom along warm waters. In this new land, Efaau impressed the leader of the local chiefdom with fireballs and turning prisoners into frogs. After showing off sufficiently, Efaau was appointed royal minister and given a nice room in the palace where the king lived. While he still nursed bitterness from being shunned, he became content with this transactional new role. He was proud of himself for forging a new possibility of a good life after being banished from his homeland.

It didn't last. Only a week later, Rome led a full out offensive against that small territory. Efaau led the successful defense with a barrage of fireballs against Rome. Still, afterwards, Efaau was banished again. This time it was because a baroness in the kingdom got sick and it was unfairly blamed on Efaau. Efaau was given a chest of gold and requested to leave. He didn't care about gold. He just wanted to belong somewhere, but he consented (and, a month later, that small kingdom fell to Rome's forces).

Traveling east from that kingdom for many months, Efaau eventually arrived in Uruk and befriended Enkida's brother, Maka. Efaau found this new master a very unlikable and bitter man, learned that he'd been beaten up by his father almost every day of his childhood and that he despised his sister. Still, this Maka offered Efaau a job while Enkida blatantly encouraged her brother to throw him out to the dogs. So, strategically, Efaau had helped Maka semi-successfully rid the kingdom of Enkida before he was magically dropped into a dumpster next to Costco.

In this new world, Efaau knew Enkida was too powerful to be ignored. She was potentially the sole threat to remaining in this wonderful new life. Enkida possessed great magic- she somehow drew him from Ur to this strange place. As she brought him here, she was likely the only one who could expel him the same way or destroy him. Still, he wondered if he could deal with her in a new way.

A customer that day talked about Enkida, "she doesn't deserve to be in jail."

"Come on," Corey pushed back, "she led a small but destructive uprising!"

"That's not the whole story though. If you knew everything, you wouldn't be so judgmental of her."

People were always talking about either Enkida or Trump lately. "No matter what her past is, she got a bunch of people to riot. Even though I agree with a lot of her cause, I say lock her up," Corey boldly disagreed again.

"She's from another world. She didn't really understand what she was doing. She's from another time," the customer pulled his long curly blonde hair out of his face before paying for his shot of wheatgrass using a bag of quarters. He was wearing a very ragged yellow tank top that accentuated bulging muscles as he drank his shot.

"You don't even know where she's from?" Efaau snarled, surprising his workmates.

The guy laughed, "listen, man, it's ridiculous. I know where she's from and you wouldn't believe me. You would not believe me. Anyway, I'll just take my shot of wheatgrass and carry on."

As he prepared the shot, Efaau looked strangely at this customer and asked Rachel, "Can I take my break?"

"Sure," she shrugged with a smile.

"And, you," Efaau asked Kle with desperation in his voice, "please tell me the story. I promise I will believe you."

A few minutes later, as Efaau headed out eagerly talk with Kle, Petra blocked his way, and whispered non-jokingly in Efaau's ear, "get that blonde dude's phone number for me and you can have my free smoothie this whole week."

Prison

Enkida was taken to a federal penitentiary in Salinas after being arrested at Charlie Hong Kong's Pasta Shop. She yielded, didn't try any magic, and didn't say a word to the lawyer who was brought in to defend her.

Life in the penitentiary was not glorious. For the first week she kept fully to herself, not saying a single thing to any guards or inmates. Her life was waking up on a hard bed, eating, walking around her cell, thinking angrily about the betrayals and losses that had scourged her in the last days, then wondering if she should just obliterate some guards and leave. Instead, she'd eat more, have an hour free time outside in the fenced area, pace around back in the cell, eat shit food, and sleep again.

A few people tried to welcome her, to encourage, "we're in this shit show together," to give her the lowdown on which prison guards were cool or not, to complain about the food, and to invite her into one of the many ethnic subcultures in the slammer (she was recruited by a Southeast Asian faction and two Latin American gangs.

Enkida silently walked away from each and every kindness. There hadn't been a trial yet, but a federal prosecutor was trying to get her twenty five years for inciting a violent mob. On top of that, the lawyer was confident he could prove she was a foreign agent.

After a week of this soul-sucking routine, a small club of four neo-nazi inmates approached Enkida with less than kind intentions.

"What are you in for?" One asked harshly.

"Look at her. She's got dreadlocks. She's a hippy, she's in here for sitting in a tree house and telling people to stop cutting it down."

"Or maybe for some illegal grow operation."

"You like trees?" the toughest one asked Enkida, mockery not hidden from her voice.

"Ya, she probably had an illegal pot farm," one concluded.

"I don't like hippies," the tough nazi made very clear.

"You don't like anyone," another one of them laughed.

"I like my Hitler and my brothers."

"Cause only your brothers would fuck you."

"Shut up, cunt."

"I asked you a question, what are you in for?" Tough glared at Enkida.. Enkida broke her silence so that these ladies would leave her alone.

"For traveling through time and starting a revolution."

"You mocking me?"

"Mocking you?" Enkida calmly shook her head, "no!"

"Ya. You're trying to rile me up, to start some shit with me and my ladies. *Traveling through time and starting a revolution.* That's a stupid answer. Like I said, I don't like hippies. But especially self-righteous tree-hugger darkies like you."

Enkida felt her pent up anger like water pushing against a dam that was about to break. She was not interested in communicating with these mutants during her 'outside free hour' in the penitentiary. "Why would I try to rile you up? Who are you? You are nothing to me," Enkida growled.

"I'm nothing to you?" the woman took a breath in and stood suddenly self-satisfied as tall as she could. She had a swastika tattoo on an arm, arms she'd spent a lot of her free time building up by lifting weights. She was getting excited about using those muscles to beat this foreign sucker. She thought *we could have a good time teaching this newbie dark-skinned piece of shit a lesson.* Enkida ignored her and looked up sadly at the sun.

"Is she a Mexican?"

"I think she's a sand nigger."

"She's definitely not American."

Enkida walked away, weary of whatever it is they were. As she turned her back and was going to the other side of the fenced-in outside area, the one with the swastika on her arm whispered, "punk that bitch. Time to rearrange her sand nigger face."

And they did. They ran and one of them swung at Enkida's back, hitting where a coyote had bit Enkida not long before. Another threw Enkida to the ground. And they each socked her. The prison guards weren't noticing. Enkida's mouth was bleeding and her arm tweaked in it shoulder. They'd have kept hitting her but Enkida whispered four magic words through her bloodied mouth, a vindictive invocation. After Enkida meekly whispered those words, the woman with the swastika tattoo croaked, "What the hell? My feet can't move.

"And my arms are stuck..." Another screamed.

The third was coughing up black blood.?" The three women who'd hit Enkida were stiffening up, like they couldn't stop all their muscles from contracting.

"What did you do to us?" One whimpered. But they didn't hit Enkida now. And the swastika-woman looked like she was starting to suffocate.

"You want to know what I did?" Enkida growled, face thoroughly bleeding and bruised. "I taught the three of you a fucking lesson," fierce intensity radiated brightly from her eyes.

"Who are you?"

"I am strength. You picked on me because you thought I was weak, because I was by myself. And I once took a vow not to use any dark spells again, but that hasn't worked out so well. So, it looks like you have unintentionally forced me to open the door for a new Enkida. You may live but you will never be the same."

"Dark spells?" one of them started to ask, but the prison guards finally arrived. The prison guards knew there had been some kind of altercation. But the prison guards couldn't figure out why the three neo-nazies were stiffening up. They knew that Enkida had been attacked by the nazi club. They knew that it had been three on one. Still, in the next hour, Enkida was put in a hole, a cell completely isolated from any interactions. The guards claimed it was for her own protection.

The hole doesn't heal or teach. It just ferments whatever evil is in you. In beating the neo-nazis, Enkida already embraced making some leap towards the dark side, but, in the hell of total isolation, a concrete box, she pulled miles deeper into the darkness. The day passed in that cube with few transitions – food being slipped through the slot in her door, a few moments to evacuate her digestive system on the pot, and lots of gray blah. In that blah, even Enkida's yearning to connect with Arito (in hopes he was truly her son) paled to near extinction.

She whispered mantras calling forces to her that she had previously renounced. She turned away from healing spirits she'd been long devoted to. The forces she called on now were ones that couldn't be completely uncalled. They were destructive forces. She kept building these forces up until she was confident she had enough power to destroy a lot of people including herself.

There was a spell that could send bad health to dozens of people across the planet. And there was a spell she learned that could make a heart collapse. She was a brave woman, largely unafraid of death. And, in that miserable cubicle of nothingness, death seemed a lively option. She built up more and more of such poison over the next hours and then days, goodness fading into a distant reality. And then she recited the first of three words which would unleash a tidal wave of curses she had built up.

She recited the second word. And, as she was starting the third and final word, as evil was quivering with excitement, with timing perfect for dramatic suspense, she heard the door to her cell unlock. She didn't finish the word. The door slid open for a guard to come in. "Nasty beating you took from

Hitler's moron youth group got you some luck. We got orders to let you out of here. So get up and come with me, please."

"Let me out of this jail?" she asked.

"Yep. Come this way."

Enkida wondered if the guard had somehow opened the wrong cell. She was not confident she was being let out of anywhere. The public defender she met with previously had told her she'd probably get at least fifteen years. She wasn't even sure what exactly that meant. Anyway, this guard continued leading her upstairs and through security gates and out to a changing room where a small box with her clothes was waiting, her leather dress and sandals.

Just outside of the changing room, Kle was waiting for her with a smile.

"What is going on?" Enkida asked.

"Your release from this prison has been arranged."

"What?" she asked without much gratitude in her voice.

"You're not appreciative?" Kle frowned.

"I want to be grateful but I'm guessing you're bringing me into another mess."

"To be honest, I felt bad for you when the SWAT team threw you on the ground. And, to be even more honest, I'm not really the one responsible for your being released. But let me tell you about it in the car."

A kid with big glasses, Kle's hired Uber driver for the day, was waiting for them outside in a clean white sedan. The driver blasted the air conditioning once they got in.

"So, how was it there?" Kle asked, sitting comfortably in the tan leather seat.

"It is a cesspool. I was about to curse the world and then destroy myself," she confessed honestly. "I am still full of so much hate energy, I don't know how I can deal with it without blowing up a great…"

"Whoah," Kle interrupted. "You liked it that much? Just chill out."

"Please tell me. How is it happening that I was released?"

"Have you ever had enemies?"

"Yes."

"What if one of your enemies had a change of heart. And they didn't want to be your enemy. We can even say they were rehabilitated."

"In Mesopotamia the saying was the only good enemy was a dead enemy. But continue..."

Kle looked unsure but continued, "this enemy had done some things to you that were very bad but they wanted you to forgive them and so used a favor trying to make it good…"

"I would forgive them. I am not like the rest of the people in Ur. I am merciful."

"Okay, so you would forgive that person?"

"Yes. Of course. As a queen I learned the dignity of forgiving those who turned to me understanding their error. I mean… any of my enemies except for one."

"Oh," Kle said with a sigh. "Who's that one?"

"Efaau. He organized my child to be taken away from me. He led my own brother against me. He had me banished from my home. He tried to get me killed with his curses. Such a venom-filled pest has no antidote. But, anyway, Efaau would never have gotten me out of prison. And he's been dead for thousands of years. I would forgive any of my other enemies, so tell me!"

"Uh, that Efaau sounds like a pretty horrible person. But, just hypothetically lets say this Efaau had a change of heart, a real change of heart, something that made him realize the error of his ways. Let's say he was repentant and he had somehow earned a favor from a powerful businessman friend named Mark Zuckerberg. And that businessman had the best lawyer money could buy. And, after your squabble with some neo-nazis, they established a legal basis for doing you a real solid."

"What?" Enkida did not look pleased.

"A lawyer got your case completely dismissed on some legal loopholes that I don't really understand."

Enkida was silent. "And why would this scum, I mean Efaau, not pick me up himself? Or are you Effau masked in magic?"

"I am not Effau but, because he knows you hate him and he knows you have good reasons to hate him, I have come for him. He fears you would not understand his change of heart, that you would lash out on him."

"What could have changed such a rotten man's heart?"

"I'm not sure exactly but, he said something about a demon being separated from his soul, drinking wheatgrass and Peanut Butter Moo'd, and his co-workers at Jamba Juice." It sounded weird, as much to Kle as Enkida.

"Working at Jamba Juice? The shitty overpriced smoothies place? Where is evil Efaau, now? Even if he got me out, I still need to destroy him."

"What about that thing about being merciful?"

"Effau is evil."

"I really don't know if he's still as evil as you think, Enkida. Strange things transform us sometimes. Either way, he's a long way from here. He went with the Santa Cruz Jamba Juice team to a festival called Burning Man. He said he wanted to get a taste of the artist community experience in the desert."

"Then the Uber driver's going on a detour to Burning Man with us," Enkida commanded clearly.

The driver interrupted, "did I just hear that you guys are hiring me to take you to Burning Man. Please say yes. I would love that. It won't be cheap though. And I am tired…"

"I will Burn Efaau at Burning Man!" Enkida proclaimed and was about to say some very grim things but the Uber driver, who couldn't hear her easily, interrupted:

"I was studying for a puppetry exam all night so I'm a little jittery from not sleeping enough."

"Puppetry?" Kle asked. He was confused, unsure what puppetry was, but hopeful a change of topic could give Enkida a chance to calm down.

"Ya. Puppetry. There's a lot to it," the Uber driver lit up with the topic he brought up.

"Tell me all about puppetry?" Kle did not want to talk about Enkida's hatred of Efaau anymore. Hearing about this puppetry was much nicer than making Enkida so scary, a cloud of darkness viscerally thickening around her.

"You know, " the uber driver was ecstatic, "when you think you're controlling a puppet, the puppets are really controlling you. The North American Puppetry exam is actually very philosophical…" The Uber driver went on excitedly about his studies with the North American Puppetry Society. A bit taken off guard by the driver's unbridled enthusiasm, Kle and Enkida listened to the international history of puppetry, the importance of knowing your puppets nuances, and the many design strategies for coming up with your puppets. He got really excited describing a documentary he'd watched about pre-WWII Jewish puppetry practices in Germany. The kid was Jewish and his grandfather had been a puppeteer. He was so immersed in what he was sharing that he didn't pay great attention to the road they were taking to get to Burning Man.

"Holy Shit!!! Watch out," Kle yelled. The Uber driver looked back at the road and swerved away from a corpse lying in the middle of the road. It was an unfortunate place for a body, right next to a steep dip off the road. The small sedan lurched into the dip and rolled on its side with a big wave of dust.

The engine buzzed to a stop, the groundless tires continuing to spin. Some birds squawked in some distant place of the desert expanse surrounding them.

The driver had hit his head on the windshield, but, because of his seat belt, the impact really hadn't been that bad. The intensity of the accident actually short circuited his jitters. He calmly climbed out of his seat and out the window from his sideways car to the ground outside.

He'd seen movies. He knew cars like this often blew up. For a tiny moment, he considered leaving his passengers trapped in the car to die. He knew he'd fucked up (by rolling off the side of the road) and they were the only witnesses to his negligence. But there's no way he would have really done that. He was too much a good person for that. And he acted very quickly to help them.

The driver pulled Enkida out first. She was mumbling, but she was conscious. And, together, they pulled the heavier Kle out. Kle hadn't been wearing his seat belt and he must have hit the roof of the car hard because he was not only unconscious, but covered with blood.

Back on the road, they saw the corpse they'd almost hit. It was an old woman who was not as dead as they thought. The corpse became animate and stood up. She was bone thin and looked like a heroin addict. She smiled at them with a self-satisfied sickliness and walked towards them. They were miles from any house. She had no business being there.

Enkida saw through this poorly placed tramp's disguise. She was a demon, a creature actually from the hell realm. Enkida knew such beasts pretended to be human to draw innocent souls into the darkest of darknesses. It took a demonic amount of grim energy to send such a being back to their hell, it was thought only a devil could send another devil of this sort back to where it came from. "She is no human. She was on the road so Kle would be killed," Enkida told the Uber driver.

"The heroin addict lying in the road? Ya, it is weird she was right there but I'm sure she wasn't waiting for anyone."

"You don't see all I see. Anyway, sometimes you have to fight darkness with darkness. It's actually good timing for me. I have gathered up more darkness than I'd ever have dared otherwise." The Uber driver didn't follow Enkida's logic. He just watched Enkida glare at this old woman walking towards them. Enkida focused the direction of her magic and chanted a few words releasing the full magnitude of the powers she'd accumulated during her vitriolic moments trapped in the hole at the prison. Nobody had ever chanted such a package of hateful spells. It was the equivalent to "going nuclear" for incantations. Enkida knew chanting this spell would so fully deplete her that she would be left for dead, but she wouldn't let such a devil cause more trouble when something could be done.

The world shook. It rocked so wildly that the Uber driver's car fell over even more so that it was upside down, the Uber driver threw his hand to his forehead groaning, "an earthquake now. What the fuck!"

The demon woman turned back at them and hissed with a tongue as long as her body snapping out of her. She knew what Enkida had done. A big chasm opened up in the ground beneath the demon. From the chasm spastic tentacles shot up and wrapped around the demon woman's legs.

"How dare you send me back?" the woman screeched, but, instead of a person there, they saw only a mess of tentacles covered with slime, shit and the nasty stink of hell. It was a mess of tentacles being grabbed by much larger tentacles. The demon clearly had no chance. It was quickly pulled down into some hellish dimension that it came from. Then the world shook again and the chasm that swallowed her closed up again. It left no hint of drama behind except these weary travelers and an upside down car.

The Uber driver thought seeing the earth swallow up a heroin junkie-turned-tentacles had been a hallucination, that he'd hit his head too hard on the windshield and was going a little wacko, "I hope I'm okay."

Enkida was so depleted she could barely move her muscles, but she chanted a couple healing words over Kle. The Uber driver looked on through a daze. Enkida knew blasting away that demon woman already took a lot from her, but letting so much evil go through her left something like a scab on her energetic body. To finish healing Kle, Enkida patted particular points around Kle's body. A healer had taught her those particular points were important to check after a healing. As she did this, Enkida stumbled across something in his jean's pocket, the ziplock bag. She pulled the bag out and found the talisman that had unleashed so much mischief in her (and others') lives. She wasn't sure if she should be angry or elated that Kle had this. "How did Kle get this?"

"The ziplock bags! They sell them at Safeway," the Uber driver tried to be helpful.

Concerned that her uber driver might start talking about puppets, Enkida ignored him and got focused again. She really had no idea how the magic of the gem would unfold this time (Enkida basically only understood the turn-on button for the very complex magical machinery hidden within this talisman). Still, Enkida held the copper object tightly and knew she would use the very last of her energy to wield this wild card again.

Wild

The festival was off the hook, with everyone dust-saturated and half-dressed. Nariah belly danced joyfully into the night with burlesque fire dancers spontaneously gathering around her, enchanted with the overwhelmingly sensual power of Nariah's wide hips. While she couldn't remember her past, she could remember how to make those subtle gyrations of her strong abdominal muscles.

Rafael and Phillip lingered nearby. They were talking passionately – first debating the historical authenticity of Noah's Ark and the next moment laughingly critiquing somebody's costume. Then they were staring into each other's eyes. It wasn't really sexual but it was love. To Rafael, this Phillip was technically a crazy person – somebody who thought he had been a direct disciple of Jesus. But he didn't care. To Phillip, this Rafael was a nonbeliever from another time. Not that either really cared about these superficial differences.

Telemachus sat sadly at the edge of the festival. It was hitting him that all his tasks were a farce- Poseidon would never make good on his promise. For no great reward, he'd devoted thousands of years to appeasing a God now seen as more of a joke than anything else. It was all dry here, barren of mermaids and underwater kingdoms. There was no possibility of a tidal wave transforming him into one of the merpeople (and uniting him with his love).

Telemachus somberly listened to the bass music thump-thump from dozens of venues across Black Rock. He thought of that mermaid's face again. He had stayed resolute and upbeat for thousands of years, but now he cried. He couldn't hold it together any longer, "I will stay in this white dustscape beyond the festival's end, starve myself to death among the turtles of this desert."

Arito was wearing a very tall sombrero while flirting with a girl he had felt drawn to, Rachel. Rachel, the manager of Jamba Juice, the one who hired Efaau and helped him get a place to stay. Even at Burning Man, Rachel was wearing a very flattering snug green Jamba Juice T-shirt. In their talk, Arito found out she, too, had spent some part of her childhood in Alaska. Within the Burning Man haze they laughed recalling experiences running from bears, seeing walruses and high school camping trips to Denali National Park.

Then a man skipped over to Rachel's side. Rachel introduced this friend to Arito, "This is Efaau. And I don't know your name?"

"I'm Arito." Arito couldn't hide the disappointment on his face, assuming Efaau was Rachel's romantic commitment, assuming his flirting was foolhardy.

"Efaau is my friend," Rachel clarified sweetly, doing her best to give Arito a chance. Efaau smiled. While he was already enjoying being *friends* with people, he'd never officially been called someone's friend. The thought made him soar. Then he saw the anklet on the boy and knew that this Arito was the boy whom he'd separated from Enkida so many thousands of years before. So, practically within the same moment, he went from a major high to a major low. He went from wondering, *Why am I so lucky to have gotten a job with such wonderful people?* to *Why did I become such a monster, letting heartlessness control me for so long?*

While Arito did have a kink in his walk, something in his voice made Rachel feel calm. He had a confident style that was unquestionably royal. And, as good feelings were clearly mutual, a few minutes later they excused themselves from Efaau to go under the shadows of a giant metal rhino structure. There they exchanged tongue-filled kisses and gentle squeezes of her warm breasts. The tender moment went on as the sun rose.

But then, in the light of morning, Arito pointed to the RV Telemachus brought him in and asked, "What is happening to that thing? I came here in that." The dragon-RV Arito was pointing to, the one Telemachus had driven him into the desert, was the first to catch the tingles of magic that had quickly blown in. Because of Telemachus's preference, the dragon-RV was parked in Burning Man's Pagan camp. He had hoped to share some Athenian and Zeus-related tales there before Poseidon fulfilled his promise.

Arito and Rachel watched the RV quiver with life and then grow real lizard scales. They both thought *maybe mushrooms were starting to kick in,* but then remembered they hadn't taken mushrooms. They'd only smoked a tiny bit of pot and that had been hours ago. By the time the RV was flapping its wings and lifting up into the sky, Arito and Rachel were far from the only ones noticing the giant lizard gleefully blazing far up into the early evening sky.

Enkida's work with the Talisman had started the magic again – a legion of bizarre (and often illegal to drive) cars flooded the skies, three-story tall VW vans, buses welded to be shaped like sharks with giant jaws open, cars artistically decorated to look like giant pirate ships complete with pyrotechnic canons, so many other mutant vehicles. People were coming down from the previous night's dancing, drugs, nudity, art and dust storms while the magic kicked in, triggered by a gem many miles away.

The car that looked like a ship suddenly seemed to set sail and flew up into the air. Dog-cars barked at cat-cars. A Hobbit house car suddenly had hobbits bouncing around in it. Valiant knights hollered from castle cars. Shark cars swam down and through the white dust. And spaceship cars shot high up towards the stars, some of which were never seen again.

Logical technophiles wondered, "is this some viciously unruly mass hallucination." More superstitious artist types wondered if Burning Man himself was showing anger for the festival's development into a commercially packaged mainstream commodity. Only Efaau considered that, hundreds of miles away, Enkida somehow had access to a sprockle jat. He didn't know anyone still had one. He'd read about them-a sprockle jat is a golden speck of pure magic from the beginning of time. It looked like a small yellow metal talisman with nine dots on it. With this talisman and a short incantation, one could unleash some of nature's most unpredictable happenings.

But even Efaau couldn't have guessed Enkida had unleashed this spell alongside dozens of untamable air currents (the gem had been enclosed and energetically mixed with the bag of winds that Telemachus, the Master of the Sea's apprentice, had gathered and given to Kle). The spell spiraled around and amplified even more because of those winds. Seven of the nine people who had intentionally (or unintentionally) been lassoed up by the original spell of the golden gem (Nariah, Telemachus, Arito, Efaau, Phillip, Zaera, and Rafael) were at Burning Man. A new chaos was drawn to them and their festival.

The scaly Dragon RV soared up into the sky and then dropped down spouting a thick stream of flame. It roared like a dragon and then hurled fire at the wooden stick figure at the center of Black Rock, the one Burning Man authorities planned to burn at the end of the festival; the Man was ablaze. People had recently taken off their ultra-fantastic "Burner" costumes. In the early morning hours, the bass beat had recently faded. Still, there was a great cacophonous mess of innumerable mutant vehicles making honking, growling, and making all sorts of noise, doing what they shouldn't be doing and waking up the Burners.

While the chaos at Burning Man was brewing, Enkida lay dying on the road in between the penitentiary and Burning Man. She was dying from having overspent herself – she had sent that demon back to hell, she did some crucial work to heal Kle, and she reopened the time-space portal again (with the incantation connected with the rarest of talismans, which Efaau called a sprockle jat.)

Kle woke up to see Enkida curled up like a fetus. He asked the Uber driver, "what happened to her?"

"She said she dealt with a demon that had been following you. She sent it back to hell. Then she did some chanting to heal you and found the bag with some copper thing in your pocket. She took out the thing and said a bunch of weird words to it. Then she passed out. I think she's dying."

"Don't say that," Kle commanded heavily. He didn't know Enkida very well but she created the opening for him to come to this world. In that sense, she was a vagina through which he was born again. She gave birth to the possibility of a new life beyond and away from the assholes from Greece he'd spent so many years trying to emulate.

As he was genuflecting on what Enkida was to him, he felt the impact of Enkida's final invocation. The time-space sequence holding everything together opened up to a gap beneath him, the non-linear vacuum of possibility, again enclosing tightly, and the Uber driver was suddenly all by himself; Enkida and Kle sucked up to some beyond.

Rafael and Phillip were being chased by a vulture shaped car with talons when they, too, felt the ground beneath them drop them through the timeless passageway. Efaau was running away from a shark car swimming through the white dust towards him. Zaera, after drinking three beers, was telling a car shaped like a penis (and growing bigger each second), "love is for idiots." As she fell through the portal, Zaera recalled Kle's descriptions of *dropping through time and space.*

Nariah belly danced right through most of the chaos with her eyes closed. When she was belly-dancing she wasn't overwhelmed by the knowledge that she didn't know who she was. Telemachus was staring at his dragon RV, flying wrathfully through the sky, when he was dropped....

Nariah, Phillip of Judea, Rafael, Telemachus, Zaera, Arito, Efaau, Enkida, and Kle. Nine dots on the talisman, nine souls carried along. They were carried by the magic of the talisman mixed with the winds from the zip lock bag. Uprooted from their current time-space continuum, these nine were hurled through a wormhole to splash down....

Mumbai Cruz

Nariah was scared of what she saw going on around her- the flying art cars, people screaming in disbelief, and a swarm of strange insects (to be clear, the insects were not particularly impacted by the magic in process. They were just there.). So, instead of focusing on all the crazy, Nariah closed her eyes and became absorbed in pulsing her belly. She gyrated with her eyes closed until she was calm. She opened her eyes just as the universe shifted with the weightless void, the timeless vacuum of no-orientation. In the complete groundlessness invoked by Enkida and the talisman, Nariah kind of realized she wasn't at Burning Man anymore.

From *there,* Nariah fell through solid air and splashed down. She couldn't remember the last time she dropped into the beach near Crow's Nest. She didn't remember being saved by Kle after that first drop. Still, the experience felt a little more familiar than it would have otherwise. Of course, like her drowned father before her, she still could not swim. But she tried to, furiously throwing her arms all over the place, kicking with all her might, and still her head sank. And Nariah was surprised by how quickly she reached down to the bottom. She thought, *I should have faith*, and, to her relief, she saw 'the light (that fluorescent-ish silver supernaturally welcoming light).' Through that vast chasm of seraphic light, Jesus's form emerged. She assumed he was there to welcome her into the glorious paradise beyond all mundane things.

No. That was wrong. By the look on Jesus's face, he was clearly not there to welcome her. His hand scratched his forehead and he was shaking his head; Nariah wondered what message Jesus was trying to convey. She strained to tune in more to Jesus, to hear his precious counsel through the deafening roar of near death's silence. Then, as if she just turned up the volume on an iPod, the messiah commanded her as loudly as a foghorn, "evil winds be gone! Nariah, remember who you are and where you come from. And, for God's sake, stop trying to swim and stand up, child. You are in pretty shallow water!" And she did. She remembered who she was, that Kle wasn't her husband and she'd been a friend of Mary Magdalene's and she'd traveled across time and space to Santa Cruz.

She also stood up, miraculously pushing her feet against the sandy ocean floor. Nariah's fully extended legs lifted her head just out of the water (and out of the heavily lit messianic vision).. She gasped and gasped, filling her lungs with fresh air. There were people on the shore, mostly dozens of kids who'd been making castles in the sand until they saw this woman appear in the cold ocean before them. She tiptoed towards the shoreline so there was water only up to her elbows. The kids looked stunned and began running away from this strange woman emerging from the sea (as if she were a monster).

Nariah gathered momentum and bounced along out of the water as the last of the kids abandoned their castles screaming away. When she was safely on dry land, Nariah realized the kids were not running just from her but, just behind her were Phillip and Rafael, the duo of stylish long-haired effeminate maleness – Fabio and Princess Charming.

As Phillip and Rafael marched out of the water, Nariah yelled to Phillip and Rafael ecstatically, "I remember everything! Absolutely everything. Jesus just visited with me underwater and healed me. He helped me stand up too."

Rafael ignored her and clung to Phillip, grabbing him with the passion of a child for its mother, sobbing, uncontrollably. New to the whole unexpected time-space portal thing, he was exceedingly disorientated by the nauseatingly big leap. Phillip just patted Rafael's back patiently and told Nariah, "Of course Jesus helped you, dear. That was a fun one."

"We're at Natural Bridges State Park beach," Rafael mumbled nervously. "But there's something very strange. This really does not look right at all…"

Telemachus dropped into a very different situation. As he submerged into the water, there was just relief, like slipping into a very comfortable bed after the longest of journeys. He felt his legs instantly wiggle the strangest of ways. Transformed, his legs weren't even legs anymore. He reached down to find a slippery, singular, long muscular fin. Instinctually, he tried all his might to waddle back *up* for air, but didn't know how to use this new appendage. The weight of it even dragged him further down like a rock.

Underwater, his mouth resisted taking a breath. But, when he finally gave up, allowing the water to fill his lungs, instead of enduring any painful drowning, the ocean rushed in sweetly as air. The saltwater flushed through his circulatory system, welcoming his transformation into a creature of the water.

He blinked his eyes for the last time, Telemachus, likewise, discovered fish-like eyes literally replacing his old set. These new eyes saw clearly even in the darkness below the waves. And, seeing not something but someone flurrying around excitedly by him in the depths, Telemachus smiled widely and swam with a full heart towards this gorgeous familiar aquatic allure zipping through the waters. Telemachus wasn't the only one who had patiently waited so long for this reunion. They'd both waited so long for each other.

Enkida was dying in the desert. The uber driver was right. Still, she already unleashed a big magic. And, after being thrown into the time-space bleep, she was restored. It's like her life was a video game simulation and she just called on another life. Zaera dropped in the same place. Zaera was sobered up. Both were almost instantly scooped up together in an old twine net. It was not a pleasant welcome into this world. The fishermen pulled Enkida and Zaera up onto their heinously grungy ship. The women gulped air frantically looking around at the men who were shocked by what they'd caught – they'd literally caught ladies. On top of that, after wailing around in the ocean, these ladies wore little more than a few revealing rags.

"A fisherman's wet dream," one of the fishermen laughed.

"They must've fallen off some yacht. Maybe they got pushed off and, uh, I don't know..." another fisherman wondered unimaginatively out loud.

Calling the fishermen's ship humble was optimistic. It was a piece of junk. At its stern, there was a small puttering diesel engine that looked about fifty years old. It made the air nauseously thick with diesel smoke. And with the dead sea life and unwashed seamen, the smell was wretched. The rest of the barge was little more than a pathetic old makeshift sheet of aluminum.

Enkida and Zaera looked around at the piles of dead fish, rusting old crab traps, and the ocean surrounding them on all sides. "Thank you so much for pulling us up in the net we fell into..." Zaera began praising her seemingly dutiful rescuers but she was interrupted.

From within one of the traps, a terrified voice roared, "help me!"

Zaera and Enkida looked inside an old crab trap and saw Arito there, reaching his arms out trying unsuccessfully to free himself.

"What are you doing in there, Arito?" Enkida screeched.

"Enkida!" Arito yelled back.

"Yes, it's me. What are you doing there?" Enkida asked, panicky.

Arito whimpered, "all the cars at Burning Man started going crazy and then everything fell away and I crashed into the water and my foot got trapped in this fucking crab cage. Just then, these guys were pulling the crab trap out of the water and pulled me out with it but, instead of helping me out of it, they pushed me even farther into this piece of shit trap. Why are you here? I only smoked pot. What's happening? I'm scared. Is this a bad trip? This is a bad trip. Please let this be a bad trip. I have totally lost it, but I'm going to wake up at Burning Man's infirmary, right? Please say this is a very lucid unpleasant hallucination that will pass. And how did you know I'm from Alaska? And why did you claim to be from thousands of years ago?"

These poor fishermen-rescuers seemed to have taken Arito prisoner. And, they were circling around the two ladies with spears and a rope (to tie them up presumably). Zaera and Enkida smelled perversion swirling in the eyes of these very sick-looking fishermen. The fishermen seemed to look at Zaera and Enkida as if they were just another fish to be gutted or sold.

"Let him out of that cage right now you silly fools," Enkida commanded the fishermen clearly. Enkida noticed how going through the portal, surprisingly, refilled all of her energy tanks. Before she "dropped" into the water of this world, she was on the verge of death, having run beyond her reserves. She was close to the vortex of Neither-Lands but now she felt as good as new, clear and strong.

Instead of freeing anybody, one of the five fishermen poked what remained of Zaera's purple skirt with his spear, apparently trying to cut through it for his viewing pleasure.

"Bastard," Zaera said and furiously pushed the spear away.

The fisherman yelled at her "don't mess with me, bitch," with an animal-like frenzy in his eyes. He was obviously on some sort of stimulant.

"Did you do this to us, Enkida?" Arito growled.

"I-I…" Enkida stuttered.

"You what!" Arito prodded sobbing angrily from his claustrophobic situation in a crab trap.

"I opened the portal again. I was hoping it would fix everything."

Arito didn't let up on her, "I don't know what type of demon you are but maybe you should stop trying to fix things."

Zaera was shocked, "You mean Kle wasn't lying about everything he told me?"

"Yes, Enkida is actually a real evil sorceress," Arito kept bashing Enkida. "She doesn't just incite riots and claim to be people's mothers. Maybe she is my mother, but in addition to bringing me into this world, she's brought me to hell!"

"Someone tell me how this can be real, what the fuck!" Zaera hysterically yelled, unsure of everything.

As Arito yelled and Zaera screeched, the fishermen were poking their spears, one eventually jabbing into the scab on Enkida's back. This scab was still fairly fresh from the coyote's bite. Another fisherman poked her breasts.

This did not go on long. Enkida decided to go dark again but this time it was only for a brief moment. Enkida pointed her hand at the fishermen and chanted three words, words she'd learned with her brother when she was a teenager.

Then the fishermen were no longer a problem. They were hopping around the floor of the ship. They were not bullying fishermen anymore. They were little brown bunnies, complete with soft whiskers, cute noses and beautiful floppy ears.

Stunned, but understanding what just happened, Arito asked, “why didn’t you turn them into fish? Poetic justice for fishermen?”

“I don’t know the fish spell. I like bunnies more than fish, anyway” Enkida confessed.

“I was so mean to Kle,” Zaera grieved out loud while instinctually picking up the darkest brown bunny and petting it for her comfort.

Enkida walked over to Arito, unlatched the cage he was in, and calmly commanded, “you start being a little nicer to me, boy? I may not be your mother but I’m not interested in taking any more of your abusive hating shit.”

Arito nodded through a traumatized obedient daze. And, as he got out her dreadlocks brushed over Arito’s face.

“Your dreadlock smells so familiar to me,” Arito mumbled.

“What about the fishermen?” Zaera asked, inhaling a fresh cool breeze intermixed with the smell of rotting dead fish.

"I don't know how to turn them back into men. They're stuck as rabbits as long as I exist," Enkida said.

Dolphins leapt around the side of the ship. The bunnies hopped around mindlessly. And Enkida, Zaera, and Arito tutted along in their little boat. They headed towards a sliver of land on the horizon. Arito revved up the smelly engine to get to the mainland faster, to figure out where and when they were.

"I'm sorry, mom," Arito said as their boat clunked along the sea.

"What?" Enkida asked Arito.

"Your dreadlocks. Their smell. I remember them. I remember being a baby and just craving that smell."

Enkida didn't respond. They bounced along through the waves towards shore, Enkida allowing herself to flood with maternal feelings for the second time in her life as their boat inched closer to the coastline. The reconciliation didn't happen as she hoped but still...

Kle cramped up in the icy cold saltwater. He knew what happened, that Enkida had unleashed the portal again. "Yay," he thought sarcastically, swimming as fast as he could. After sucking in enough air, he screamed at the sky, "come on Zeus. Not again!"

Kle saw land on the far distance of the horizon. It was too far. There was no way he could swim that far through the chilly water. As usual, Zeus didn't seem to respond with much help, so Kle pleaded with another god, "Poseidon, God of the sea, have mercy on me. I hate Odysseus too."

Seemingly more responsive, Kle saw a shark fin headed his way. Perhaps it was a mercy, the shark could eat him and finish this nightmare. Kle waded and waited for the shark's mouth to show its teeth and grab some appendage from his body. Instead, the finned monster calmly drew close to Kle. Kle saw it was not a vicious shark but an enthusiastic dolphin! And it circled around Kle playfully, even repeatedly brushing up against him. Dolphins can't talk but this one seemed to scream out, "get on my back, Kle. I will take you to that place you need to be."

Kle had always considered dolphins suspicious, Greek lore claims them to be servants of Poseidon. Still, he felt things had somehow changed between him and the god of the sea, Poseidon. "Have we made peace, dear King of all the Waters? Am I right to assume you send a gift now or am I deluded by a trick?"

There was no answer. Still, Kle saw no option but to climb on the back of this dolphin, a Hercules cowboy on the back of his water horse.

And this rodeo pair took off, whisking through the waters, Kle feeling like he was flying. The sun and ocean water washed against Kle's skin. He remained on the dolphin's back as the sun climbed higher and warmer and what was a sliver of coastline grew until Kle saw familiar sights. There were the hills behind Santa Cruz, the rollercoasters of the Boardwalk as well as the arcade building Kle once feared to be Poseidon's fortified temple.

Near Steamer's Lane, the surf break leading up to the lighthouse, the dolphin slowed. They neared the wharf adjacent to the boardwalk. It was a sunny day but these generally popular spots were not teeming with people. There were no surfers on the waves, tourists on the wharf, kids at the arcade, or cars buzzing along the road. Kle could see this was not the world he just left.

Horses carried men armed with rifles along the wharf, at the entrance to the arcade. Dozens of armed men could be spotted along the coastline. And there was a motor boat pulling onto the shore, with three people. Kle had to squint to see who the three people were. When he strained enough, he recognized them: Enkida, Arito, and his Zaera. Zaera!

Kle was blasted from being so rejected by Zaera but he still loved her. And now she drew him towards the shoreline. As the dolphin slowed even more, Kle leapt from it to swim himself the rest of the way. Making sure he was heading the right direction, he lifted his head up. At that precise moment he saw Enkida hurl something into the sky. Not only that but, with this object coming from at least a hundred feet away, he put up his hand to protect his head from it. Instead, he caught it. It was the small metal talisman. Still eager to see Zaera, he threw himself back into swimming.

Enkida knew she had saved her son, finally won him over with magic she never thought would prove too useful – the bunny spell (it only worked on particularly weak minded fools). Even Zaera, this red-headed princess, had gone from hater to a fan. Enkida was drunk with the gloriously conclusive results of her magic.

With these thoughts of self-admiration swirling blissfully through Enkida's head, she didn't notice the morphed shoreline they bounced towards. She saw the roller coaster and the wharf but she overlooked the horses carrying armed men. Arito and Zaera were too enchanted by the seemingly innocent fishermen-turned-hopping bunnies to gaze at the shoreline with much attention.

The Big Dipper roller coaster's wood was rotting, paint chipping, and nobody was on it. There was no music, no beeping of arcade games, no howls from people enjoying any rides. Enkida, Arito, and Zaera guessed they were in the future but didn't know how far. It was so quiet they could hear leaves rustling along the empty beaches.

Enkida slumped to the ground, "I've failed again, misled by this damned gem's magic. Every time I use it, things get even worse." She took the gem from her pocket and deliberately hurled it as far out into the sea as she could manage. She didn't even see Kle out there. She didn't notice him easily catching the small object that had been in his possession not long before.

Arito mercifully put his arms around Enkida. He no longer fed his anger. He was grateful to be out of the crab trap. Anyway, he was well versed in knowing the world is just fucked sometimes. Zaera came up and pat Enkida's back, saying "whatever the fuck that's been done, we're here for a reason now." Zaera even felt electrified by the possibility of a purpose for her in this seemingly post-apocalyptic Santa Cruz.

Instead of benign leaves rustling across the sand, a car's engine rumbled towards them. Down from Beach Hill, a black recently washed SUV limousine rumbled smoothly towards the Boardwalk. The door opened and there sat the most hateful character from Enkida's past, her brother, Maka.

At Natural Bridges State Beach, Nariah, Phillip and Rafael swaggered like wet dogs out of the water. They walked past the kids' abandoned sand castles into what looked like a busy military encampment set up at Natural Bridges State Park. There were dozens of tan army tents, many accompanied by poles in the sand with American flags atop them. There were four giant wooden crosses at the corners of the encampment. And, of course, there were people. Most carried rifles or supplies and looked busy, the men wore fancy-ish business suits and the women with seemingly inappropriate tightly fitting white dresses down to their ankles.

The children who'd been playing in the sand ran to their mothers. One of these children grabbed his mom and pointed at the newcomers. The mom screeched at the sight of these bedraggled time travelers, "Invaders! Foreigners!"

Within seconds, the whole encampment, hundreds of people, were surrounding Nariah, Phillip, and Rafael, pointing their rifles, and chewing their cheeks anxiously. A leader among this militia, a considerably older version of the fire and brimstone preacher Nariah saw when she first got to Santa Cruz, spoke "ye non-believers, if I see clearly – a whore and two faggots. How dare you come to stain the purity of the Lord's army, gathered here awaiting the rapture. We stand as true Americans, what is it you want?'

"We just dropped in here," Phillip explained. "We don't mean to bother you."

"You don't mean to bother us?"

"No, of course not," Rafael responded demurely.

The preacher wasn't impressed, "have you come to preach communism, Liberal wussy-ism! Jesus demands we bring the sword against sinners like you. He demands Christ's Army reports for duty. Today our master hands us the sword." He went on and on, getting worked up about the sinful untrustworthy nature of these arrivals.

"I really don't understand how any of what you're saying has anything to do with Jesus," Phillip said perplexed.

"That's because you either haven't read the good book or you haven't understood it properly," the preacher snapped.

Nariah remembered listening to this preacher after arriving in Santa Cruz the first time. She had been too confused, too self-questioning to say anything. She'd even half-believed it was a bad dream. This time was different; she was fed up. It didn't help that some of "Christ's army," men in suits carrying rifles, were scornfully pushing Rafael and Phillip back towards the cold water, as if they should be drowned without reason. It didn't help that a few women were spitting on her as some in Judea would do so many years before. Nariah was a soft bumbling sort of lady, the type of person that preferred to peaceably blend in or encourage, never to offend. But now she was offended, inferno level offended. The preacher went on, "It's time to proclaim the good news, Jews, gays, and socialists…"

Nariah exploded. Accepting she might be shot down dead on the sand, she roared back: "How dare you call yourself Christ's army? Jesus was the most peace-loving man that ever lived. He was humble, simple, whole. You know nothing about him or what he taught. He wasn't American, a homophobe, or capitalist. He was Jewish! You all are broken believers, ideologically bent on protecting your small-minded interests as some holy directive. Well, you're wrapped in fear. It's not God or me that curses you. You live in shadows, you curse yourselves. Your ignorant hatred is the hell you already live in! You don't need to wait for the next life to see it."

To the woman who had spit on her, she commanded, "DO NOT DARE SPIT ON ME AGAIN!" And, turning to the men who had been pushing Rafael and Phillip into the ocean, her words were the most forceful, "STOP PUSHING MY GENTLE FRIENDS!" The men did stop. And the whole 'army of Christ' collapsed to the ground sobbing, their skin flushed red in shame. Many shook spastically, others ripped anxiously at their own hair. Just as Jesus had radiated a ferocious presence at the merchant abusing Mary Magdalene so long before, Nariah had now lived that fierce example. She did the *one thing* she'd identified to Rafael at the Tannery, she stood strong for the gentle souls.

Those in this camp were more afraid than they'd ever been. They felt awakened, as if they'd been undead zombies, and it was very scary for them to notice what they'd become. They could suddenly feel the painful vulnerability of human nature. They were sickened by themselves. "Who are you," the man who'd been preaching asked with shaky knees. Where he'd been so proud, he looked as fragile as a thin piece of paper.

"I am Nariah. And I AM HERE FOR THE GENTLE SOULS!" While she didn't say it gently, the gentleness was understood.

"She's here for the gentle souls," a murmuring rippled all through to the back of the encampment.

"Can we become gentle souls?" The man who'd been playing leader of this mob-parade squeamishly requested, having been somehow convinced of Nariah's trueness.

"If you stand up to those trying to crush gentle souls. And if you find gentleness inside you," Nariah responded clearly.

"Then you are here to lead us in revolt against Maka," the woman who had just spit on Nariah asked.

"Who's Maka?" Rafael asked.

"Maka?!" the woman looked surprised that Rafael did not know who Maka was, "the new king of Santa Cruz, of course. Maka's whole world is about crushing the gentle souls. He used to be our ally."

Ambition

Kle clenched the small talisman he caught tightly in his hand. And he kept swimming as hard as he could. While swimming furiously, his mind drifted into its usual tendency of comparing himself to others, to remembering how he didn't measure up in the world. He recalled that no Greek city would have chosen Kle to represent them in the Olympic games. Even though he always tried his best in things, he remembered how shunned he'd felt among all Greeks.

Kle wondered what he could have done differently, what in himself was so flawed as to deserve such disdain, to be dismissed in all things. He knew he'd made some questionable choices as a trader, his abilities in business limited. He knew he could be clumsy and inarticulate in negotiations or even when talking with ladies. He knew he wasn't the strongest, smartest or most charismatic.

Still, the Greek swam towards shore, occasionally peeking up to see Zaera's beauty. He remembered the mornings he had woken up with that red hair over his naked chest in her Santa Cruz condo. He remembered how she pushed him to follow through on his idea for a workshop instead of dismissing his enthusiasm as stupid. She'd even insisted he teach her javelin, mythology and some of the wisdom from the course. She didn't ridicule it all like Kle knew his Greek peers would have done.

Kle had felt at home with Zaera. Still, she'd suddenly kicked him out of her life, a rejection that hurled him into grotesque shadows of an underworld he never sought to visit again. That rejection hurt more than all the abuses endured from his boat mates. Kle didn't want to go through such pain again but, again, he swam on towards red-headed sweet Zaera. Kle kicked and reached his arms forward through the cool water until he heard an engine growl. Then he peeked up from the water to see an SUV limo drive up to Zaera, Enkida, and Arito. Dozens of men on horseback carrying rifles, practically a small militia, had emerged from the shadows at the same time.

Concerned Zaera was in danger, Kle put his head down and swam even harder...until he heard a gun go off and looked up again. It took a few moments to see over the swells. By the time he saw the shore clearly, neither Zaera or Enkida could be seen but there was a long trail of blood leading to the limo, someone had apparently shot and dragged the women (dead or alive) into the luxury vehicle. Arito was screaming on the beach, leaping in the air to avoid bullets.

From the limo, someone yelled, "be quick with that retard! And after killing him, head right back to Felton. We have to deal with our new cargo." The limo didn't wait for an answer. It sped off, followed by a small parade of diligent soldiers on horseback.

Kle had just seen Zaera, his dearest love. As he should have expected, he'd been too slow, allowing her to be killed or abducted because of his physical inadequacy. He had been so close to the shore but completely too late, again falling far short of the hero he always aspired to be.

Hoping he could somehow catch up with the black limousine, Kle put his head down and swam on as hard as he could, racing until out of the water. The final rifleman on horseback was still trying to shoot Arito. The shooter seemed awkward, unfamiliar and very incompetent with his gun. Kle sprinted as fast as he could and ripped the man with the gun from his horse. The goon slammed down to the ground. And Kle flung his fist into the jaw of this man (who had quickly shifted from being predator to prey). Kle punched three more times before realizing he knew the bloodied face below him.

"Alos?" Kle recognized the man. Alos was the worst of his boat mates from Greece, the man who'd taunted him most.

"Kle?"

"What are you doing? Who was the man telling you what to do?"

"King Maka."

"Who? Why were you listening to him?"

"I made a deal with King Maka. He pays me to serve him. I'm guessing you're not being paid to be such a foolish ass with me! Now get off me, you gawky piece of useless sheep shit."

"Who is King Maka?"

"A very rich man, and my generous benefactor if I can kill that retard with wobbly legs before I go back to Maka's fortress."

"The man with wobbly legs is my friend, as were those two ladies. Leave the man with wobbly legs alone and tell me where they've taken those ladies."

"You are not my commander, Kle. Since we lost you in Tiberias, you seem to have developed a false sense of confidence, fool."

Kle started to get up, yielding to Alos due to some negative habit in his self-esteem. He just asked meekly, "please tell me where this man's fortress is."

"Fuck yourself, you cockeyed bitch," Alos refused.

As if Kle woke back up to something very important, he remembered his passion to save Zaera, turned around, and swung his fist again full force into the face of Alos, knocking his old arch-nemesis out cold.

From Crazy to Crazy!

"My dear sister," Maka calmly greeted Enkida from the SUV.

"Ishtar, let me out of this madness," Enkida could not believe Maka had managed to bulldoze back into her life.

"You want out of this madness. I will grant you this," Maka told one of his guards, "shoot them."

Enkida and Zaera were shot before being dragged into the back of the limo. Arito watched his mother taken away from him for the second time because of his uncle, Maka.

After seeing his mother shot, dragged into the car, and drived away, Arito assumed he would be killed quickly. Fortunately, the one charged with killing him turned out to be a particularly unskilled shooter. Arito managed to dance over at least five bullets. And then Kle showed up. Arito saw Kle run like lightning, knocking this final goon from his horse. And then Kle beat the goon senselessly on the ground.

Arito helped Kle tie up the goon. A few minutes later, as Alos, their prisoner, began regaining consciousness, Kle sincerely asked Arito, "should we kill him?"

"Uh, I don't know. I've never killed someone before," Arito answered.

"He's from my land."

"What do you mean?" Arito didn't understand.

"He's from ancient Greece. The magic of the talisman must have somehow drawn him here. He, more than any other, taunted me and painted me as a loser to everyone I knew before I fell into the future with Enkida and Nariah."

"Wow. People have been assholes since the beginning of history."

"Tell me about it! This guy argued against me coming on my last expedition. He took every opportunity to point out to the others that I was just a heavy burden to their trip. Part of me would be very happy to kill this pile of shit tied we've tied up."

Arito added a little hesitantly, "this shithead shot my mother. He might have killed her. He was trying to kill me just a few minutes ago. Killing him is probably a good idea. Still, I wonder if that's heroic or good… *I always thought the real hero is the one who has mercy when he has a chance to give mercy– even for his enemies.*"

"The real hero is the one who gives mercy when he has a chance. That sounds good but this guy's a real asshole?" Kle said.

"I'm the asshole!" Alos snapped weakly from his bloodied mouth. "I might have been an asshole with you but you deserved it!"

"What!" Kle objected to his prisoner, "how could you even think I ever deserved your crap? I never taunted you, Alos."

"You're the god of assholes. You used to constantly prance around arrogantly, showing off how musically talented you were. And when I asked you to teach me how to play a single damned tune on your stupid flute, you said, 'I don't know how to teach music. It's just in me' as if you alone among us mortals could have Apollo's gift of music."

"I don't know how to teach the music."

"Anyway, much more that you lost so much of my wealth. On my first expedition together we'd have returned aristocrats if not for what you paid out for some old scrolls. Maybe those scrolls would have value in other worlds but among our people they were fire kindling. Instead of becoming aristocrats, we returned without even enough to pay back those who'd invested in our trip. It was embarrassing. I was constantly harassed by my cousins because everyone knew I'd been party to such a failed expedition. I never told anyone outside of our crew it was all your damned fault."

"You're the one working for some tyrant to get rich now, willing to kill anyone like a pathetic mercenary. Maybe getting wealthy is too important to you," Kle was pissed but a little conflicted now. He never thought of himself as arrogant about his music and he never really considered how much his failures affected the lives of the other men in his expeditions.

Alos wasn't tolerating this condemnation, "I was dropped in this world by no fault of my own. Some messed up magic brought me here. And Maka was the only one willing to help me. He gave me food and a place to sleep. He protected me and assured me anyone he hurts is a danger to the world, murderers. Those women they took away must be murderers. Kle, I'm sorry you think I'm an asshole but if you could see through my eyes for just one minute, you would recognize you're blind to what an ass you are."

"Enkida and I aren't murderers," Arito snapped at Alos. "She might be a little crazy, a little over eager to get things done. But, no, your Maka lied to you. I don't believe Enkida's a murderer and I know I am not. Your master, Maka, has a dark obscured vision and uses you as his tool."

Alos was quiet and then responded, "perhaps I am wrong." He paused and added, "it is true most of Maka's other guards are drug addicts, infested with sick minds. Yes, maybe I am wrong."

"Then even you understand we can't free you," Kle said.

"If I vow to help you, will you spare my life?" Alos offered.

"The problem is we could never trust you," Arito objected.

"I know Alos. While he is completely an asshole, he is a man of his word. I have seen him keep his word, even when it worked against him. I've seen it countless times... I have never known him to lie. Do you vow upon the holy virginity of our goddess, Athena, that you will be our ally and not betray us?" Kle asked. Kle was not pulled on by compassion as much as a yearning to collaborate for Zaera's safety and freedom.

A medieval castle just popped up in Santa Cruz County's Henry Cowell State Park (a place celebrated by the people of Santa Cruz for its grove of giant old growth redwood trees reaching nearly 300 feet high). One day it wasn't there and the next day it was there. The massive fortress that spontaneously popped up in the parking lot of Henry Cowell State Park was made of rough gray stone five stories high. It was exquisite, as if it had been carefully scooped up from the highlands of Scotland in the 1300's and laid down perfectly intact upon Henry Cowell's parking lot asphalt.

Only seconds before it happened, Maka had been sitting on his own throne in ancient Mesopotamia. Things shifted and he slipped a few inches through time and space to find himself on the floor of the central room in this Euro-style medieval castle which manifested in the hills above Santa Cruz.

There was a throne but Maka was not sitting on it. Instead, a light skinned man with red beard and red hair smiled peacefully from this fortress's royal seat.

Maka, quickly realizing he'd have to adapt to whatever happened to him, said humbly, "good King, where am I?"

"I have only just arrived here too, friend. I am not king. I am pretty sure this is just a dream and you are nothing but a figment of my imagination," Arthur replied. "I hope to use whatever happens in this dream as fodder for my next book's magic."

"You're a magician? Did you bring me here, friend?" Maka carefully asked.

"Well, I teach cooking and writing. To call me a magician might be a bit of a stretch. And I'm sorry but I have now idea what is creating you in my imagination," Arthur laughed.

Maka frowned deeply, his humble facade melting, "then get off the throne!"

Still convinced this was a dream, Arthur replied, "you're rather rude. What's up your butt, buddy?"

"I am a patient man but not eager to repeat myself," Maka snarled. "I am a king. I was born a king. Will always be a king. I am a great sorcerer too. Put those together and I am power. Power is not questioned or insulted. You will remove your fat ass from my chair and serve me as an obedient pawn in whatever game I play or you will be crushed. Is that clear, you pathetic piece of scum?"

A cool draft blew through the hall. Arthur could not remember such a lucid dream. He wasn't so sure about the whole sleep thing. Still, he stood from the chair, turned around, slapped his own butt, saying, "kiss my ass."

Maka had led attacks against many armies but no enemy has ever calmly invited him to kiss their ass. Maka was not interested in anyone's ass being kissed except for his own. He pulled back his hands, said some words of power, and flung his arms forward. He invoked one of the oldest spells in human history, that which turns its recipient into stone. Arthur no longer appeared as a friendly heartfelt friend. He was a solid unliving stone.

After taking care of Arthur, and thus claiming the throne as his own, Maka searched the castle and found seventeen massive bags of white powder in the dungeon basement of the castle. It can never be said where the bags came from, only that the power of the gem somehow drew this large supply of cocaine into the castle Maka was dropped in.

While most of the incantations Maka had learned over the years were oriented to hurting others, at that moment Maka drew on a method of "seeing" the nature of a plant substance (something his sister, Enkida, had once taught him!). And, through this knack, he concluded these bags of white powder were full of a stimulating intoxicant, something his mind now called cocaine.

In the next few days, Maka discovered the world around him was called Santa Cruz and it was threatened by a plague, political divisiveness, and massive fires. Maka, very resourcefully, made an acquaintance from nearby Lompico who was interested in helping to sell the white powder. That's how the enterprise began. At first, he gave small free samples of the white powder to hungry ghost-like souls who passed by his castle. If they were prone to addiction, they returned as ardent customers. The most reliable customers became his salespeople, bodyguards and spies. To his credit, he adapted quickly to the reality of his new home.

Maka was an equal opportunity employer, not caring if his subject had been computer engineers, janitors, or artists. One virtua- he didn't care about their race, religion, or sexual orientation. He just valued whether they were willing to give him gain, to be brutish hammers to forge the kingdom he wanted to build. With bricks of cocaine he began building his new life (and Maka knew better than to try even a tiny bit of this white poison himself.)

Over the course of one year, Maka further evolved to sell a wide variety of products from his castle (some illegal, some not). His castle became much more than a very unexplainable tourist attraction standing in what had been the parking lot of a state park. From this castle, people purchased heroin and crystal meth. Then, after continuing to grow in understanding of the market, one could buy organic food in those stone walls (the food was branded organic but wasn't really!). Then Maka broadened his scheming to T shirts with semi-funny slogans, tanning salon machines, and prostitution. Maka converted that castle into a truly bustling red, black (and gray) market nexus. Inspired by the reality show industry, Maka even financed a TV show called Santa Cruzandia (ripping off the name from Portlandia). The show focused on the drama between the drug addicts who lived in his castle. The show and its grotesque interactions was quickly sponsored by Netflix.

With the pandemic, fires, and general political chaos of the world; local law enforcement had become underfunded and overstretched. Recognizing this, Maka used a portion of his income to bribe most members of the department, effectively establishing his immunity from prosecution. After just six months this was successful enough for Maka to be considered the most significant leader within Santa Cruz County. In the face of pushback, Maka made alliances by promising local prominent business people greater profit so long as they were allegiant to him. He donated funds to some religious groups, encouraging them to become militant against 'demonic heretical anti-nationalist hippies' as a demonstration of 'righteous devotion to the cause of Security and Christ's Salvation.'

He knew little about Christ but recognized people could be convinced to do insane things when this Christ's name was used. Very dramatically, Maka successfully lobbied to make it illegal to surf and skate (claiming the waters weren't clean enough for surfing and skating damaged the sidewalks). And whenever a resurgence of the plague seemed to have a plague, he used this as an excuse to enforce long term stay at home orders and the wearing of masks (to discourage the emergence of any charismatic challenges to his authority).

As his power solidified, Maka's guards continued to be well supplied with whatever intoxicants they craved, businesses not affiliated with Maka became over-regulated and closed (leaving many homeless), the pro-Maka group called Christ's Army (who looked to Maka as their inspiration and guiding force) acted as an increasingly influential type of morality police through the county, and flattering photoshopped pictures of Maka in front of his castle were displayed on countless billboards in the area. Through these changes, lots of people (and their money) fled the County concerned about its direction.

The Battle

Enkida and Zaera's injured bodies slumped over each other in the back seat of Maka's SUV limo. Their wrists were bound by zip ties and they bled all over the car's nice gray leather upholstery. Zaera's gunshot wound was in her shoulder, Enkida's in her gut. A black and white camouflage wearing twitchy oversized bodyguard sat at the left and right of them. Maka sat by himself in the chair opposite them, smugly as if it were his throne. As they drove off, Maka glared silently for a few minutes at Enkida until finally bursting out, "how did you do it?"

"How did I do what, Maka," Enkida responded weakly.

"How did you pull me into this world? How did you escape being hunted by Efaau's curses? How are you still alive," he screamed furiously.

"I swear I'll tell you if you set my friend free," Enkida confessed honestly. She seemed out of breath and blood kept seeping from her gut.

"OK, my sister. We have a deal," and he told his goons, "slow down and push the one with red hair out."

The car slowed down and when it was going about 10 mph, the bodyguards pushed Zaera out of the vehicle. To Enkida, it looked like Zaera landed on her bleeding shoulder.

"I..., " Enkida hesitated.

"Tell me or we quickly go in reverse and run your friend over."

"I used a talisman."

"Good, Enkida. Very good," he smiled. "Now give it to me."

"I don't have it anymore."

"Liar!."

"Search my mind. I'm telling you the truth."

Maka was quiet for a few moments, searching Enkida's mind just as she encouraged. Then he roared, "you threw it into the ocean! You fool!"

Then he told his friend, "run her friend over. Crush her!"

The chauffeur looked in the rearview mirror and responded, "forgive me but she's gone, Boss."

Maka grimaced and waved his chauffeur onwards to the castle.

Rafael, Phillip, and Nariah were followed by hundreds of zealous "soldiers" from "Christ's Army," the clan of hyper-nationalist zealots who'd found themselves redeemed through Nariah's passion for aiding Gentle Souls. "The castle has a lot of armed guards," someone from Christ's Army told Nariah, Phillip, and Rafael.

"We won't be able to overtake it with sheer force then," Nariah mused.

"I agree," Phillip concurred. "We'll have to find another way."

"So," Rafael continued with unexpected leadership, "to topple this tyrant, we need to use disorientation."

"What do you mean," Phillip asked.

"We have to go balls out," Rafael clarified.

"Cannon balls?" Phillip grimaced; he hated how the use of violence had not been eradicated since the days of Jesus.

"No, dear Phillip, I mean nut sacks and all," Rafael offered.

"What?" Nariah squealed. It took a bit of explaining but, considering their position as newfound leaders of this previously militant hyper-conservative but now loyal-to-the-cause of Gentle Souls cult, Rafael thought engaging an armed castle with a mob of naked people might have the smoothest (albeit very risky) result. The plan was to disarm or re-direct aggressors with the ridiculous vulnerability of mass nudity. Phillip thought the image of an unclothed army invoked a gesture of re-claiming the garden of Eden. Nariah thought it re-asserted the innocence of her nudity from before the traumas of prostitution.

Nudity means something different to everybody. To many, being naked has a connotation of being dirty. There's shame. Rafael is the kind of person who confronts shame as boldly as Frodo confronted Mordor or Martin Luther King Jr. confronted racial inequality. Rafael never fit in and he long accepted he would never fit any idolized mold within society. Thus, his motto of life was, "boldly make friends with shame!"

"Okay," Nariah, the emerging general, agreed to the proposal. And after Nariah asked them, Christ's Army also agreed. So not far from Natural Bridges State Park, they disrobed and, more naked than a legion of bears, they marched down Mission Blvd. They went past Brazil restaurant, west side's aikido dojo, and past the old Catholic mission. All along the way, random Santa Cruz people took their clothes off and joined the march (inspired either by the nudity or the cause of overthrowing Maka's hateful tyranny).

They all turned up River Street, passing Pro Build, Central Home Supply and the Tannery. They kept going and headed into the cool shade of a trail redwoods not far off Highway Nine. There they met their first wave of Maka's deranged guards. The guards had semi-automatic guns and were dressed in stylish but useless black and white camouflage. They were so confused by this vast ocean of naked people trekking through the woods that they just removed their combat fatigues and followed along as well, assuming it was what must be done. When the growing mass of flesh met more guards, the initial ones explained "we need to protect these people. They're naked. And we need to be naked, too. It's what's happening."

"Uh, okay," the others grunted in agreement. Anyway, in addition to the naked enchantment, they were too high to object. By the time Nariah, Phillip, Rafael, and the parade arrived at the castle in Henry Cowell State Park's parking lot, more guards were naked and protecting the parade of disrobed persons than the number of guards on duty at the fortress. And, because of that, it might have been a wholly non-violent takeover of the castle had not a single guard standing atop one of the fortress's walls freaked out and shot a spastic bullet directly at Rafael.

The bullet slashed angrily into Rafael's lower abdomen. Blood splattered and Rafael collapsed onto the dirt. There had been so much hope. It had been a powerful demonstration of non-violent protest. But this revolution was seemingly crushed with a single bullet. Rafael, who had proposed a strategy which would injure no one, was now bleeding with what seemed to be a lethal hit. Every man and woman in Christ's army gasped, many wondering if following this plan was a mistake, wondering if they would now be slaughtered. The thousands of redwood trees around them were silent but seemed to grieve to spilling of gentle blood before them.

"Maybe I will meet your Jesus now," Rafael croaked to Phillip weakly.

"Snap out of it," Phillip responded. "You have a lot more work to do before that." Phillip, who lived in the light of a unique holiness, casually reached into Rafael's gut, pulled the bullet from his insides, and held his bloodied hand over the wound as if inviting it to heal. He commanded, "wound, become whole." In a matter of seconds, the bleeding stopped and the wound closed up. Rafael stood back up, dazed look on his face.

The naked army's collective consciousness inhaled deeply, their convictions rebounded amplified, and they broke out in song to "Amazing Grace," the chorus of Leonard Cohen's version of "Hallelujah," and "How Great Thou Art," all while holding each other's hands and wrestling down guards who showed physical resistance to their movement. The drawbridge was peaceably lowered by a guard inspired by the bold nature of these newcomers. Nariah, Phillip, and their legion walked into the heart of the castle, the throne room, wearing nothing. They were an endless wave of unstoppable nakedness.

Maka was not impressed. With his throne room overflowing with breasts, asses and genitals, he laughed, throwing his hands into the air, "I surrender to this, uh, herd of sheep stumbling into the slaughterhouse. I assume that is what you all want?"

Nariah saw the stone imprint of Arthur, her dear culinary instructor and friend, at the side of Maka's throne. She was shaken but was far from the bumbling follower she'd been not long before. She commanded, "we are the gentle ones and you have oppressed us for too long. Come down from your self-centered throne of venom."

"Quiet, you wobbling fool!" Maka stood up from his chair, waved his arms around the air gathering power. Then he chanted, "matrasa, lokmanya, trevastya," and then threw his arms violently forward.

There was no delay in impact. All the naked people in the hall were suddenly held. Maka unleashed all demons in their heads. You couldn't see these demons. Each naked person just suddenly faced (heard) their most hateful, self-critical, depressing thoughts. Their most negative thoughts were unbearably loud in their heads. At the beach, Nariah's furious presence had turned on the most wholesome light, freeing those hypnotized by greed, misguided loyalties, and judgment. Now Maka's force worked to completely reverse this movement, to do the opposite with these same people; enlivening the very worst internal pattern in everyone.

They thought things such as, "if I'd only been smarter or more devoted, creative, talented, giving, etc." They saw their bodies, their faces, their selves as hideous masses of ugliness. They saw vast gaps of inadequacy in themselves. They saw their lives as unlucky, hopeless, destined for gloom. They recalled every goodness as empty gestures. Suddenly, it seemed that more dominant than any merciful god was a hateful, uncaring force. Life just sucked.

Maka smiled, watching these naked people contorting, struggling desperately to cover themselves, twisting and groaning all sorts of things like, "I am unforgivable," "I am a failure," or "I am disgusting." Maka knew they would not be able to handle it, in short order they would submit to his dark power's control. Nariah fell to the ground remembering being a whore for soldiers sent to Tiberias from Rome. Some of the soldiers beat her before her "work." Many from the local Judean community shamed her. She felt a nauseous wave of self-disgust, hatred for her parents for not protecting her from life's harshness, fury even with Jesus for letting her be so pathetically unimportant among the entourage around him. Nothing had light in it.

Rafael recalled being beat up by his father innumerable times for being "too effeminate." He remembered his high school's football team holding him down and painting 'I'm a fag' across his chest. He remembered being homeless, drunk for weeks on end, and alone for even longer. He remembered trying to kill himself before finding *his people* out west.

Phillip doubted everything. Having been established in faith for so long it was like a million teeth being pulled from his mouth at one time. He saw humanity, with all its sinfulness, as a nasty sickness that should be purged from earth. He saw his own calmness as weak complicity. He saw himself as letting God down. Each person in the horde of nakedness was hit by the full force of latent shadow from their own minds.

Maka enjoyed squeezing those before him with his dark energies. And he'd have kept it going for another couple hours, long enough to completely break them, make them unable to even put a few words together. He wanted to destroy, to make a blubbering bunch of idiots out of these assailants to his throne, his power. His heart swelled, so much subservience would be great fun to exploit, an army of real zombies! To him, it was perfect. Nariah tried to draw on that mustard seed of faith Jesus talked about. She searched inside herself for a drop of trust, clenched her fists and face trying to resist the negativity of Maka's grim tentacles. And then she was drawn back into horrific memories.

Enkida lay on the dirt floor of the dark dungeon, blood still oozing from her wound. She knew a guard was waiting at the top of the medieval stone staircase down to this dungeon. "I was so close," she told the cold walls of her prison. "And, again, I didn't pay enough attention to the possibility of enemies. Why didn't I learn? Now Arito's probably dead and I will be soon too. I was so close…"

"Then let us get you closer," she heard a familiar voice. And then, outside the bars of her imprisonment stood a shadowed form.

"Who are you," Enkida asked.

"Somebody who has wronged you countless times and only asks now that you let him try to right his wrongs."

"Efaau," as distrusting and hateful as she was towards him, she was too weak to do any magic, too trapped to even swing from the bars a fist at him. "Please do not trick me again as I die. Give me that one favor."

"I am not lying. I am here trying to redeem myself," Efaau lit a cell phone flashlight and Enkida saw his face

"I see no beard or mustache. Your robe is gone. Even your hair is short. What kind of trick do you play on me now, evil one?"

"Enkida, I was a monster with you. I have had to change some things on my outside to get a job in this land. And, because of certain people in this place, I have changed on the inside too. I'd never had a friend and that's why I was so willing to brutalize your life for my advantage."

Enkida groaned but then said, "how did you get down here? I didn't hear a struggle. It seems you have been allowed in, that you are still working with my hateful brother, that you are still conniving."

Like a child, Efaau ran enthusiastically but quietly back up the steps of the dungeon and came back a minute later dragging a guard. The guard was snoring and, even though he'd just been dragged down many steps of a stone staircase, he didn't awaken, "I just put him into a deep sleep. I may not want to use my craft for dark purposes anymore but I will still use what spells work in this world as I choose."

"If you weren't just deceiving me again, you'd let me out," Enkida snarled.

"I will but, please, I heard you speaking to yourself. I know you were just lost in thought about how you haven't been diligent enough with keeping up your guard. I am asking you to ignore that lesson and give the world more, not less, trust. I swear I will do what I can to protect you from Maka and help us escape. Just please don't hurt me."

"And if I don't agree?" Enkida, even now, was uncompromisingly honest.

"I will still release you. I have done too much evil to you to leave you here among the rats. But I have other hopes and plead with you to give them a chance," Enkida could see

Efaau's eyes, she could also peer into many of the brutal secrets of his past.

Nariah wriggled on the ground under Maka's tortuous enchantment as she looked up to see Enkida emerge from a passageway. Enkida looked beat up, her gut covered with blood from a wound but she stood proud and glorious. At her side Enkida busily began waving her arms around in what were magical gestures for countering Maka's heinous control.

A surge of gratitude washed through Nariah, almost instantly. She was suddenly unshackled from the nihilistic rivers controlling her mind. Likewise, the mass of hundreds of naked bodies cried almost in unison, feeling unbound from their deepest regrets and anxieties.

"Enkida," Maka roared. "How did you escape again?"

"A new friend," Efaau responded stepping forth. Efaau had scrape marks across his face (which he had allowed) but, other than that, he was intact.

"Efaau! You return to my sphere but, instead of an ally, it looks as if you have helped my enemy, the enemy you repeatedly promised to rid me of.. And you try to challenge me! I am not forgiving towards traitors!"

"Not forgiving to traitors! I have not seen you forgiving to anyone. In Uruk, you disposed of anyone who you found distasteful. Even in my brief time here, while walking to your castle, I saw your moving car hurl out a woman as if she were trash. I have seen how your guards were bound to you through addictions. I am fully awakened to what you are and what I was. I was a traitor to myself when I served you..

"Then you and Enkida are the poison in our midst," Maka snarled.

"Your hatred is a poison in your mind. It sickened that long dead kingdom of Uruk. Free yourself from this poison. Become a new person. Nourish yourself with fresh thinking. Celebrate a new chapter by drinking fresh juice with me!" Efaau sincerely invited Maka to live another way.

Maka, on the other hand, squinted his eyes and smiled, calmly letting them know, "one of Enkida's friends delivered a little talisman to me. Enkida used this troublesome little talisman to make all our lives so messy, to create so many twists and turns in time and space."

And Maka opened his fist, within it a small talisman glistened brightly, nine tiny dots on it "A few minutes ago three visitors surprised me with their arrival. Such lovely young men. One had worked for me, Alos. Another was an over-eager Greek, an aspiring hero named Kle. And the last walked strangely and had very familiar eyes. This one mentioned Enkida over and over again. I believe he called himself Arito. He said, 'I'm here to save my mommy.' Was he that boy I took from you so long ago, the one that disappeared from our land shortly later?"

"Where is he?" Enkida asked, wide eyed.

"Dear sister, your child is fine for the moment. They're all happy as a hare. Speaking of hares, perhaps we should discuss our differences over a meal this evening. We can make some rabbit stew?" Maka pulled three squirming rabbits from a sack that had been sitting at his side. Alos, Arito, and Kle had not successfully overtaken Maka after emerging from the secret passage to his throne (which Alos had shown them). Enkida learned the spell which turned those fishermen into rabbits from her brother. She knew who the rabbits next to Maka were. Efaau knew who those rabbits were. Zaera knew who those rabbits were.

"You've stolen so much from me, all because I felt too much mercy to kill your wife when it may have been wise. I was too weak. I did not hesitate out of spite. I am sorry but, please!" Enkida was crying and screaming.

"Thank you for reminding me about your error. It chills my heart and should chill yours too," Maka grimaced and hurled a vicious frozen spell towards Enkida. It was a spell Efaau had taught him, the spell Efaau had used long before, the one that got him banished from his small community of origin in ancient Europe.

Efaau could see the spell hurl across the room. And, before it hit Enkida, Efaau selflessly leapt into it. This frozen spell turned Efaau into an un-living block of ice.

Maka swirled his arms, gathering as much more darkness as he could. Then he threw his arms back, and flung a massive ball of energy, a force that effectively deletes its recipient, removes them from the time-space continuum Maka believed he had been wronged and, because of that, he did not hesitate in trying to completely undo Enkida's existence.

Before a drop of this "go-away" spell landed upon her, Enkida threw up a protection shield around herself. This force field held back the terrifying ball of go-away but to keep it up is a terrible drain; it cannot hold back any spell for long (and Enkida was already very weak). Enkida knew there was only a few moments of strength before she was overtaken.

The naked people, Nariah, Phillip, and Rafael were too disoriented to do anything. Efaau was frozen onto the side of the castle. The three rabbits were sadly unhelpful.

Still, while so focused on finishing this vital task of getting rid of Enkida, Maka didn't notice one new arrival in the hall, a red headed young woman angrily walked in. Along the way, she grabbed a medieval style spear hooked onto a castle wall. Kle had loved teaching her to throw a spear (when she took Zeus's Holotropic Spatial Seminar). Now, true to what she learned, Zaera quickly pulled her spear back and hurled it with graceful Olympiad form. Even Athena, the ancient goddess, would have been wowed by the perfection of Zaera's form.

The spear arched up so that it nearly hit the high ceiling of the throne room. It looked effortless, as if it was something she'd done a million times. Then the spear glided down, hurling towards its goal. Enkida's energetic shield was fading. She was almost completely spent.

Then Maka saw it, the spear aiming to pierce completely through his heart. Reflexively, Maka lifted up his hand as if to protect himself. The spear sliced through his hand and then his sternum through to the decadent throne behind him. As he stopped pushing his magical castration spell on Enkida, it boomeranged back on him- if you fling a spell and it doesn't land, it returns right back to you. He was forced to receive the spell he flung. In being deleted, every place his powers were still at work, were now undone.

Pagans and Prophets, Preachers and Teachers

With the frozen spell now undone (along with Maka's existence in the modern world), Efaau's corpse collapsed to the castle's hard ground. He was unmoving.

Phillip, the renowned apostle of a carpenter from Nazareth, approached Efaau's cold form. Then Phillip closed his eyes and gently put his hand upon the center of Efaau's deflated chest. As Phillip stood there, a large tear dropped from his eye onto Efaau's motionless forehead. Phillip was very familiar with miracles. As he stood there, warmth surged through Efaau, his heart fluttering and then beating fairly normally again. He gasped for air but remained untalking, not all well but much less dead. Three rough medieval blankets in the castle were found and wrapped around Efaau's still cool but now shivering body.

In addition to the frozen spell, witht Maka's magic undone Arthur was suddenly not turned to stone. He collapsed to the ground and, right away, went into an epileptic fit. While his body flung itself every which way around the large throne room, Alos, Kle, and Arito were released from being rabbits. Still used to being rabbits, they hopped around innocently for a few moments before looking around in a daze at the man wildly shaking at their side, at the countless naked people in the hall, at Zaera's proud warrior-goddess form, Nariah the reluctant general, Enkida's now warming bloodied gut, and Phillip still in an otherworldly zon from having just performed a miracle. They took it all in, their rabbit consciousness trying to mesh back with human complexity.

Even following this most ridiculous culmination of events, time must find a way to go on… They all had to figure out what one does after dealing with whatever it is we think of as our main problems, or when we get what we desire. Either we get smug and shrink away, get depressed, or creatively conjure up new problems and purpose.

After recovering from his fit and getting back up, Arthur was, again, unsure if this was a dream. In a daze, Arthur picked up a small piece of copper he saw on the floor. Then he pushed Maka's pierced body from the throne. The corpse dropped onto the cold floor and he took the seat himself. It was a perfect King Arthur namesake moment. Over the next few days, the still somewhat puritanical but now reformed nationalist-zealots cleaned the castle of all drugs and grime (the castle was later considered "gifted" to Roaring Camp Railroads and transformed into a local family friendly amusement/ tourist attraction). After their work on the castle, the once militant anti-taxation nationalistic salvation seekers from Natural Bridges State Park left the fortress and walked deep into San Lorenzo Valley together…

This tribe did put clothes back on. To be clear, it was not the business suits and fancy dresses that had uniformed them before. They wore loose fitting cloth which suggested the discovery of a more delicate inner-nature. Still, this group remained a tribe and, together, they homesteaded (illegally) a track of burned down forest above Bonny Doon. And, instead of a personality cult holding the full focus connecting them now, each of them diligently cultivated the spirit of gentleness within themselves through Tai Chi, working with crafts, contact dance, and a myriad of other new age modalities. Unquestionably inspired by Nariah, they each discovered a unique expression of service, art, meditation or whatever nourished their authentic inner-calm and gentleness...

During Maka's rise to power, there had been a surge of fires, a plague, political unrest, and general turmoil. While a lot of magic had been brewed, all these issues were not magically and instantly undone. Santa Cruz still needed a lot of healing.

In local politics, Santa Cruz found new leadership in Arthur. Moved by his moments on a throne, the culinary chef/ writer ran for Santa Cruz city council and won. As a leader, he worked hard to root out all the corruption that Maka had implanted into the police infrastructure. He helped re-establish Santa Cruz as a realm where compassion, non-dogmatic spirituality, reasonable taxation, environmental awareness, and a great love for creativity re-emerged as the core values of local culture. Good Times had a front page article on, "How Benevolent King Arthur Revived our Round Table."

Kle married Zaera (with Arito and Alos at his side as groomsmen/ former rabbits). At the wedding, Zaera wore a fantastically edgy glow in the dark blue and green wedding dress designed by the increasingly prominent fashion conquistador Rafael (who was now being called left and right to design). After a somber quiet period of defrosting, Efaau was supported in opening up a juice bar. And his juice bar later expanded into a natural foods restaurant. His restaurant catered Kle and Zaera's wedding. And Nariah grew to be recognized far and wide as a sage-woman, enlightening people across all religious affiliations (or lack of affiliation) to a Higher Reality of Love. Nariah even officiated the well-attended union of Kle and Zaera's love. Nariah's online sermons would go on to kickstart change in the Christian world globally, many saying her influence "forged Christianity into something more resembling Christ's original message." Nariah used much of her online viral success's to start a non-profit fighting sex trafficking and helping prostitutes get out of that trade (or receive therapy if they chose to remain in it.)

After the wedding, Kle and Zaera co-taught the newly developed "Zeus AND ATHENA'S Holotropic Spatial Seminars" together on the new age west coast circuit – going from Los Angeles up to Seattle and everywhere in between. Their workshop was celebrated as "self-help led by people who are not pretending to be spiritual, people who show us how lust, fear, anger, and joy can all harmoniously co-exist.:" They even participated in a hilarious interview on the Daily Show with Trevor Noah discussing Kle's book on his assumed-to-be-fictional past. Their marriage was not without its challenges, both of them being hot-headed and principled down to the core. Still, they endured and were even blessed with the arrival of Althaia and Calliope, twin girls. Then a whole other series of quests and adventures began for this family unit.

Over many months of recovering from this traumatic period of her life, Enkida lived in a small house overlooking the concrete boat in Aptos. She was regularly visited by Phillip, who would sit and talk to her about healing. He occasionally gave her healing sessions, a laying on of hands which she claimed "washed away sufferings" and connected her with "a wellspring of peace.." Arito visited her with the most frequency. He openly acknowledged her as his mother. And he loved hearing about his cultural heritage in stories of ancient Mesopotamia. On his own, he tried following a career as a spoken word artist. At some point he transitioned to working as a successful sound engineer.

Enkida did not miss the power or adoration of being a ruler in Uruk (or from leading a foolhardy revolution in Santa Cruz). Nor did she not miss the heat of Mesopotamia. But it took time to really settle into the modern world with its fast automobiles, vast internet, complicated rat race, and money driven economy. Hers had been a fire that had burned as brightly as the sun, perhaps she had overcooked herself. She was learning to be a steady flame. Enkida's demeanor revealed a more reserved (even anti-social) woman. Still, over the course of time, she re-discovered wholeness.

After a few years, there was a sort of reunion evening, when most of this story's central players gathered around an orange-glowing bonfire at Moran beach one evening. With Enkida was Arito, Kle, Zaera, Nariah, Arthur, Philip, and Rafael. While Efaau had redeemed himself, he was still a sore sight in her eyes; she was not ready for casual visits with him. Enkida poured a special (and tasty) calming concoction (made with whiskey, basil, and saffron) into cups for them all. After drinking his cup, Phillip, who looked even younger, smiled and encouraged Enkida, "you should see people in need of healing and offer your wisdom."

"I am too broken to heal others," Enkida declined.

"The true healer is completely broken open," Phillip encouraged. The sun was going down as they stared out at the waves.

"What do I have to give except my tiredness?"

"Enkida, you have gone far into the darkness. And you have emerged from that darkness with vast knowledge."

"Phillip, I am not like you. I am too stained."

"We are all stained but, in the realm of healing, you are very much like me. You are a vast vessel, filled with a knowing radiant darkness.... Anyway, you have to pay your bills and being a healer would probably work out better than going back to the whole monarch-tyrant thing," he smiled playfully.

"I will think about it, Phillip."

Phillip paused and then put in, "it's time for me to return to the past and fulfill my role with Jesus."

"You will leave us?" Rafael objected.

"I choose to fulfill promises. I would leave you comforted if I was confident Enkida's healing gifts will be shared. Enkida, please teach people of your ancient Mesopotamian healing practices, your herbal lore, massage practices, and chants. Many people come to this land of Santa Cruz for healing, as it welcomes outcasts."

"This is definitely where ridiculous people find their ridiculousness celebrated," Arito put in.

"And where people from seemingly unwanted lands find safe harbor," Kle added, smiling at Zaera.

Before she could object again something distracted their conversation… splashing out in the waves, Enkida and Phillip noticed something flipping around out in the water. Zaera smiled, "is that a merman and mermaid swimming?" Alongside two big splashes, it did look like a man and a woman with fins. They seemed to come even closer to the shoreline and linger happily there. Even from a distance, they looked content. And then Enkida heard the eerie song-squeal of these strange creatures. A moment later they were gone, only the splashing of the waves remaining.

"When I was a lion," Phillip began, "I was impressed by how ferociously you hit me when we first met.

"Huh," Enkida didn't get it right away, that he had been her lion.

Instead of saying any more, Phillip stood up and stepped through an invisible doorway on the beach before disappearing.

After his disappearance, Enkida did as Phillip suggested. She opened up a healing shop called Pagans and Prophets. And she thought this transformation into running a healing business was the final big transition of her life, that she would quickly fade into a quirky old eccentric that people giggled at behind her back. Enkida had no idea about the boats which were already floating into Santa Cruz from various portals. She didn't yet know the talisman's magic was not done, that the boats were arriving with new conundrums. Enkida didn't know how much Arito still needed her, how important her healing with Efaau still was, or how much Althaia and Calliope, Zaera and Kle's daughters, would need her help. Enkida didn't realize purpose waited for her very close by!

Made in the USA
Las Vegas, NV
19 January 2024

84552177R00204